Standing Alone

Standing Alone

The Mysteries of Bella Rose Estate
Book #4

Phyllis   Dewey

Copyright © 2022 Phyllis Dewey
ISBN   978-1-7364347-7-2

Dedication

Standing Alone is dedicated to my former co-worker Steven. When Steven heard that I was a writer and had already published two books, he asked me if he was in any of them. I told him he was not – yet. He was relieved but became wary of saying anything around me for fear I would put him into one of my stories. I also heard through mutual friends that he envied me.

There is nothing to be envious about, Steven. This book is not only dedicated to you, and I have used your name for one of my newest characters, but this message is for you and to everyone who ever wanted to write a book or who is in the process of writing one. Keep Going! Keep writing. Enjoy the process, and may your stories soon be available for others to experience.

Prologue

Bella Rose Estates had become well known both near and far by friends and strangers alike. Life for the expanding Fairchild family had found a normal pace. The secrets and truths discovered were now safely kept by those who knew them. The family had settled down to enjoy their lives, and new happiness filled the manor's walls.

Miles away, in another state, Barbara's life had been anything but normal since her childhood. Every time she thought life was changing for the better, something seemed to happen and tossed her world into another downhill spiral. She found herself repeatedly standing alone and left searching for a better life.

Now she was standing by someone who may change her future and show her that life is full of amazing people and love. Someone who vowed to never leave.

Could something or someone change her life so that she would never have to stand alone again? Would she finally see that dreams come true? Or would her nightmare never end?

Chapter One

Fear of Darkness

In silent stillness, Barbara gazed through the clouded picture window in the living room, watching the darkness steal the light of day. Mesmerized, she stood frozen in space, watching the tree branches waving goodbye to the colors of autumn as their leaves descended and scattered across the freshly mowed lawn—the last mowing of the year.

Nighttime elevated Barbara's fear of loneliness while she reflected on her day. The night's approaching darkness captured her senses every time she was alone, but she felt the grip was even tighter this night. Another day had passed where no one had called, no one had stopped in, and no letters had arrived. It seemed as though no one cared. Possibly, no one knew.

The sound of two quick beeps transformed her mind into reality. She bade goodbye to the day, closing the solid gray blackout curtains against the fears that came with the decreasing light. Retracting into her tiny, outdated kitchen, she cautiously stepped across the chipped tiles of the aged floor to pour herself a cup of plain, strong black coffee. It would be another sleepless night with or without the caffeine in her system. The sounds from the coffee maker had become her joy. The blend of the aroma with the taste of strong bitterness would keep her company and give her comfort until morning. It was her only companion most days.

Barbara would never forget this night. The night of her final goodbye. When morning dawned, her life would be transformed—in ways she never dreamed possible.

I digress—to before…

Chapter Two

Thirteen

Barbara sat up in her twin bed. Her only possession, a ragged, old quilt, slipped from her shoulders. Afraid to move her body, she shifted her eyes to see if there was a beam of light sneaking in through the small crack under her bedroom door.

She took a deep breath, sat up straight, placed her feet on the floor, and stood. Wrapping her quilt around her to keep warm, she shuffled in bare feet to the lone window in her room. The curtains were drawn, masking the truth that daylight had begun to awaken the world outside. She moved one cloth panel and squinted to see past the fog that blocked a clear view of freedom.

Today she would become a full-blown teenager—an age she had desired to be for as long as she could remember. Somehow she hoped her life would change when she reached that magical number. Yet, as she peered out the window, she realized that not only would her life not change, but she also doubted there would be any celebration in her honor to commemorate such an accomplishment.

Barbara sighed, shrugged her shoulders, and closed the curtain panel, making sure to position it as it had been before she touched it. Any alteration to her room would bring punishment. She saw the light stream in from the hallway across her floor and rushed to climb back into her bed. She laid back and closed her eyes as her door opened.

Renee walked past Barbara's bed and spread the cotton panel apart with one quick swoosh. The metal rings attached to the curtains scraped against the black iron rod and caused Barbara to jerk in her bed. She opened her eyes and faced Renee. Forcing a smile to greet her mother, she sat up.

"Good morning, Barbara. Time to rise and shine; we have a busy day ahead of us."

"Yes, Mother. Good morning."

Renee left the room to let her child get ready for the pre-planned day—just the two of them. Renee poured herself another cup of coffee while she waited for her now thirteen-year-old to join her in the kitchen. She was trying to limit caffeine, but three cups were still less than the four or five she normally consumed before nine in the morning. It was a beginning.

They were in the middle of downtown two hours later with their arms full of packages. Barbara admired how her mother could get everything she needed so quickly when they shopped together, but how long it took for Renee to shop when she went alone.

They made no other stops after Renee had purchased everything on her list. She gave no indication to Barbara that she had even remembered what day it was. When Renee reached their house, they noticed a strange car parked in the driveway before she turned in. Renee sped up and drove past the house instead of turning in. She drove another quarter mile past her house before parking in a church parking lot.

"Why did you go past the house?" Barbara asked as they passed it. She turned her head to look back through the vehicle's side mirror.

"Sorry, I was not ready to face those people."

"Who are they?"

"Those people are with the children's services. They are there to do a check on you. Honestly, they are there to check up on me about you."

"I think you are doing a great job; why are you afraid of seeing them?"

"Because." Renee stopped speaking for a moment. She had to gather her thoughts. "Because my time is up to have you stay with me."

"What do you mean your time is up? I thought you were my foster mother!" Barbara was reeling, and tears instantly flowed down her cheeks.

"I am your foster mother. Or I was for a while. I got a call the other day that another family wanted to take you in, and the agency believes you will be a better fit with them." Renee had moved around in her seat to face the daughter she had come to love.

Barbara wiped her tears and stared at her. How could this woman do this to her? What was wrong with her that Renee did not want her anymore?

"Listen, my child, I know this looks like I don't want you anymore. I do. But the truth is you would be better off with the other couple. Yes, a couple, instead of a single me."

"But I like living with you. You just called me your child! I don't care if you are married or not."

"Thanks for that, kiddo." Renee smiled, although the conversation was breaking her heart. She could not tell this beautiful young girl the truth. Renee had to convince Barbara that it was in her best interest to live with another family. "When the agency found this couple who wanted to pursue adoption, they knew you were the right fit. I do not have the means to adopt you. They do."

"I don't want to be adopted! I want to stay with you!" Barbara turned her face to look out her window as more tears fell. She sobbed while she thought. Renee's life was not perfect, but it was the best Renee had known. She knew what to expect, even when Renee punished her.

"I know you do. It is not up to either of us at this point. You have to go with these people."

"I'll say I want to live with you. I'll beg the agency to let me stay. I'll run away and come back to live with you."

"My dear sweet, Barbara. I know you do not like change, but this one will be for the best." Renee started the car's engine and drove back to her house. Her heart broke as she listened to Barbara's sobs.

The strange car in the driveway was still there when Renee pulled in beside it. She forced herself to smile through her heartache.

"Miss Renee Bowers?" The case manager, who had been waiting beside his SUV, greeted her as Renee opened her driver's side door. My name is Charles, and this is Jenna. The lady with him stood on the other side of the SUV.

"Yes, sir, I am Renee Bowers. And this is my, this is Barbara." Renee was not sure how to introduce her. Barbara had climbed out of the car and clung to her foster mother.

"Miss Bowers, you know why I am here. It is time. Do you have this child's things packed and ready to go?"

"Not yet. And *she* has a name; it is Barbara, not *this child*. We had some errands to run this morning. I just now told her what was going on. As you can see, she does not want to go."

"You know the rules. We have a family who desires to adopt her. Therefore your services are no longer needed for this little girl. As we agreed on the phone the other day, it is time for her to come with us." The lady gave Renee a look that only she understood. It had been a part of their previous phone conversation. Renee knew there was nothing she could do to stop it.

"I know, and I understand. That is one of the drawbacks of being a foster parent. Saying goodbye is not always easy. This time it is difficult for both of us. I remind you; she is not a little girl; she is a very sweet young lady. She turned thirteen today – in case you didn't know." Renee watched as the other case manager walked around the front of the SUV.

Barbara looked up at Renee and smiled. Yes, she was a young lady now, and she realized that Renee had remembered her birthday after all. Her hopes for a party were ruined.

Renee looked at Barbara. "Honey, we need to go with this lady to your room and pack your things while I speak with this gentleman."

Barbara pulled away from her and ran into the house, slamming the front door behind her. Renee and the case managers from the agency followed.

"Barbara, I know you do not want to go with someone new. I know you feel comfortable living here with me after our years together. You knew from day one that I could only be your foster mom and nothing more. I had told you over the years that one day someone would come along and may want to adopt you."

"Yes, you did, but I never believed you! And the older I got, the more I knew no one would want an older child. I mean, who would want me? Other than you, of course." Barbara clung to her stuffed teddy bear that had been her only constant for as long as she could remember.

"I know I also told you that most people did not adopt older children. It is my fault that you took me seriously and assumed no one would want you. But, my dear, sweet child, someone does. And I think that is a blessing for you. You will no longer have to worry about moving to another family."

"I don't understand how anyone would want me."

"Oh, Barbara, you are an amazing young lady. You may not see it, but you are maturing, and this new family will help you become the person you are meant to be. I cannot do that for you."

"I don't understand. We are a team. You have been there for me since I was a little girl. Why the change?" Barbara was slowly gathering her things as she had been told to do, but the tears were still trailing down her face.

"In time, you will." That was all Renee could say. Barbara could never know the truth.

Again --- another before...

Chapter Three

The Beginning

Annie rushed to answer the door when she heard the first chime of the doorbell. She knew who she expected—the little girl who needed a new home. As a foster parent, she always looked forward to this day. The day a new needy child joined her family. She hoped she could give this one the love needed to have a better life. The agency had told her that the toddler was a four-year-old little girl named Barbara and that her parents had died in a car accident.

Opening the door, she found a little girl clinging to the social worker. Her little arms wrapped around the lady's neck. Lady held a small bag in her free hand. The bag held all of the toddler's belongings. Annie recognized this scene all too well. It saddened her each time because she understood that another child had to say goodbye to the only life she may have ever known.

Please, come in." Annie took the bag from the young lady and motioned for her to enter. Annie and her husband, Kyle, had transformed the house into a safe, comfortable, four-bedroom home, ready to accommodate up to six children if they were chosen to be foster parents for more than one at a time. It also allowed them to accept siblings. They had been through the training repeatedly and passed all the tests and home visits over the previous five years. This little girl would be their tenth toddler. They had previously fostered children ranging in age from infants to teenagers. Annie loved them all, but the toddlers held a special place in her heart. They were in such need of a caring and loving family, one that she and Kyle were more than capable and willing to provide.

"Thank you, Annie. My name is Chris, and this little one is Barbara," she said while attempting to peel the child's hand away from her neck.

Barbara let loose and turned her tear-stained face to look at Annie. Her eyes held deep sadness. Annie reached out to take her from Chris. Barbara immediately twisted away and clung tighter to the lady who had been by her side for the last twenty-four hours. The person that had made her feel safe since a stranger had informed her that her parents were gone. She did not understand what that meant but knew she had not seen her mother or father in the last few days. This nice lady had held her. Wiped her tears, fed her a hamburger and French fries, bathed her, combed her hair, and rocked her to sleep the night before.

Annie and Chris walked into the living room and sat on the light gray upholstered sofa. Barbara never let loose of Chris. The open space, illuminated by a large window facing the street, made the room inviting. An abstract area rug covering almost half of the hardwood floor complimented the furniture. Barbara loosened her grip after everyone else sat down, and she sat on her own with her leg still touching the lady's leg. She opened her eyes to look around and spotted the toy box in the corner. Chris and Annie smiled as Barbara then wiggled her way to the floor and walked to the box of toys, picking up a true-to-life baby doll dressed in an infant's pink onesie. Barbara listened to the grownups talk as she sat on the floor with her new friend, stroking the doll's hair and rocking her in her lap.

Chris talked with Annie for over an hour. They had been friends long before their foster care connection, making it easier for them to work together. Chris was confident that Annie and Kyle were the perfect couple to help Barbara. Chris explained that they did not know a lot about Barbara other than she had been dropped off with the explanation that her parents had both died and no family member wanted to take her. A man had dropped her off with a note attached to her shirt saying her name was Barbara. The man had not even stayed long enough to ask any questions. There was no further indication of who her parents had been.

Annie knew what it was like to lose both parents. Hers had died in a fire when she was a teenager. Annie had shared her story when she and Kyle applied to be foster parents. She thought her experience would benefit someone else one day. That day had arrived—again.

During their conversation, Chris and Annie sat on the floor with Barbara. They told Barbara that she would be staying there and could play with all the toys. Barbara cried when she heard that the lady who had brought her was leaving. She jumped up and wrapped her arms around Chris. Annie reached out for the toddler and helped Chris escape the child's grasp. Annie understood what the precious child was going through and planned to do all she could to help this child deal with this life change.

The door closed, and life as Barbara knew it was about to change—again.

The next morning Barbara awoke confused. She looked around the room and felt alone. Until she heard voices coming from the other part of the house. The voices she heard were of other children. Her senses woke up enough to hear laughter and what sounded like fun, so she got out of bed and opened her door. What she saw made her smile. She had not been around other children her age that were happy before. She wanted to join them but hesitated. One of the older boys came over to her and reached for her hand. "Come with me; Mom has breakfast waiting for you. Then you can come to play with us." He gently pulled Barbara into the kitchen while Annie cleaned the table of dishes and glasses.

"Ah, good morning Barbara. I see you have met Randy. He is staying with us like you are. He's been here for about six months. Randy, can you get some juice for Barbara while I make her breakfast?"

"Sure can, Ms. Annie." Randy held a chair for Barbara to sit down and walked to the refrigerator to get the juice out. He carefully watched as his new friend sat quietly, not making a sound. Randy knew Barbara would open up in her own time; they all did. He had been in foster care long enough to know how it all worked. Randy was waiting for someone to adopt him but realized that people didn't want to adopt a child as old as him. He was almost a teenager at age twelve.

In time Barbara did settle in with her foster family. She enjoyed playing with the other children. Annie took special care of each of them. Annie's husband worked hard away from home but did his best to spend time with them each evening and helped Annie around the house. It seemed like a perfect family.

Until one day, after Barbara had been living there a while, Kyle didn't return home. Barbara was busy doing things and playing around the house as she always did but sensed something was wrong. That night at the dinner table, Annie explained that Kyle had to take a job out of state, and for the time being, they would have to move into a place that her mother had so they could all stay together. None of the children understood the reason behind that, especially Barbara and the other smaller ones. Randy understood but didn't say what was on his mind. He knew Kyle was not coming back.

The next day Annie met with a case manager at the agency to talk to her. The next thing Barbara knew, Randy and two of the older children were packing their belongings and leaving with Chris, the counselor who had brought her there. Barbara ran to Randy and hugged him. They had become close while she was there, and she didn't want him

15

to leave. She relied on him to help her. She liked him. He was the first person who seemed to care about her. And then, he was gone. Just as others in her life had done—they left her.

Annie spent the rest of that day packing the belongings of Barbara and Wendy. Wendy was the only other child Annie was allowed to keep. Annie also packed her personal belongings. Barbara helped pack as much as she could for her young age. She helped even though she didn't understand what was happening. Little did she know that this moment in her life would be a pivotal moment. Again it would change her life.

Two days later, Annie loaded her car with suitcases, boxes, and two little girls and drove away from the home she had known for the last fifteen years with Kyle. She hid the tears that flowed down her cheek but never looked back.

Barbara watched the landscape change as her foster mother drove away from her beautiful home. The open fields changed to woods. The sunshine became hidden by tree branches that hovered across the road forming a tunnel. The road became curvier, requiring Annie to slow down to manage the turns. After a while, Wendy and Barbara fell asleep as Annie continued to drive. They woke up when they felt the car slow down.

Barbara spotted a creek along the road and smiled when she noticed the water cascade over a small rock, forming a miniature waterfall. She became excited when Annie slowed the car and turned into a short driveway, parking the car in front of a small single-wide trailer.

Barbara looked around as Annie got out of the car and went to the trailer to open it. Barbara unbuckled her seat belt and climbed out. She saw a swing in the front yard. Flowers were in bloom along the edging in front of the trailer. There were more flowers and bushes in a separate flower bed in the middle of the yard. She heard water flowing, and when she looked around, she saw the creek was wider there than when she had seen it earlier. It was pretty there, except for the trailer. It wasn't anything like the house they had left. It was not bad; it was not the beautiful home they had left behind.

Annie returned to the car, collected the suitcases, and invited the girls to join her inside the trailer. It was to be their home for a while.

Barbara woke up in her new bed as morning dawned. The abrupt move to the trailer had been a shock, but the bed was comfortable. She may be little, but she already knew a comfortable bed when she had one. Plus, she had a bed to herself for the first time she could ever remember.

She peeked across the room to see her foster sister, still sleeping in the other twin bed. Her bed was situated by the window. Wendy's was close to the bedroom door.

Barbara knelt on her bed and peered out the window. She watched the fog lifting from the creek as the dim light of day gave way to sunshine. Her only thought was hoping she could play in the water later.

As Barbara was daydreaming, the bedroom door opened slowly. She smiled as her foster mother walked in. Annie had been her guardian for over a year already. She had enjoyed being with her and Kyle and the other kids. Now, she wondered what was going to happen. She knew Annie wasn't happy these last few weeks. Maybe being by a creek would cheer her up.

Annie tiptoed over to Barbara's bed and sat down. She reached out to hold her little girl. Barbara scooted over and cuddled in her arms. A smile shared between them made them both feel better.

"Good morning, Little One. How did you sleep?" Annie asked.

"I like my new bed! Can I play in the creek today?" Leave it to a child to be honest about the important things in life.

17

Annie held her out from her and smiled. "We will see. We have some work to do first today."

Wendy stirred in her bed across the room and opened her eyes. She stretched, crawled out of her bed, and joined Barbara and Annie. She knew and understood it was just the three of them now, and they would have to stay close.

Annie held her two little girls against her body. This move was not what she wanted. She would have preferred to stay in her home, but it was all she had under the circumstances. She would have to make the most of it. A tear started to form. She wiped her eyes, pretending to be tired. "Time to get up and get busy today, girls. We have a lot to do. And a creek to explore." She winked at Barbara.

The girls jumped out of bed and helped Annie get up. To them, this was a new adventure, and they were going to have fun.

Annie made them breakfast of cold cereal and toast. She poured them each a small glass of orange juice. Annie frowned as she placed the orange juice back inside the refrigerator. She would have to go grocery shopping today. Their sudden move had left her little time to stock up on all the groceries she would need. The girls may be little, but they loved to eat.

A more in-depth look at the inside of the trailer and her shoulders hung low. There was a lot she had to get done. Cleaning, shopping, making the girls feel at home. The most important thing was to make this a home. She knew, with her move, that the children's case manager would be stopping by at any time. That was the risk of being a foster parent. She was always under the watchful eye of big brother. When she had Kyle helping, it was easier. Now that he was gone and she had to let the older boys go, it would not be easy. She had been fortunate to have been able to keep the girls. She shook her head. Why had she been able to keep them? She must be doing something right.

Barbara and Wendy played outside a lot in the first several days they were there. They helped Annie as much as they could, and she let them play outside for a reward. Also, to give her alone time to get more tasks completed. The little girls learned the rules for being close to the creek and their boundaries around the trailer.

One day, as the girls were playing, they noticed a boy across the road. He was outside tossing a ball against the side of his house. A few minutes later, an older man came out of the house and yelled at him. They knew he had gotten in trouble because the boy stopped playing with the ball and walked inside as the man guided him by his shoulder. The boy looked at the ground as he was escorted inside.

It wasn't until two days later that they saw the boy again. This time he was playing quietly in his front yard. Wendy and Barbara watched him from their yard and wondered if they could play together. Wendy ran inside and asked Annie if they could go across the road and play with the little boy. Annie looked out the window and permitted them to talk to him. She didn't know anything about the neighbors, but what trouble could little kids get into at that age? It was a small, almost isolated location, and Annie was not afraid of or aware of any danger.

"Hi, boy," Wendy called from the edge of her yard. "Can you come over and play on our swing?"

"I'd better not. My uncle might get mad."

"Can we come over there?" Barbara asked as she started to walk across the road.

"I guess so. At least until he sees you."

Barbara and Wendy carefully looked both ways and crossed the road. They sat on either side of the boy on the large rock in his yard. He had just been playing with a stick in the dirt but stopped when the girls approached him.

"What's your name?" Wendy asked.

"I'm Benjamin. What're your names?"

"I'm Wendy, and this is my little sister, Barbara."

"Hi. You just moved in, didn't you? I watched you from my bedroom window when you unloaded the car the other day. My uncle wouldn't let me out of the house when you moved in. Said it was best to keep our distance until he got to know you and your parents."

"It's just us two and Mom. Dad left us about a month ago, which is why we ended up here. We used to live in a nice, big house."

"We used to have two big brothers, too," Barbara added after being quiet for a moment.

"Where are your brothers?"

"They had to be returned to foster care. Mom could only take us with her," Wendy answered. She had picked up a stick and was drawing in the dirt as Benjamin was. Barbara was sitting on the ground watching her sister and this boy talk and play. Always the shy one, she usually let the older kids lead the way. At least the boy seemed older than she was, and she was shy around him for some reason.

"So, why are you here? You say you have a large house. Why not stay there?"

"We lost the house."

"How do you lose a big house?" Benjamin didn't understand that concept.

"Our Dad kept it.

Oh, so your dad left you?

"Our foster Dad did. We never knew our real father or mother."

"How can you not know them?"

"We're foster kids. Her parents died, my father left us, and my mother couldn't take care of us. So here we are."

"Sorry 'bout that."

"It's okay. We're used to it by now."

"Okay. So you're not real sisters?"

"No, only foster sisters. She's almost two years younger than me. I'm six. How old are you?"

"I'm five. I live here with David. None of the rest of my family is alive, so I have him."

"Oh, so you're a foster kid, or did he adopt you?"

"No, he didn't adopt me, although he says he will. I keep waiting. He takes good care of me, I guess. I don't know for sure."

"Do you go to the creek to play?" Barbara was ready to play. She didn't understand their need to talk so much. She wanted to play, not talk.

"I can't. I'm not allowed to go there on my own."

"You won't be alone. We're going with you," Barbara said as she stood up and started walking to the creek. "Come on; we'll all go together.

Wendy stood up and placed her little stick against the rock. Benjamin stood up and looked back toward the house where he lived. "I guess I could go for a little while. Until he misses me.

Life for Benjamin wasn't that great, but he was not about to tell these little girls. Wendy might be six years old, but she didn't look it. She looked younger. He didn't want to get either parent mad at them. He may be little, but he understood what a parent could do to a child when they misbehaved.

Together, the trio quietly walked down the dirt path to the creek.

An hour later, the kids heard their names being called. They heard Annie calling for Barbara and Wendy. Benjamin heard his uncle calling his name.

"I think we are in trouble," Benjamin said as he climbed onto the bank on the opposite side of the creek from their homes.

"I think so too. I've never heard Annie sound so mad." Wendy grabbed Barbara's hand and pulled her back across the shallow creek toward their home. She would not let Annie get any madder than she already sounded. She knew that sound all too well from her previous homes. It was never a good outcome to let the adults get that angry.

"Where are you going? You scared? What are they going to do to you?" Benjamin sounded big and brave. Inside he was the one shaking. He knew what David would do to him. Running away may be his best bet. He stood up and was walking further away when he heard Barbara scream. He turned just as he saw her fall into the creek.

Wendy grabbed for her little sister. The water was flowing faster than it had been when they first crossed. Wendy had misled them in their attempt to rush home, and they were near a deep pond. Benjamin rushed to the edge of the creek and jumped in. He swam to where Barbara was and grabbed her shirt. Pulling her to the shore and making sure her head stayed up. As he reached the safety of the shore, he looked up and saw his uncle and the woman he assumed was Annie reaching in to lift Barbara from the water and his grasp. He knew she would be safe but didn't want to let go. Something about this little girl intrigued him.

Barbara and Benjamin were about the same age from what he knew. She had dark hair as he did, and her eyes were such a shade of blue he was instantly drawn to them. He was only five, and barely that, but he was big and strong for his age. He had learned to be strong. Living with the man he called his uncle was not the easiest thing to do. And he often referred to him as David when someone asked him. There were days that he had to fight his way past him to survive. The man drank far too often and way too much. Benjamin knew that it was best to stay away from him when the man drank.

Benjamin watched as Annie wrapped her arms around the two girls. She yelled something at David and him and stomped away to the trailer. Now it was his turn to face the wrath of his uncle. What he got was not at all what he expected.

"Young man, you need to be more careful! You are big for your age, and those little girls could have drowned out there. Had it not been for you, she may have done just that. Thank you for acting so quickly. I am proud of you." The man wrapped his arm around Benjamin's shoulder and walked him slowly to their house. Benjamin just looked up at him as they walked into the living room. "Who are you?" He thought. Why was he suddenly acting so calm and, well, sober?"

Wendy and Barbara were treated to fresh towels to dry off. Annie was so angry with them that she was silent. Annie was doing her best to keep the girls safe so they would not be taken away from her, and then they took off and almost died! She was furious but didn't want the girls to know how upset she was. She wanted them to make friends. Just maybe not with the boy across the road. From what she knew about the area, though, he may be the only friend around for them to choose from.

By the next day, Annie had calmed down regarding her girls and her decision to ban them from seeing the little boy next door. He had been the one to save Barbara, and she would be forever grateful for that. She would have to talk to Benjamin's father. They had both been so upset about their children the day before that they had only exchanged names. The man's name was David.

Annie saw David working in his yard early the next afternoon. She took a deep breath and walked across the road. She still blamed him and Benjamin for her girls walking off her property. The fear of losing them had been unimaginable.

"Hi, David. How are you today?" Annie asked in a calm voice. She hid her anger well.

David looked up and saw Annie. He blinked and took a deep breath. "Hi, Annie. Are the girls alright? That was such a scare yesterday. I made sure I punished Benjamin for it."

"It may not have been all his fault. My girls asked if they could play in the creek when we moved here, and they saw it. They may have innocently invited him, telling him they were allowed to play there."

"I appreciate you trying to take the blame away from him. He is only five and just turned five not long ago, even though he is big for his age. And he already likes to break all the rules he can since he's been with me."

"Benjamin isn't your son?"

"No, I have guardianship of him ever since his parents died."

"So sorry about his parents. Are you a family member? I only ask because I am a foster parent to those two girls, and neither have any living relatives. You said guardianship, not foster, so I assume you are related."

"Yes, his father was my brother. It was a tragic day when both his parents died. No one can prepare for that."

"No, they can't. I have had other foster children in my life, and some of their stories and circumstances are so sad. I do my best to love them all, but I can only do so much. So far, all of those I have fostered have gone on to be adopted. These two will be soon, too, I'm sure."

"You are amazing to do that with so many kids. My wife and I had a hard time with just this one."

"Oh, is your wife here with you? I have not seen her."

"No, soon after Benjamin arrived to live with us, she walked out. She wanted to have her own biological children and could not handle raising my brother's child. She never did like that man, and she said the child would remind her of him all the time. I don't understand that from her. She won't explain it further, so I finally let it drop. She's already married to someone else. Sorry, I get carried away sometimes when someone asks me about her. I still love her, you know. We had a good life together, but she couldn't handle the family connection I had with my

24

brother. He would have done the same thing for me if the roles had been reversed. I know he would have."

"I understand. Blood relatives have a connection like no other, for the most part. Some don't get along."

"So, what is your story? Why in the world did you move into that trailer? The woman who owned it just up and left one day. No one has been here to take care of it since."

Annie shook her head. "That woman is my mother. Don't apologize for your comment. I agree with how you feel. I was shocked when she packed up and left it and moved across the country. She said she needed a change and that if I ever needed a place to stay, just come here. I am not in touch with her often, but I did manage to call her when I needed a place. She said to come and take it over."

"So that woman was your mother? Wow. Someday I will learn to keep my mouth shut from voicing my opinions without more information."

"Don't be silly. You didn't know. Now, for the rest of my story of why I needed to move here. My husband walked out on the kids and me. I had to give the older boys back to the agency as I could not house all the kids. I am lucky they let me keep the two girls. In time I am sure I will lose them too. I mean, look at that place." Annie pointed to the trailer and the yard that was in disrepair. There was so much work to be done; she had no idea how to get it all cleaned up before the girl's case manager visited her.

"I can help you clean it up. Even Benjamin can help some. Even if it is to play with the girls and keep them out of our way."

"Thank you, David, but that is not necessary."

"I insist. Tomorrow I will come over, and you can show me what needs to be done."

"Okay, it may be more than you are willing to tackle. I'm warning you. And you are free to quit on me at any time. I spent many years standing alone and doing things for myself before I met and married Kyle. That may be why they let me keep the girls. They know I can do the job and love them if nothing else."

"You are some strong woman. I'll give you that. Tell you what. First thing tomorrow morning, we will be over to see what all needs to be done. You have coffee ready and maybe juice for the boy, and we will get busy.

Chapter Four

Memories

Barbara sat in her dining room, enjoying a cup of coffee. She knew something was up the moment she opened her eyes that morning. It took a sip of her favorite hot morning beverage to realize the date.

She raised her left hand to her right eye to stop a tear falling down her cheek. Today was an anniversary—one of the many she had experienced during her early childhood years. This one was the one that changed her life forever.

The memories of all she had endured rushed in, crowding her mind. All those goodbyes. All the tears and anger, the insecurities that took over with daily fears every time she saw a strange car pull up and park nearby or an unexpected phone call. Here she was, anticipating another goodbye, as she always did when life seemed to be going well.

Barbara shook her head to clear her mind after taking the last sip of still-hot coffee. She placed the empty mug inside the dishwasher and closed the door. She walked down the hall and into her bedroom to get dressed and ready to face whatever the day brought. She knew her plans but realized those could change instantly. Her life had been full of sudden changes.

Instead of getting ready for the day, she lay back down on her bed. Thoughts, memories, and sadness engulfed her and flung her toward a state of depression—again.

Today was going to be a special day. She had chosen this date so that this date in the future would be a happy memory. Today, she was marrying Joshua. She closed her eyes and tried to smile, envisioning her happy and perfect future.

She fell asleep as tears dampened her pillow. She never heard the doorbell chime. Or was that part of her memories?

Chapter Five

Something Missing

Barbara awoke to the aroma of fresh flowers. She opened her eyes and saw the beautiful bouquet arranged in an etched crystal vase sitting on her nightstand. Red roses, white carnations, and baby's breath were intermixed with various greenery. She smiled as she eased herself up to sit in her bed. She wiped her eyes and remembered her tears as she had accidentally fallen asleep the night before.

There, waiting for her at the foot of her bed, was Steven, her loving husband she still considered her groom. He walked to her side of the bed and reached for her hand. Steven gently pulled her up and hugged her close, and as she stood in his embrace, she knew he would never let her go. Knowing this eased any fears she had.

An argument earlier had sent him out the door, causing Barbara to fear the worst. All her life, people continued to leave her. She felt that someday it would happen again and that even her husband would walk away at some point. Yet, here he was—holding her in his arms with a gentle grip that said it would be okay and he was not leaving. She felt loved. Felt happy and her tears this time were of joy, contentment, and love as he calmly spoke to her.

"I am so sorry for the harsh words I said earlier. I knew they were harmful as soon as I uttered them. I realized too late the memories they would evoke. I walked away to give you time to think. I knew, at that moment, you would not welcome an instant apology because you had heard them all your life. Walking out on you was also stupid of me. Too many others have walked out on you, and they never returned. I was not going to be another one. You know I will never leave you."

Barbara watched his eyes as he spoke. She felt him gently holding her hands and listened with fear as he continued. She knew more promises were coming. Could she believe anything he said? He had never lied to her, but he had never walked out on her before either.

"Barbara, I want you to know that I am committed to you and us. It is best to walk away for a brief time to gather my thoughts so that I don't say something that I will regret. It does not mean that I am running away from you or leaving you alone as many others have. I love you. I hope you know that and believe that I will stay by your side through thick and thin and forever."

She smiled as she leaned in and met his kiss. She trusted him. She loved him, and she finally felt safe and secure with him in her life. She understood him.

Several years earlier, when they had first met, she had no thoughts of trusting him further than she could have thrown him. He was just another man to her—one that eventually would leave. He was a man who was not worthy of her trust. She certainly had no intentions of falling in love! He was simply a guy to spend time with along with her other friends as they all went out in groups. Then one of her girlfriends suggested she take a step out of her comfort zone and ask him out on a real one-on-one date. She was hesitant, but the more she thought about it, the more she thought it was a good idea. What harm could there be in simply asking? From that first official date on, they were inseparable. They were married two years later. She doubted she would ever tell him it had not been her idea to ask him out.

There were a few times during their early marriage when they disagreed on something or when Steven raised his voice that reminded her of her marriage to Joshua.

Joshua had known Barbara since she joined his foster family. They had become fast friends as young kids, and by their late teens, they realized it was more. They loved each other. They were not related; they had spent several years growing up together. They were so close it was obvious they would fall in love and marry one day. No one questioned it.

Soon after they married, Barbara noticed a change in Joshua. He no longer was the fun-loving person she had known for so many years. They tried to work things out, even attending marriage counseling. Then Joshua told her one day that for both their sakes, he was leaving. She sensed he realized he was not good for her and had abused her. At least he realized that he needed to get away and keep her safe—from him. She did not understand how he could leave her when he knew the pain of people walking out of his life as they had done hers during each of their years in foster care. As much as she hated him for leaving, she eventually accepted and was grateful that he had walked away instead of abusing her more.

However, he was just another person who left her at the time. Maybe she would be better off if she just accepted life independently. Maybe there was something about her. Maybe she was the one causing everyone to leave.

Then Steven came into her life and changed that thought.

Again, she was having doubts, but Steven quickly erased them from her mind. He was good to her. He made her happy. Her friends even noticed a sparkle in her eye that had never been there before.

Steven took his wife's hand and guided her into the kitchen, where he had breakfast waiting for her. She sat down and accepted a fresh cup of coffee from him. Laying next to her plate was an envelope. She looked up at her husband with a curious look and asked what it was.

"Open it," he said as he sat down in the chair next to her and sipped his coffee.

Barbara opened the envelope and took out the formal-looking letter.

"Dear Mrs. Howard,

My name is Randall Williams, an attorney in East Tennessee. I have been doing some family research for a client of mine, which has led me to you. If it is at all possible, I would like to meet with you at your earliest convenience to discuss my findings.

The only thing I am at liberty to say in this letter is that it concerns your biological family history. It is information that I am sure you will appreciate hearing.

Please get in touch with me at the phone number or email listed below to schedule a time for us to meet.

Thank you for your time. I am looking forward to meeting with you and your husband.

Randall Williams, ESQ."

Barbara looked up at Steven and handed him the letter. When she looked at his face, she realized that somehow he knew what the letter said and grabbed it back before he had time to finish reading it.

"Something tells me you know what this is all about. Do you?" She held the letter up to him.

"I might. What does it say?" Steven tried to act innocent.

Barbara handed the letter back to him and took another drink of her coffee. She was curious what this Randall person could be talking about. What could he possibly know about her past? Who was his client? And why now?

Steven read the letter and then knew it was time to tell the love of his life what he had been up to over the last few months. He set the letter down on the table.

"Yes, I knew the letter was coming. I did not know when, but I knew it was in the works." He watched Barbara for her reaction. When she continued to stare at him motionless, he continued.

"You see, when we began seeing each other, I knew something was missing in your life. You smiled, there was a light in your eye, but there was a darkness hidden behind both. Your eyes had a light but no sparkle. Your smile formed, but not automatically. I started to ask you about your past, and when you finally started to open up and share that with me, I knew I had to do something to bring back the joy that I was certain had been there at one point. I don't know how long ago that was, but you must have been happy at some point in your life."

"I am happy, Steven. You are correct that it has taken me a long time to find happiness again, but I found it in you." Barbara rebutted. She reached over and touched his arm.

"Yes, you seem happy, but I still saw the darkness and wanted to try to fix it for you. I took the liberty to contact as many people leading back into your past as I legally could."

"How? I thought all those details were confidential?"

"Most of the records are. But I found a few people willing to take the risk and offer help. Some took a risk with their jobs to help me help you. They had a strong connection to you and still think about you."

"That is hard to believe. How could anyone still love me? More so, how could I love a lot of them? So many of them treated me horribly over the years. Promises they were unable to keep. Emotions they refused to show. And a couple were downright mean and were only after the money."

"I did get that impression from a few of them and had to retract and try a different tactic. In the end, Mr. Williams connected the dots, going as far back as possible. I think you are going to appreciate what he has found out."

"What has he found out?"

"I think we need to contact him and set up an appointment for him to come here to tell you what information he has. All I know is that he has made a connection. He has not given me any other details."

"Okay. I hope it is something good. You wouldn't let anything bad come my way, would you? You know so much about my past; I am not sure I could handle something negative ruining what happiness I have had in you."

"No, I won't let anything bad come near you." He reached over and put his arms around her shoulders. He had heard enough about her past that he certainly did not want Randall, or anyone, bringing more bad news to bring her into depths of depression.

Chapter Six

Information

The doorbell chimed, and Steven walked to the front door and let Attorney Williams inside. He and Barbara had been waiting for him ever since their discussion a couple of weeks earlier, prompted by Mr. William's letter. He led Mr. Williams to the living room, then went to get his wife, who was busy in the kitchen.

Barbara was anxious to meet this stranger who seemed to know about her life. She had so much family history in her past that his information could be about anything. Good news? Bad news? What else could go wrong with her family background? She had finally put most of it behind her and did not think about most of it anymore.

Barbara offered Mr. Williams a cup of coffee or water to drink. He accepted a cup of coffee, adding that he took it black. He was not planning to stay too long but knew it was always polite to accept a beverage when offered at someone's home.

Barbara suggested they sit at the dining room table to talk. Steven carried the mugs of coffee while Barbara carried a plate of homemade cookies to enjoy while they spoke. Randall found it impossible to resist a warm chocolate chip cookie.

When they all sat down, Barbara began the conversation, getting directly to the point of his visit. "What information do you have? Is it good news or bad news? If you know my family history at all, you know I am prepared for just about anything." She reached for Steven's hand to hold. She wanted the security of the best thing that had ever happened in her life—her husband.

"Mrs. Howard, the news I have for you is something that I do not think you are aware of. I have documentation that indicates that you were taken to an orphanage when you were an infant," he began.

"Yes, that is true, I was taken to an orphanage, but I was a toddler at the time. You see, my parents died in a car wreck. I went through several foster homes and finally was adopted many years later." Barbara corrected him. "Sorry, I just want the true story to be stated."

"That is fine. Whatever age you were at the time, it has come to my attention that there is more to your story and your family history. As an attorney who works closely with family situations on legal matters and my newest client, I have discovered valuable details that involve you. It involves the time before being placed in the orphanage."

"Before being placed into the orphanage? What have you found? I have searched over the years for more information and found nothing. I've always felt there was more to know. There was always an empty feeling deep inside, you know?"

"I have heard that similar story from other adoptive families over the years. Adoptions were not my normal practice, but I did handle enough to become familiar with the adoptee's emotions."

"I have always felt there was a missing piece in my life. Not just a fact that both my parents died in that car accident, and I never knew them. It is more of a feeling of a missing physical piece in my life. Like there was someone else in my life before that frightful day of the accident."

"And that, Mrs. Howard, is what I have news about." Randall reached into his briefcase and pulled out a file.

"Please, call me Barbara. Not many people call me by my married name. I like a more personal touch, even from strangers."

"Barbara, it is."

Randall opened the file and pulled out the top paper. He handed it to the beautiful lady who sat in front of him with wide-open eyes as a child expecting a long-awaited and requested Christmas gift.

"This paper indicates that you have a brother."

Barbara took the paper and gazed at it. She looked up at Randall, then at Steven. Her eyes were wide in disbelief. She looked back down at the paper in her hand. She could not read a single word of the typed print. Her eyes had instantly swelled in tears when she heard the word, *brother*.

"I have a what?" Barbara wiped the tears that had automatically started to flow down her cheeks. Had she heard correctly?

"You have a brother. His name is Ben. He is not only your brother—he is your twin brother."

"A twin? How is that possible? Why did I not know this until now?"

"Barbara, at the time of your parent's death, your brother was in the car with them, but you were not. For whatever reason, you were with your aunt at the time. So when the accident happened, the rescue squad never looked for you to begin with as there was no indication of another person. However, your aunt never came forward during that time to tell others about the connection. No one said a word about you during that time, nor since."

"How could other friends and family not know another child was involved in the family?" Steven asked. He was all ears even more than Barbara was. This news was fascinating.

"For that, we do not have an answer. And we may never have an answer. We found this out only because the relative passed away and left this information in the papers with her will in the bank vault. I was the one who handled her last will and testament but had no idea about what other papers she put into the folder before placing them into the bank vault. Her will only specified that there were other important documents included. I never question my clients about what other items they include separately."

Barbara's eyes had cleared enough for her to read the paper. After reading the first paragraph to herself, she started over again and read it aloud. Her husband deserved to know what was going on as much as she did. She temporarily forgot Randall or even Steven were in the room, also listening.

To whom it may concern,

I write this letter with a sound mind and spirit mixed with sorrow and apology. It has come that time, albeit possibly far too late, for me to admit what some might call a crime that I committed. I do not think it is punishable by death, although my death has occurred if you are reading this letter that was left with my will.

You see, many years ago, my sister asked me to babysit her little girl while she and her husband took their son, Ben, on an errand of some sort. I honestly do not remember what the purpose of the trip was. While they were driving, they were involved in a car accident, and my sister and her husband died instantly. Ben survived, but with no information about him, he was immediately placed with children's services. I heard about the accident on the news. I knew there would be an investigation. I also knew what I should have done. But I didn't. I packed up my niece, who I named Barbara, and ran. I ran to another state. Far enough away to be in hiding. Close enough to keep in the loop the news provided. I learned that

Ben was placed with his uncle, David. David had not been in touch with the family for many years and barely knew his family because of it. All the information he received was that he was Ben's only living relative that they could find, and since he was blood, it was best to be together. There was never a connection made to little Barbara or me for whatever reason.

I know you are already asking why I did not contact the authorities of David. Here is where the crime might have occurred. I was selfish. I always had been when it came to my sister. I envied her for everything she ever got that was right in this world, and I always felt like I got the shaft, so to speak. She had everything. I had nothing.

The day she died, I cried, but it was tears of joy because I now had possession of something that was hers, and I was not about to let it go. I was going to keep Barbara all to myself. No one was going to find us or find out about us.

A day after the horrific accident, I packed up all that I could fit into my car, strapped Barbara into the back seat, and drove away. I planned to stay away. But a few years later, I was broke with no home and no place to go. I panicked again with no family except Barbara and no light at the end of the tunnel I had worked myself into. I returned to her birthplace and placed her on the steps of an orphanage. I knew she was still young enough that they would take her in and care for her. The only information I *left was her name and a close birthdate, but not exactly her real one. I did not want her to be traced to me or to that horrible day she lost everything. I hoped her few years with me would be the ones she remembered with happiness.*

I know now that it all was a BIG mistake. A lie I had lived with all the rest of my life. And a secret I have told no one— until now.

I kept track of Ben over the years from a great distance. He has done well for himself despite the heartache of childhood. He found a wonderful girl to love, and last I knew, he is the father of two adorable little boys.

I hope that this information I provide will help you, Barbara, find your long-lost brother. I don't know how he will react to the knowledge that he has a sister, but I hope that in time, and when you meet, you can not only become close like you should have been all your lives but that somehow, somewhere, deep in your hearts you both can forgive me. If that is not the case, I completely understand. I know that it has weighed heavily on my heart for most of my adult life, and I regret having done it.

Barbara, Ben lives in the great state of Tennessee. He lives and works at Bella Rose Estate, which his wife's family owns. His wife, Heather, and he have two boys, Marc and Maddex.

I hope and pray that you can locate him and create a bond. I am so sorry for contributing to all the sadness in your life. I

have followed you over the years as well.
Even after my life turned around for the
better and I could have reached out to you, I
knew it was too late, and you were much
better off not knowing about me. I do regret
not being able to tell you about your family.
Please, if you can, forgive me.
I've always loved you…
even though I had no right
Jane

Barbara turned the paper over, looking for more. There was no more to the letter. Underneath the letter was her original birth certificate with a sticky note on top. Barbara placed the letter aside and picked up the document, carefully lifting the sticky note.

Barbara looked closely at the birth certificate.

Name: Beverly Ann Kane
Parents: Benjamin Thomas Kane and Jean Kane
Date of Birth: August 17, 1975
Place of Birth: Asheville, NC

Barbara stared at the paper. "My name is Beverly Ann," she said matter of factually. "I knew I never felt comfortable with the name Barbara but never realized there would be a reason for it."

She stood as if transfixed and walked to the front window. Just then, the antique grandfather clock in the hallway chimed at two o'clock. She jumped when it began and brought herself back to reality. She walked back to her chair.

"So, now what do I do? What can I do? Do you know how I can locate this Ben person? My brother—twin brother?"

Randall had been listening to her as she read the letter. He was almost as shocked as she was. It was justified for her to be in shock. Who wouldn't be? But he was also stunned by the detail of it. It was such a small world. He took a deep breath.

"Barbara, or maybe I should call you Beverly Ann. I have more news."

"No, please continue to call me Barbara. I may not have always liked it, but it will take me a while to get used to the other name if I ever use it."

"Barbara. You may not believe this, then again, with all that you just found out, this may not be a shock to hear. But, I know not only where Ben is, I know him." He stopped talking while it sank into Barbara's thoughts.

"What do you mean, you know him? You know of him since you know where he lives?"

"No, I personally know Ben. I know him and his family quite well." Randall took a deep breath, stood up, and began to pace.

"You see, all those details of who he is and who his family is….leads me to believe Ben is none other than my brother-in-law." Randall stopped talking.

"Your brother-in-law? How?"

"I know that Ben had been searching for his family members or anyone who could tell him about the day he lost his parents. He has been searching for years. Although he has not been searching for any siblings, he has been searching for his father. Ben is the client I mentioned earlier.

"Why would he be searching for his father? If he is my twin brother, our father died at the same time our mother died—in that car wreck."

"That's just it. Ben thinks his, rather your, father is still alive."

"What would make him think such a thing? Wasn't it a fact that he died at the scene?"

"Well, from what I recall him talking about, Ben can remember his mother going from screaming to silence all those years ago, but he never recalls his father being in the car, nor how he died. He said he doesn't remember going to the funeral of either of them. He admits he was young, and it might be that he was too young to picture the funeral or that the people who were caring for him at the time didn't take him."

"I certainly do not remember any funeral. I was not even along for the ride that day for some reason."

"That reason was so you could be with me," Steven said quietly to her as he put his arm around her shoulders. "You were meant to be here today. And even though we might never know why it took so long to reconnect, this might be the perfect timing to find your brother."

"Brother. I have a brother out there somewhere." Barbara smiled as her eyes drifted into space and an imagination no one else could see. A longing no one else could feel or know she was feeling. Another feeling of goodbye. Again one she had no control over. Maybe this time, there would be a goodbye to all her goodbyes. She thought it had come when she found Steven. Maybe this was another one to show her that life can be good after all. One just had to live through a lot of pain sometimes first. That made the joys and happiness all the more powerful and amazing.

Chapter Seven

Anticipation

The house was quiet. Barbara sat alone, staring at the photograph of the distant mountains. She could not believe the beauty of the place in the picture. A tear fell from her eye. She was about to meet her brother. A sibling she never knew she had until a couple of months earlier.

Steven had been by her side every step of the way. He wanted her to be happy and knew that this connection would make her life complete and would give her a feeling of belonging that she never had, even with him in her life. He always sensed something was missing. Ben was the missing piece. Steven was so glad he had done the research and found his wife's connection. Seeing her face when she discovered that she had a brother and a family was priceless. It was worth all the things he had kept from his wife. It was worth every suspicion she had about him while he was so secretive. It had not been easy to pull off. They normally talked and shared everything.

Barbara and Steven had spent the few weeks after Randall's visit mentally preparing for meeting Ben. They had sent word to Ben through Randall, as he requested they call him, due to his family connection. The message was brief. Barbara had decided to keep it simple and let this man, who might be her brother, know that she wanted to at least talk with him. She would see how that went before she agreed to meet him in person.

Steven did not quite understand why she was cautious but did not push her to meet this stranger. The more he thought about it over the next several days, the more he thought he understood. His beautiful wife had been hurt enough in her life. Everyone she had met and had taken the time to get to know, love, and trust had walked out of her life. Everyone that was, except him. He, Steven Howard, was not about to walk away. He was in for life. His life or her life, it did not matter. He made a vow to her on their wedding day and to himself even before he proposed that he was not stepping away from her no matter what hardship came their way.

Ben had immediately responded with a few details about his life that he hoped would ease her mind and to at least think they were siblings. He knew he was not one hundred percent sure, but this finding had been the closest he had ever come, and it was worth the effort to find out for sure. He knew he could be disappointed in the end, but it was a risk he was willing to take.

Barbara read his email response and sent him a few more questions. Once Ben answered those, Barbara told Steven that she was ready to meet with Ben. The man who could be her missing link.

Steven called his travel agent, and they made arrangements to make the short trip. Car rental and all. If he thought it would be more impressive, he would have hired a driver, but he did not want to be overbearing to this family—after all, his wife had come from a humble if not difficult beginning. It was he who had made something of his life and could afford just about anything they wanted. His wife, however, never wanted to flaunt what they could have and enjoyed living a modest, comfortable life.

Barbara and Ben sent a few extra emails to each other and agreed to meet.

The highway carried them into a new world where she would meet her brother. Steven hoped it would change his wife for the better and make her happy. How could it not be a positive experience? An adventure back in time. A breakthrough of a life that was, one that could have been, and one that may be in the future. It was all going to be up to Barbara and Ben to make it be whatever it was meant to be.

Steven glanced at his wife from time to time as he drove along the highway for the last twenty-five miles. He could only imagine what was on her mind. He dared not ask her for fear of taking her out of her zone. Early on in their relationship, he had learned when she looked the way she did as they drove that it was best to let her be in that state for a while. It was not always a good state for her to be in, but she most often needed to experience it. She later would reveal what she had been thinking or what she had been reliving inside her mind. Although he knew there were other times he didn't notice the mesmerizing look, he accepted that he never knew what was on her mind. It was more than a man not understanding a woman. His dilemma was not about understanding where her mind went, and he was smart enough not to ask.

After several hours, traffic jams, and a few short stops along the way, Barbara and Steven arrived at a small inn named Walton's Inn. The inn was named in memory of the man who was the first to arrive in this little area. After just stopping to look around at the beauty it offered from all directions, this man called this place home. Mr. Walton helped build the beginning of what had become a stopping spot in the south. It was now home to many who cherished the area and learned to preserve the beauty. It was a quaint town with people who honored its history and where they cherished their neighbors.

Their room overlooked the valley below. The sunset that met them was breathtaking. Barbara thought that if the beauty were any indication of what was to come, she would never forget this time in her life. She hoped it was half of what she dreamed it would be. Even half of what she dreamed would be more than she expected.

Ben was sitting at home as the miles had clicked away for Steven and Barbara. He could not believe his luck finding the missing piece to his life. At least part of it. A piece he had not even been searching for, a piece that he didn't know existed. He had been searching for a missing parent; instead, he found a sister he didn't know he had.

He would continue the search for his family until he found the truth. He hoped what he suspected would be true. It was also his biggest fear. It was finding this woman who could be his sister; that was a bonus. He hoped that she had some answers to his questions. From what he briefly knew of her, she knew less than he did about the details of their separation.

Then there was the dread that she was not the answer he needed. Ben shook his head and looked at the clock. He took a deep breath. His sister would soon be at her first stop before they met the next day. He had the urge to drive out to meet her when she arrived but realized that could jeopardize their relationship.

Heather came into the room and saw Ben staring out the front window. "You know that she is not coming until tomorrow. Staring out the window won't help bring her here faster," Heather walked up behind him and put her arms around him. She loved doing this to him. It was nice when they hugged each other, but her tender touch of loving him in this way meant a lot to both of them. It was a silent passion, full of love without saying it in so many words. She had begun doing it after they reunited after the car accident that almost ended their marriage so many years earlier. She smiled as she sensed his love for her in return when he placed his hands on hers and held them firmly in his. He smiled as he brought his mind back to the present, feeling the love from his wife. She was the best thing in his life. Finding his sister would still be a close second.

Chapter Eight

The Meeting

The next morning's drive to Bella Rose Estate did not take long from Walton Inn. The small town led quickly to the main road and included a picturesque view of the mountains and pastures. The life of the large city was long forgotten here. Peaceful and calm were more of what lay around them. Barbara smiled as they drove. For some reason, she felt at home.

Steven turned onto the driveway of Bella Rose Estate. The road was lined with rose bushes and trees. A rustic fence, the length of the driveway helped support the roses and other plants. Steven slowed the car to almost a stop and asked Barbara if she was ready to meet her brother and the rest of her family.

"Yes, I am more than ready. It has been far too long. I should have never been kept from Ben. Now is our chance to be a real family. At least it is my chance. I know he already has a family, and I have you and your family, but there is just something about having a brother. I realize I don't even know him yet, and he could be someone I don't want to know, but from our correspondence, and then with what Randall said, I think it is all good."

"Okay, here we go. The last chance for you to change your mind."

"No, I'm good. I've waited long enough for this."

As Steven turned the last curve to the manor, they saw people sitting on the front porch. As their car reached the parking area, Barbara watched as one person stood up and took a few steps away from the others. She saw his smile and instantly knew that it was Ben. That man, standing tall, with a wide smile, was her brother! She was almost out of the car before Steven brought it to a stop.

Ben stood still and watched as a beautiful, tall lady with dark red hair walked toward him. He knew that was his sister. His smile grew as he walked down the steps to meet her. A slow walk was the furthest thing from either of their minds. Ben and Barbara rushed toward each other and fell into a hug as neither had ever had. Tears flowed down their cheeks. After several minutes they pulled away and looked at each other in silence with the biggest smiles.

Steven had remained near his car to let his wife and Ben greet each other. When they separated, he walked to the steps to meet him. Ben's family also stood back and waited. This moment was for the siblings, not them.

Ben reached for his sister's hand as Steven caught up with them. "You must be my brother-in-law." He continued to hold Barbara's hand as he reached out and hugged him. "Thank you for bringing her to me." A tear slipped down his cheek as he looked again at her.

"It is my pleasure to meet you and my honor to bring the two of you together." Steven hugged Ben, then pulled away as the rest of Ben's family had joined them, and it became one big group hug complete with tears and everyone talking at once.

The family group gradually found their way to separate, and everyone walked to the porch floor and the manor. Barbara was still in awe of it all and could not stop looking at her brother. Her mind was trying to figure out what he looked like as a child but could not remember him at all from that age. They had grown up together for a few years, but being pulled apart so young had left her with few memories. She hoped Ben would remember more than she did.

As was the family's way, Sara led them all into the kitchen to sit around the island. She knew a full tour of the place would be later. For now, it was time for excited chatter and indulging in fresh coffee and Andy's famous chocolate chip cookies. As Andy poured the coffee for everyone, he smiled at that chatter he heard and remembered the sound from when he had returned home as the prodigal son.

As they began to sip coffee and nibble on the cookies, everyone stopped talking, and the room fell silent. For the first time in thirty minutes, no one had any words. They were all looking at Ben and Barbara. When Ben asked what everyone was looking at, he was met with Heather grabbing a mirror from a drawer close by and turning it so Ben and Barbara could see for themselves. There was no denying it—they were twins.

Each sibling had a birthmark above their left eye that faded into their eyebrow. Each had a dimple in their right cheek and had the same eyes and nose shape. What didn't reveal itself in the mirror was that they both stood the same way, held their coffee mugs the same, and took their coffee the same way—black.

After dinner, Ben and Barbara separated themselves from the rest of the family. Ben took his sister for a walk along the trail below the manor. The path led them to an overlook, revealing beautiful mountains in the distance and a deep valley below. While they walked, they talked. They knew little about each other, but each sensed an instant connection that only twins have. Even those that have never spent time together. Ben felt it was something deeper than that.

"This area is beautiful! You have been blessed." Barbara said as they stood at the edge, looking out.

"Yes, I have been blessed, but I always felt something was missing. Have you ever felt that way?"

"All my life. Most of my memories are not good memories. I am even sure some things I have been through I have blocked from my thoughts. I remember that every time I turned around since I was a little girl and my, or our,

52

parents died, I had to stand alone. People always left me. I felt like I was the reason they left. I was the reason no one wanted me. I was damaged goods. At least that is what I thought for most of my life until Steven entered my life and changed everything."

"I am glad you have Steven. I was blessed when I found Heather too. She has kept me sane all these years. Well, for the most part. There was a time when things were not going well for us, but I came to my senses and made things right. During that time in my life, I realized something was missing or something was not right with my past. I could feel it."

Ben and Barbara had turned from looking at the mountains and were looking at each other.

"I was the same way. I always thought it was the fact that being in all the foster homes made me feel like an outcast and that I had no family that loved me. When I was adopted, I felt more loved, but I still felt something was missing. I never dreamed it was the fact that I had a brother! When did you find out you were not alone? That you had a biological family?"

"It was during my therapy sessions around the time I had walked out on my wife. I had breakthroughs that had nothing to do with my marriage through talking with Joe. Joe helped me bring those to light, and from there, he, and my family, helped me search for the truth."

Ben and Barbara began to walk back to the manor as the sun was setting. He wanted to take her to the gazebo to sit and watch the beauty of the sunset. A scene that Ben had enjoyed for several years. Now he could share it with his sister.

Barbara watched her brother lead the way. She was mesmerized by him. He looked so familiar. It was more than the fact that they were twins. There was just something about him that reminded her of a different time in her life. She could not pinpoint it. She had lived so many places, met so many people, and had many foster brothers and sisters over the years. There was no way to know if she had ever met him. Plus, how could she have? They lived in different worlds. He had been raised by one family and into one lifestyle. She had been raised in another for most of her life. She had lived in nice homes and not-so-nice homes. She lived with good people and not such good people. Each one had taught her something new, and each one had shown her different aspects of life and living. When she met Steven, all the good in life came to the forefront, and he had given her the best life she had ever imagined or dared to have dreamed of. She had been happy. And now, a dream she had never imagined was unfolding before her.

"Are you coming?" Ben asked as he looked back and noticed Barbara had fallen back.

"Oh, yes, sorry, I was just in never-never land. I was thinking, as I tend to do too much sometimes. Do you ever get lost in your thoughts?" she said as she caught up with him.

"Often. It's easy to do here with these views. I come here almost every day when the weather is nice and sit for a while and watch the world go past. My mind is often in never, never land."

The two of them sat down on the bench inside the gazebo. In silence, they watched the last rays of the sun fall to the earth and the light of the moon's glow show in the sky.

As they walked back to the manor, they began to talk again. "Do you have any good memories from your childhood?" Ben asked.

"Yes, one I do remember started as a bad experience but turned out okay for a while. Before being adopted, especially before Steven, most of my life was a mixture of good times and bad. I assume most people's lives are that way. I would hope that no one has a life that is all bad. There are good things along the way in every life situation.

Or at least there was in my life. What about your life? Good and bad?"

"Yes, I had mostly good. There were a few bad times along the way, but time and therapy took care of those. Tell me about the bad that turned to good."

"That is a long story. I will save it for another day. Your family may be wondering where we are, and Steven may be driving them nuts."

"Ha! It is more like my family driving him nuts." They both laughed and were laughing when they entered the kitchen of the manor.

"Where have the two of you been? Not that we were worried or anything." Sara said as she heard the door open.

"First, we walked the path to the overlook, and then I took my sister to watch the sunset at the gazebo. Have all of you driven Steven crazy yet?"

"They have not," Steven replied. "I have enjoyed getting to know my wife's family." He walked over to Barbara and put his arm around her. "I did miss you, though."

"I missed you too, but it's been fun to get to know my brother. And by start, I mean that. We have a lot of catching up to do." Barbara reached out and took Ben's hand. "He is my missing piece."

Ben put his arm around his sister. She was his missing piece, too. She was also right; they had a lot of catching up to do.

It was late, and everyone agreed it was time to call it a night. Steven and Barbara said their farewells and headed back to Walton Inn for the night. They were going to meet the rest of the family at the manor for brunch the next day.

Barbara could not sleep that night after she met Ben. There was something about him. It felt like more than the fact that he was her twin. Every time she closed her eyes, she visualized watching him walk towards the gazebo. What was it about him? What memory did it conjure up? She finally fell asleep, and in her dream, she saw it.

Chapter Nine

Small World

Steven woke early to find Barbara sitting on the back deck of their room, looking over the pond. He noticed the peaceful beauty of the calm waters and heard the birds singing from the branches in the trees and the frogs croaking from the pond. The sun was beginning to shine in the sky. It was going to be another beautiful day. He knew she had not slept well and could tell by her stance that she was deep in thought. He returned to the apartment and started the coffee pot. He would leave her alone for a little while longer. He smiled as he watched her.

Her beauty showed to all who noticed her. Yet, she was a troubled soul deep inside, and he knew it. He had known it from the moment he met her. Her blue eyes still held a look of longing. One that he could not erase, no matter how hard he had tried over the years. He wanted to make her life perfect. He had always wanted the best for her. Now, he hoped some of that would change. Locating her brother may have been the answer. The coffee pot beeped and brought him back to the present. He poured two mugs of fresh coffee and walked out to join Barbara.

He handed her a mug and her eyes refocused on the present moment. Briefly, he noticed her distant gaze. One he had seen many times before. The lost look meant she was searching. Searching deep inside or out into the universe for answers. He wondered what had drawn her so far away this time.

"Good morning, my love," Steven said as he said down.

"Good morning, Love. Thank you for the coffee. I could certainly use it this morning."

"I noticed you didn't sleep well last night. Too excited to sleep?"

"No. It was more than that." She took a sip of the hot coffee. "I sensed something about Ben yesterday almost as soon as I met him. Later, when we walked to the gazebo, I watched him walk in front of me, and that sense grew more intense. I could not put my finger on it at the time, but I think I have figured something out." She took another sip and was quiet.

"What is it? Something good or something bad?"

"I'm not sure. It could be either one if I am correct. Maybe more sad or even cruel if my assumptions prove true."

"Oh, this sounds intriguing. What is it?" Steven sat up taller and leaned toward Barbara.

"I need to talk to Ben about it." She reached over and touched Steven's arm. I know you want to know what is in my mind, even after all these years when I tend to keep things inside, but this time I need to talk to Ben first."

"Okay. Well, we are going over there for brunch later this morning. Can it wait until then, or do we need to go over sooner?"

"No, it can wait. But I want to write a few things down on my notes on my phone, so I don't forget to ask the questions or talk about details."

"Details? As in memories?"

"Yes, and that is all you are getting out of me right now." She stood up and walked into their suite with her coffee. She needed to make those notes and then take a shower. There was a lot to talk about today with her brother. Her twin. Her friend.

Ben woke early and sat on the front porch of his home. He listened as the world woke up. He had slept well the night before, which had surprised him. He was so excited about meeting his sister that he anticipated not sleeping at all. Instead, he dreamed. It was a strange dream. One he could not explain. It made no sense to him. And since he was no good at interpreting dreams, he tried to let them go, as most dreams fade away upon waking. This one hung on. It was still lingering when he joined the rest of the family in the manor's kitchen for brunch. He could not stop smiling when he saw Barbara. He hoped that meeting her had not been a dream that had faded. Indeed it was not a dream. She was there. His missing piece was found.

"Good morning, Brother," Barbara said when she saw Ben walk in. She and Steven had arrived a few minutes before and were already enjoying a cup of fresh coffee that Andy had offered them. The aroma of breakfast cooking in the kitchen had drawn them in. How could anyone resist that?

"Good morning, Little Sis," Ben said and hugged her.

"Who are you calling, little sis? I could be your big sister. Ever think of that?"

"Well, no. To me, you have always been thought of and referred to as my little sister. Maybe that is because I always wanted a little sister or brother, but I'm happy with a sister." He winked at her.

"Whatever we are at the time of our birth doesn't matter. We can fight over it if we ever find out when we were born into this world."

"Deal."

Andy interrupted everyone by telling them it was time to sit for brunch. He had laid out a feast before them.

After eating, Ben and Barbara excused themselves and went for another walk.

"Hey, Ben," she began as they slowly walked along the path. "I have something to ask you. It is something about when we were young children." She hesitated.

"Okay, ask away. Was it from when our parents were still alive or later? We were quite young when they died, and I'm not sure I remember much about that time in my life. However, I do remember Mom some. How about you?"

"I don't remember Mom much at all. Nor Dad, for that matter. No, this is about when we would have been about four years old. Maybe five."

"Tell me what you are thinking or what you remember. If it was after our parents died, how am I involved? The authorities separated us right after the accident. I'm not sure where you are going with this."

"Yes, they did separate us, but I think we knew each other at one point later on. Not as family, but as friends maybe."

"Whoa. How is that possible?" Where did you live?"

"Funny, with all the foster homes I was in, I lived a lot of places and met many people along the way. But one of those locations stuck with me for several reasons, and now it may be an additional reason I never considered, nor had reason to consider, until now."

They had reached the bench of the overlook and sat down. Barbara sat facing her brother with her leg under her. Ben looked into her eyes, wondering what was behind them.

"Do you remember where you lived when you were about five? It could have been earlier, but chances are you don't recall that far back—most people don't."

"Hardly. Do you think you can fill me in? But how can you fill me in as to where I lived? You weren't there." He drew his head back in suspicion of who this person in front of him was at the moment. How would she know where he lived at that age?

"Do you remember ever living by a creek? In a small house with a trailer on the property next to it? Where to get to the creek, you had to walk along a gravel path between the two properties?" She waited for him to respond.

Ben looked out over the overlook to the mountains and then back at this woman. His mind was confused. His memory was traveling back as far as he could remember. His eyes were focusing on the memories stored in his head. Nothing was coming to mind. He remembered living in a couple of places as a child with the man and briefly a woman who had raised him. But the image of a creek was not coming up.

Barbara continued when she realized he didn't recall anything. "Two little girls lived in the trailer with a woman named Annie. The girls loved playing in the creek on the swing and with the other kids in the area. All of us hung around together. Anything coming clear yet?"

Ben looked at her. His eyes widened. A tear automatically fell from his eye. His emotions engulfed his words. He could visualize the creek. He saw the little kids playing, running around, jumping in the creek, swinging on the swing. He started to smile at the memory of the little girls as his playmates. They were the only ones his uncle had allowed him to spend time with when they lived there. He always wondered why that was but never questioned him even after growing up.

He automatically shuddered. He could feel the cold water around him. He remembered jumping into the water after one of the girls who had fallen into the water. Ben looked at Barbara.

"You? Were you one of the girls? Wait! You were the girl in the water?" Ben's voice raised as he made the connection.

"I am sure you were the boy across the road. When we first connected through Randall, he had done some research; I also did some searching. You are the only child we were allowed to be around all the time when we lived there. We played with the other kids in the area occasionally, but you were the only one we were with every day."

Ben's eyes darkened as he remembered the day the little girls were taken away.

"Why did you ever leave? I liked having you and your sister next door. I had been alone up until that time in my childhood. My uncle only let me play with certain people, and you were one of them. I never asked him why he felt you were safe to be around. I never questioned why the other ones were not. Maybe he knew who you were and figured we would never figure out the truth at our young age. Did your mother ever tell you who I was?"

"No, no one ever said anything about it. I never suspected it. Heck, I knew I was a foster child at that age but only knew that my parents had been killed. There was never any word that I had a sibling somewhere, let alone why we would have been separated."

Barbara sat back and took in the image before her. Here he was, a living and breathing brother. She now had family out there. She wondered why Annie had never let her know who the boy was. Maybe Annie did not know. Did Ben's uncle know?

Ben reached over and hugged his sister! They sat there with tears flowing down their faces. A world that had separated them had just come to a close. It was a connection that had been so close all those years ago that neither knew. Now a mixture of the pain of years apart, the joy of finding each other and coming together—and questions not verbalized. He could not get his eyes off his sister.

Chapter Ten

Lives Compared

Barbara and Ben had spent the day together, walking the grounds close to the manor and the Bella Rose property and talking. They were finding out about each other's past life—the life they each had experienced as children. With the miles between them and the different ways they were raised, they found how different or alike they were. It was amazing how much they were alike, considering how many years they lived apart and didn't know about each other. Even their facial expressions and their body movements were similar. And their eyes looked the same. It was hard to imagine now that they may never have met and discovered this bond. To be placed in different homes, different environments, yet to have met that one time when they both lived by the creek seemed surreal now.

For several minutes they just looked at each other. Each with their own thoughts and memories. Each trying to think of how things would have been different if they had connected at that age, at the creek property.

"Can you imagine?" Ben broke the silence.

"If we had known?" Barbara shook her head. "How our lives would have been so different now."

"We would have been raised by your uncle, I would assume."

Ben's eyes rolled. "I'm not sure that would have been such a great thing."

"Why?"

"You don't remember all that happened while you lived there, do you?"

"I was four or five. No, I don't remember everything. I had so much stuff happen in my younger life that I tried to remember only the best parts. When I think of the bad experiences, I get lost inside myself, and it takes a few days to pull myself back out. So what happened?"

"Let's just say that my uncle was not the easiest man to live with. He used to punish me for no reason. Forced me to stay inside a lot. Rarely let me have playtime and even more rare to be around other kids other than at school. So summers it was just he and I and, well, let me just say, I did not enjoy my childhood like most kids do."

"So sorry. No, all I remember is when we all went to the creek to play." Barbara fell silent. Ben noticed her facial expression change.

"What is it?" Ben asked.

"I do remember the day you pulled me from the creek. When we got back to the trailer and you to your house, that man grabbed you by your shoulder and forced you inside."

"That he did. And that was not all, nor was that the only time."

"What else happened? If I remember, it was several days before you came back out to play."

"Yes, it was. He was not one for spankings. He was one for using his belt. Or, on occasion, as I got older, he would smack me or even punch me in the face. Like I said, it was not all fun back then."

"I wonder if any of that would have changed for you if we had stayed living there longer? Do you think we would have found out we were siblings if Annie hadn't lost her ability to keep Wendy and me?"

"We can only imagine and wish things would have changed. It would have been nice to have a sister. But if we had both lived with him, who knows how he would have been to the two of us, not just me. No, things happen for a reason and in their own time. I found it best to let God handle it all, if possible. I ask him every day to lead me where I need to be for that day."

"You have a strong faith in God."

"I didn't use to. Heather got me to believe more after we got married. How about you? Do you and Steven go to any church where you live?"

"No, not at the moment. I used to be involved with a little one when I was a teenager after I was adopted. I miss those days."

"Maybe if you and Steven move here, we can find a new church to attend."

"You are assuming we are moving here?"

"I would love for you to live close! We could spend a lot of time together."

"That we could. But Steven has his career at home. I do not think we will be moving here." Barbara looked around. She loved what she had seen of the area, and a part of her would love to move where the winters are calmer. Plus, the bonus of being near her brother appealed to her.

They continued to talk about their time at the creek for a little longer before joining the family back at the manor. They had plans for the rest of the day to spend it with family, and Steven wanted to just drive around the area for a couple of hours to see what was around.

Ben and Barbara agreed to meet up the next day. Ben wanted to show her the work he had done at the manor. He had long decided that his talents must have come from his biological parents because, even though he had picked up a few skills and some talents from his uncle, Ben had talents that the man he had lived with all his young life did not have. Ben had no way of knowing what his ancestors had been like and what they did. Maybe that would explain a lot if he only knew. This meeting with his twin sister may answer questions neither one had even thought to ask.

Ben turned around to watch her walk away. He knew so little about her and even less about her husband.

Chapter Eleven

Steven's Story

While Barbara and Ben were spending time together, Steven reflected on his past. He saw the joy in his wife's face and the wonderment in her eyes from when they arrived. The anticipation he saw in Barbara brought joy to his heart. He knew she had a missing piece in her life, and he was thankful that he could give her closure to the gap that had filled her life. Her life had been full of rejection, sadness, disappointment, and heartache. He had taken it upon himself to give her the happiness she deserved.

Now he found himself with spare time, and his thoughts reverted to the path his life had taken that brought him to where he was now. He had a past that he kept secret. A secret that few people, including Barbara, knew. He had always been honest with her as much as he could be. His past did not alter where he was now. There was no chance of it catching up with him and causing issues. He had burned all of those bridges as soon as he had turned his life around. Turning it around had come with a price. One he now was grateful to have paid. A price that had cost him to say goodbye to a perfect life—in the beginning. He had done his best over the years to forget about it—until now. Now, it crept in and seemed to haunt him.

Steven had spent his late teens and early adult life on his own. He had moved away from his parents and family as soon as he could. His home life as a child left scars. Both emotional and a few physical scars. Scars were acquired from the fights at school. He tried to stop them, but the more he tried to stop the fighting, the worse it became.

Finally, he was the one who got kicked out of school in his sophomore year, while the ones he fought were allowed to stay. So, he packed his bags one night and left home. His father told him to find a life. His mother pleaded with him to stay. He chose to leave and search for a better life. Little did he know it would take falling further down into the trenches of living before his life would improve.

At age sixteen, he was fortunate to look much older and found work when he arrived in Seattle. He not only managed to run to a different town, but he also found a different state. His first job was as a bell boy at a hotel. It was a great job for my first job. He had lied his way into it, but that didn't matter. He was making good money; the hotel let him stay there, and things were going well. He even looked into returning to school.

Within six months, he made new friends with kids in the neighborhood. A new way of life began. His friends introduced him to alcohol and then to drugs. He lost his great job and was forced to move in with one of his friends. He found a new job but soon lost that one as well. He was getting into fights for no reason. He ended up sleeping on the streets, and his dream of a perfect life soon was the last thing on his mind. His only goal was to survive the streets one day at a time. He knew his life was never going to improve. He had lost touch with his parents.

Then one day, while waiting at the pier for the ferry, he started talking to a man standing next to him. The man asked him where he was from—that was all it took. Steven broke down in tears. Instead of walking away from Steven, the man put his arm around him and let Steven cry.

"Son, we've all had times in our life we are not proud of, times that leave us in pain. Let me hear your story."

Steven was so embarrassed by his tears that he could not face this stranger. He wiped his tears on his shirt sleeve and backed away.

"No need to back away. I'm here for you. Nothing more than listening to you and seeing if I can help you."

Steven had heard all the horror stories on the streets of how bad people were and how they only wanted to use some kids. For some reason, he did not get that vibe from this man. He felt genuine concern coming from him.

As the ferry arrived and the two of them took their place with the other walkers to cross the river, he began to talk. To Steven's surprise, the man listened. He watched Steven as he spoke. The man did not let anything or anyone take his focus away. When they reached the other side, the man invited him to join him for lunch, telling Steven he had an idea.

That was the day Steven's life changed. The man, Owen Granger, took him under his wing. He moved Steven into a studio apartment, gave him a legal job for his age, set him up to return to school to get his diploma, and introduced him to better people.

In two years, Steven had cleaned up his life, gotten his high school diploma, became a bartender at an upscale restaurant in Seattle, and was always determined to be there to help anyone who was having a rough time in life.

His job as a barista, his attention to customer service, and the ease of getting to know people eventually led to an even better job on the East Coast of the United States. He did not even hesitate when Owen offered him the corporate position for one of his companies. Owen told him he earned it.

It was that move that brought him to meet Barbara. However, the promotion was not why he moved to the East coast. Before Steven could take Owen up on his offer, all the good that had come to Steven ended. Steven befriended a man and tried to help him, but his gesture of goodwill backfired that time.

Steven shook his head to erase those memories. He knew those were all behind him. The good bridges were burned as well as the bad ones. After he departed Seattle, his life took on a much more positive role.

Chapter Twelve

Nightmares

The evening had come to a close. Barbara and Steven had returned to their hotel room even though Ben had invited them to stay at the manor. Barbara was not ready to be that close to Ben. She needed her space to think. Steven understood this and was quiet as they drove the short distance to the hotel. He wanted to give her the space and quiet she needed to digest her new life, recall as much as possible, and bring closure to her past. He knew it had not been the best life by far. Yet, he was proud of how successful she had become, despite the hardships of her upbringing.

Steven pulled into the parking lot at Walton's Inn. He had not asked Barbara anything about her day with Ben. He knew she would have to digest it on her own. For her to share such intimate details was not her forte. She kept to herself until she had all or at least enough answers to satisfy everyone, especially herself. Truth be known, she had walked away with more questions than she had gained answers to the questions she originally had. Barbara felt she needed a blank notebook to write her thoughts, even to keep up with herself.

Steven poured her a tall glass of wine after they had settled in the private sitting room of their hotel suite. He was hoping to help her remember something important. A connection with her past, a memory of something, a sudden realization that would help her and Ben find the answers they needed. He knew enough about their situation to know that there were a lot of missing pieces.

While they each sipped their wine in silence, Steven watched his wife. Her eyes were searching. Her mind must be a thousand miles away in thought because she never heard her phone ring. Steven let it go to voicemail. If it were important, the caller would call him.

Steven took another sip of his wine as his phone rang. He grabbed his phone to answer it before Barbara could come out of the trance.

"Hello," Steven answered quietly as he stepped into the bedroom area away from Barbara. "Yes, Ben, what's up?" He listened as Ben spoke.

"And here I thought it was something important." Steven laughed quietly. "Did you call Barbara's phone first?" He looked around the corner to see Barbara stand up and walk toward him.

"Who is on the phone?" she asked, taking the last sip of her wine.

"It's Ben." He replied as he listened to Ben on the other end.

"Ah, okay. Anything important?"

Steven held up his hand to silence her as he got all the details he needed from Ben. After he said goodbye, he turned to Barbara.

"Ben tried calling you, and when you didn't answer, he called me. He has invited us to have brunch with him and the family tomorrow at the Café downtown. He said it was a family tradition of sorts to take all the family there when they were in town. I told him we would meet them there. Sorry, I was shussing you, but I needed to get the address and other details."

"That's ok. I know how you are." She was standing by his side and reached over and kissed his cheek. "You are the best; do you know that?"

"Of course, I know that." He took her wine glass from her as he kissed her forehead. He went into the kitchenette, poured more wine into her glass, and refilled his. Holding his free hand, Barbara led them back into the sitting room.

"I've been doing some inner searching." She said as she sat down with her leg under her.

"I could tell by the way you were so zoned out when the phones rang. Did you come up with anything else that would be helpful for you and Ben?"

"The only thing I have come up with is more of the time I spent with my foster mom, Annie. I remember being in the trailer by the creek and playing with who now we know was my brother. I also remember how the man he lived with was so strict with him. Ben was not allowed to be outside much. When we played together, it was usually under that man's watchful eye. I remember the man and Annie talking at the fence sometimes. They got along, but it was very distant. Like they knew each other but didn't get to know each other more than they had to as neighbors."

"How long did you live there? I know you told me a while ago, and it seems it was not that long."

"No, it wasn't. I don't think we were there for more than a year, maybe two." Barbara turned her head to stare out the window.

Steven watched her and didn't say another word. He sipped his wine and made mental notes of what she had been telling him. He would do his best to piece it altogether if he could. As an outsider of sorts, he may be able to notice something neither Ben nor his wife did. There had to be a back story to the real reason they were separated after the accident and why Barbara was not in the car that morning. He wanted to find out why the lady she was first given to had kept quiet about the connection to Ben. It was clear to anyone that the accident should have led to a search to find family members for Ben.

Barbara shook her head. She had to clear her thoughts. The images she was seeing were disturbing. She had become accustomed to bad treatment from her elders, but this image was not what she expected. She would save those questions for Ben when they talked the next day. She was hopeful that what she saw was not fact. She turned to face her husband.

"Whoa. You were lost in thought there for a while. Are you ok?" He noticed her facial expression. It was different than he had ever noticed before."

"Yes, I am ok. I just remembered a few things that I have to talk with Ben about before discussing them with anyone else. I hope what I saw in my mind is not what happened."

"That bad?"

"Maybe, I hope not." She finished her wine in one long gulp. This development may require a whole bottle, she thought.

"I think I need to get some rest—if I can sleep."

Steven took her empty wine glass and his into the kitchenette and turned to follow her into their bedroom. He would be by her side no matter what was revealed between her and Ben.

Barbara snuggled into Steven's arm as they lay on the king-size bed. She hoped sleep would engulf her and erase the images. She fell asleep while Steven was caressing her hair. She loved when he did that. There was just something about that act that brought her comfort.

In the middle of the night, Steven heard Barbara scream. He sat straight up in bed and reached for her. She was not right by his side. She was on the other side of the king-size bed, holding her head and rocking back and forth. Then her arms were thrashing about as if she was fighting someone off her. Steven rushed to her side and got hit by her swing as he sat beside her. He ignored the pain and grabbed her arms to hold her still. She fought him off. He held her tighter. She continued to scream and yell as she attempted to punch something invisible to him.

Just as fast as she had begun to scream, there was silence. She stopped punching the air. She was motionless. Steven let loose of his grasp and looked at her face. Her eyes were open and bloodshot, but he knew she was not there in the here and now. She was still miles and miles away. He realized she was asleep. Whatever she had been afraid of was in her nightmare. He put his arm around her shoulder, gently eased her back onto the bed, and placed her head on the pillow. He stood by her and pulled the covers up to her shoulders so she would not get cold as she continued to sleep. Whatever she had envisioned in her subconscious could not have been pleasant. Steven hoped she would have no recollection of it when she awoke.

Chapter Thirteen

A Sense Within

Ben woke up and looked at the clock on the nightstand by his side of the bed. It was only three in the morning. He gently rolled to his side and saw Heather still sound asleep. He carefully moved the covers off him and slid out of bed. He did not want to disturb his wife. Something had awakened him from a deep sleep and disturbed him. He could not put his finger on it, but something was happening. Maybe not to him, but to someone. He opened their bedroom door, and after stepping into the hall, he closed it without making a sound. Not only did he not want to wake up his wife, but he also did not want to wake up his boys. He knew it would take forever to get them settled back down.

Ben walked to the kitchen and looked out through the window behind the sink. All he could see was darkness. Not even a star could be seen in the sky from his vantage point. He moved to the living room so he could go outside. Something was wrong, somewhere.

He grabbed a flashlight from the table by the door and walked out onto the front porch. He looked out into the darkness and could see nothing out of the ordinary. He lifted the flashlight to see if he could see more. There was nothing out there that he could see.

He walked back inside and closed the door. The house was still quiet, yet he knew something had caused him to wake up. He checked on his boys before going back to bed, thinking it was just a dream. As he closed his eyes and drifted back to sleep, he heard it again. This time he was sure it was not a dream. He knew he heard a scream. He opened his eyes, knowing that he had quickly fallen back to sleep. All he heard was silence. He shook his head to clear the dream. He was sure that it had been a dream both times. Yet he also knew it was rare to dream the same thing twice, especially during the same night. He brushed it off, rolled over, and closed his eyes one more time.

Three hours later, Ben woke up to the sounds of his alarm. He turned off the alarm and sat up. He was about to get out of bed when he remembered the incident in the middle of the night. After going back to bed, he had not dreamed of anything else and decided not to mention it to Heather. He got up and took his shower. He would be meeting his twin sister in a few hours and had things to get done before the family met at the Café. He was anxious for everyone to get to know Barbara better. He knew his extended family would like her enough to take her in as part of them. His only concern was if she would like them. Neither one of them had had much of a true family growing up. He had been an only child. Barbara had been with several foster families before being adopted, but it wasn't until being adopted as an older child that she felt part of a true home situation. He hoped that day's meeting would go as well as the initial meeting had.

Heather joined Ben in the kitchen for coffee. The boys were sleeping in a little longer than normal, and they would take advantage of it. Heather walked over to Ben and hugged him from behind him. He bent back to meet her hug. There had always been a connection between them. It was these gentle touches that meant the most to him. Just the random touches. The random words of love they had shared most of their lives. He would never forget when they almost divorced and how her love for him kept that from happening. He had learned from her to appreciate the little things in life and see the positives that occur every day.

"What's on your mind, Ben?" You look a million miles away."

"Oh, nothing," he lied. "Just hoping all goes well at brunch today as we get to know Barbara more. I still am having a hard time wrapping my mind around the facts we are discovering about our lives."

"I understand that. Who could have guessed you had a sister, let alone a twin. Did you ever suspect such a thing?"

"I always felt something was missing in my life; I just never thought it was this. I thought it was more about my parents. And to be honest, I still think there is something odd about our parents. I think Barbara feels it too. We have so many questions between us. I hope we can get it all resolved and both be able to move on in our lives."

"Do you think that not knowing has somehow held you back in your life?"

"I didn't, not until recently. And it's not that I would change anything about my life and what I am doing. I think there may be so much more that I could be doing. If my life had been like most people's lives—well, I don't know what would be different."

"And who is to say that your life isn't right where it belongs? I know it seems like it would have been better if you and your birth parents and your sister had been together throughout your life but look at it this way. The life you had growing up led you here and to our family and me. Who knows where you would be if you had lived a different life?"

"Yes, you are right. I know we are put on a path from the day we are born and that God has a plan for us. I just wish I had known about my sister sooner."

"And that goes back to the idea that everything happens for a reason and in its own time. We are all right where we are supposed to be at this time in all our lives. You don't know how life would have been for all of us if you had known about her sooner. Maybe it would not have been as positive as it seems to be. Steven is her second husband. Maybe the first one would not have supported her to meet us. Maybe it just would not have worked during that time in her life. She seems happy with her life."

"Again, you are right. What would I do without you to keep me thinking the way I should?"

"See, if things were different, you would not have me in your life, and you would be a mess." Heather put her arms around her husband. He reached around her and held her close.

"I love you. You know that. My life would be a mess without you in it." Ben kissed her on her forehead. He truly was grateful for her. Life had not always been easy for them. Yet together, they had endured it all.

Marc, their oldest son, interrupted their embrace. They opened their arms to include him in a family hug when they saw him. He welcomed it and reached his hands in the air for Ben to lift him. He was just too big to lift anymore, so Ben sat down on the floor and let him climb on his lap. A minute later, Maddex had joined them, and the three males were rolling on the floor. Heather watched from her vantage point with a smile on her face. Her family was perfect, and she hoped Ben would soon feel the same way about his newfound family.

Barbara and Steven woke up to the sun streaming through the window. Barbara sat up, stretched her arms, and yawned. Today was a new day—a new adventure for her. Her life had taken on a new life. One that she was welcomed with open arms.

Steven opened his eyes to see his wife rise out of bed. His mind wondered if finding her brother would prove to be as positive as it was starting to be. He had gone to great lengths to make it all happen. He only saw a good conclusion that included the final piece's placement in the puzzle of her life. Before getting out of bed, he reached over into his nightstand drawer. He had placed a surprise for Barbara there. Not only had he been able to find Ben, but he had also been able to find what he hoped would be a treasure for her and her brother. He had researched her past and connected to people even she may have forgotten. He lifted it and carefully placed it under his jacket so he would remember to take it with him to brunch.

Chapter Fourteen

Café Tradition

Terri welcomed everyone to the Downtown Café. She had recently purchased it and had made it her mission to greet each customer that came to her establishment. It added a personal touch to her regulars and made a good impression on the new guests. She treated each person equally even though she did have her favorites. And the owners of Bella Rose Estate happened to be one of her favorite families.

Ben and Heather were the first to arrive at the Café and told Terri they would need the back section for their lunch as the whole family, plus two would be joining them. Terri was happy to oblige and led them to the backroom she had added on when she bought the place. Terri knew her locals would appreciate a quieter meeting place for lunch meetings and, as this indicated, also for family gatherings. She worked with the local wedding venue to have the café offered for small wedding receptions and bridal dinners and stayed open for such occasions.

Randall and Sara soon joined them and said that Andy and Karen were parking their car. Steven and Barbara were slowly walking up the sidewalk as they saw Andy and Karen walking across the street. The four of them entered the café together and joined the rest of the family. Barbara was amazed at the warm welcome from the lady at the front door and mentioned it when they were seated.

"That would be Terri. I've heard that she's made a great impression on the locals," Randall replied to her comment.

"I heard that too," Sara added. "I'm so glad. I would hate it if this place were not here anymore. Coming here has been a family tradition for as long as I can remember. If we are not gathering in our kitchen at the manor, we are gathering here."

"Very true. And when I don't feel like cooking." Andy added.

Barbara laughed. "I will keep that in mind for when we are here. The food must be good."

"It is. Simple, elegant, and delicious." Sara looked at the menu. "Terri has added more meals to the menu. We need to try some of these."

"I say we each order something different and then share so we each can sample almost everything and choose our favorite," Heather said as she adjusted Maddex in his booster seat.

"Sounds like a good idea to me," Steven agreed.

While they were placing their orders, Ben kept watching his sister. Just a week ago, he knew so little about her. He hoped to learn all about her over the next week before her planned trip to return home. Maybe she would learn enough about all of them to want to move closer and join the family. Although this family was not the one he had grown up with, he had felt a belonging from the first time he took Heather out on a date. He felt a smile form. His life had changed so much over the years. He hoped this change would also be a positive one. How could it not? This change was his sister! The only true bloodline of his past. He would make the most of it no matter what.

The family talked while they ate, and everyone was asking Barbara questions faster than she could answer them. Following dessert, Steven reached behind him and pulled out the item he had hidden since leaving the hotel room. He handed it to Barbara. "While so many of you are asking questions about my lovely wife and some she can't answer, I hope this will help her and you, Ben, figure out your past lives."

Everyone looked at the photo album Barbara had in her hands. She looked at Steven and then at Ben. Each man was sitting next to her. She felt loved by having them both in her life now. She moved her plate and set the album down on the table between Ben and her. They looked at each other as Ben opened the cover. The first photo was of them as babies in a carriage. Both were looking up, smiling at whoever was taking the picture. They could not have been more than a few months old.

"Where did you get this photo?" Barbara asked, looking at her husband.

"It took a lot of investigative work, let me tell you. So much of your life was kept confidential after your parents died, and you spent years in foster care before finally being adopted. But, I have my connections and found several people willing to help me when I shared your story. One person I have contact with even wants to write your story."

"Write my story?" Barbara asked.

"Write the story of both of you. How you were separated, grew up not knowing about each other, and how you have reconnected and are now living happily ever after." Randall explained.

Ben found his humorous side. "That is to say, we do live happily ever after. We may find we hate each other. That would not make a good book. Or at least change it into a drama or even a thriller." He laughed. "Just kidding. I hope." He added.

Barbara reached up and punched his upper arm. "Yep, we are related. I thought it could become the newest best-selling thriller if we didn't like each other. These mountains are ripe for hiding people."

Sara shook her head as she looked at Heather and Andy. "Oh, you just don't know much about how to hide people. All for the right reasons in our case, of course. Just wait until you find out about the family you now belong to."

Ben smiled. He caught the inclusion of his twin into this family. He liked that idea. Not only had they taken him in when he married Heather, but they were also now taking in

84

a part of his family. He could not have asked for a better life.

"Oh? You will have to share that story sometime."

"We will. It is a part of who we are and what Bella Rose is now known for—its history." Sara smiled as she sipped the last coffee in her cup that she had ordered when everyone else had ordered dessert.

Ben and Barbara were slowly turning the pages of the photo album. The first several pages were of them as babies with their parents. The smiles they all had gave the impression that they were a happy and loving family.

"I wonder what took place to change everything so drastically before the accident?"

"What do you mean? What changed?"

"Well, something had to have happened to make it so that you were not in the car that day with me. Look at all these photos. We are always together. Why were we not together that day?"

"Good question."

"I don't know what happened, but I know that is something we will investigate," Ben responded.

Randall raised his hand slightly. He had been quiet for most of the meal as the family talked. Now it was his turn to offer what he could. "I can suggest a private investigator who can help you find some answers."

Ben looked up and then at his sister. He raised his eyebrows in a silent question. Then he asked, "What do you think? Do you want to pursue our back story and the reasons, or be thankful for the here and now and move forward?"

"I want to find out as many details as I can. The life I had was horrible, and I would like to know why it had to be that way. I know you had some rough patches along the way too. Don't you want to know more?" Barbara assumed he would want to know as much as she did about their life's story.

"Yes, I do. I have had this part of my life hidden from me for far too long. I felt there was a missing piece for so many years. It is time to connect the dots of our lives and see where they meet, how they fell apart, and now, how they are mending."

"I like the way you think, brother." Barbara reached over for Ben's hand. She held it for a few minutes and smiled. Her life was feeling complete.

"I say we take this photo album back to the manor and look at it together. I am sure the rest of our family will understand. We can tell them the highlights as we find them."

"You two have a lot to discover. I plan to wander around town and enjoy some of the sights while you two get to know each other. Don't worry about me at all while we are here. This trip is all about the two of you." Steven told them.

"Thank you, Babe. You are so sweet and understanding."

"I am glad to be in your life and be able to help you."

"I agree with Steven. We can handle the manor work while you two figure out how you got here."

"Thank you, Sara; you are a lifesaver. Maybe literally."

Terri entered their space and asked if she could do anything for them, anything else she could bring them to eat or drink.

"No, we are getting ready to leave. Sorry for occupying this space for so long." Randall said as he reached for the bill Terri had in her hand.

"It was my pleasure. I overheard part of what you are doing. Is it true that you and Ben are twins? And that you have not seen each other since you were about four years old?" Terri directed the question to Barbara.

"Yes, that is true. That is why my husband and I are in town. By the way, the food here is amazing.

"Thank you, ma'am."

"Oh, please, call me Barbara. And this is my husband, Steven."

"I have a feeling you may be seeing a lot of us while we are here," Steven added, reaching to shake Terri's hand.

"I would be honored. You are welcome here anytime." Terri took the payment from Randall and walked away.

Terri returned with the change as they were getting up to leave. "It was so nice to see you all again and to meet you, Steven, and Barbara. I hope to see you soon. If there is anything I can do for you, you know where I am. I am always here."

"Yes, you are always here. I think you need to take a day off once in a while." Randall said. He knew she was always here as his office was just a block away, and his fellow attorneys and some of his clientele stopped in often to eat there.

"Maybe someday I will be able to. For now, this is my baby and my life." Terri heard her name called from the kitchen. "Duty calls." She said as she walked away and headed for the kitchen, wondering what the issue was now. They rarely needed her help.

"Let's all head back to the manor and give Ben and Barbara some time to talk."

"Sounds good to me. Can we use the kitchen island for a while? I hear that it is the family gathering place."

"Of course, you can. I won't need the kitchen until the morning for the guests. I can brew you a fresh pot of coffee if you want."

"Thank you." Barbara reached her arm into Steven's. "Are you okay with that, Babe?"

"Yes, I am. I will find other things to do. I may go back to the hotel and take a nap."

"Nonsense. You can join us at the house if you like." Andy offered as he looked at Karen. "You don't mind, do you, Dear?"

"I insist. We can get to know each other. I have a feeling we all will be one big, happy family. Bigger, happy family. We keep growing, don't we?" She asked as she winked at Andy.

"That we do. And so far we are a big happy family. Surprising how life threw us all together over the years."

"You never know what the future has in store for you," Karen said, directed at Steven. "I learned a long time ago to go with the flow. This family taught me when they welcomed me without hesitation or question. You are welcomed in the same way."

"I appreciate that. Thank you," Steven said as he and Barbara walked outside and joined the rest of the family already waiting.

It did not take long for brother and sister to seclude themselves in the kitchen gathering place. It may have been more comfortable in the manor's great room, but they did not want to interfere with the guests.

Steven joined Karen and Andy in their home while he wondered what the photos he had compiled from his contacts would bring to the love of his life and her twin. He was impressed with how it was going so far. All Steven wanted to do was to bring joy to her. While they were eating, he saw a joy in her eyes he had never witnessed before. His plan was working.

Chapter Fifteen

Discoveries

Ben and Barbara settled in the kitchen after everyone else went home. Andy had set out snacks for the guest returning from their day trips around the area. That had been a ritual he started when he became the chef. The guests appreciated it as they often gathered in the great room to visit with the other guests and share their experiences and adventures of the day.

Once left alone with a fresh pot of coffee, Ben opened the photo album as they both took a deep breath. It was amazing how alike the twins were, considering their past lives.

The first set of photos was of the two of them when they were babies and then continued on to their toddler years. The photos often included their parents. As they looked closer at the photos, they noticed that as time went on, it was just them, or them with other children, but not their parents. Or it was with just one parent. It was easy enough to explain, as maybe the other parent was taking the picture.

"Do you notice something about these pictures?" Barbara asked as she flipped back a few pages.

"Not that comes to mind. What have you noticed?"

"Look at our father. As we age, he is in less and less of the family pictures."

"I noticed but figured it was him taking the photos and unable to be in them?"

"But each one is like that by the time we are about two." She turned the pages back and forth to their different ages.

"Interesting, I admit." Ben turned the page to the next group. The photos on the next page were just of Barbara.

"Hey, where did I go?" Ben asked and laughed at the same time.

"What age were we on that page?"

"Three maybe."

"Ben, that was after the accident." She flipped briefly through several more pages. The rest were just of her and her foster families, but none had Ben in them. Then she landed on a page several pages further in the album.

Ben noticed she had stopped flipping so fast and looked at the page she had left open. "Wait! Is that me?" They both leaned in closer to see the details.

"That is me, for sure, and yes, I think that is you." Barbara sat back as her mind tried to take in the scene within the photo.

"When and where was that taken?"

"Remember when we each lived near the creek?"

"Yes, that time when I rescued you from drowning in the creek," I remember. He looked closer at the photo. It was at that location. The place he had lived with the man he treated as his father but called his uncle most of his life.

They both sat there looking at the photo and taking in all the details. Then they looked at the photos that followed. Ben bent down for a close look at a photo that had him and the man who had raised him. His eyes opened wide as he took the book from under Barbara's nose and flipped back to the beginning.

"Sis, look at this! He pointed to the photo of them together as a family, specifically their father. Then he flipped to the last page they were examining. "Do you notice anything strange?"

Barbara smiled and just looked at him.

"What?" He asked.

"You called me Sis."

Ben hesitated. " Well, you are my sister."

"I know. I like being called Sis. It makes me feel more a part of the family."

"You are family. Not only my sister, but whether you know it or like it, you are now a part of a much larger family. They all have taken you in as their own."

"I don't think I've ever felt that much love—except the love from Steven. He changed my life. And he is still changing it." She bent and took a closer look at both pages. The photos had faded over time, and it was hard to see the small details.

Suddenly she sat up, eyes opened wide, and looked at Ben. "No. That isn't, is it?"

"No, not what you are thinking, I don't think. But I do think our past and the mystery of it is now deeper."

"But, how, why, and why did you never know? And why?" She suddenly had more questions on her mind than she could dwell on for answers.

"I agree; how, why, what, and when?" A tear escaped as he turned to hide it.

"Ben, what are you thinking?"

"I think we need to keep looking and address this discovery later. There may be more clues ahead." He reached over and turned to the next page. This one was just of her, but they both recognized the trailer in the background.

"I am now confused. Who was the man who raised you? He looks just like."

"I know. I was never really told anything about him or his life. I just took him to be just a man who adopted me. These photos raise a whole new set of questions." Ben said as he stared at the clearest photo.

"I agree. And if he is who we think he is, did he know who I was? Did Annie know who you were? Did the two of them agree to keep a secret? And if either of them knew anything, why keep the secret? Why not tell us?" Barbara raised the questions.

Ben sat back against the island stool. He felt the world he had known fall apart inside. He felt anger building up.

To stop it from rising to the top, he stood up. "I need to go outside for a few minutes."

"Okay." Barbara watched her brother walk out as he wiped his eyes. Was it tears of anger, realization, or tears full of more questions and disbelief? She was so confused. She decided to keep looking through the photos alone.

Ben walked outside, taking his time to step one foot in front of the other. How could the man who raised him remain quiet all those years? The similarities between the man and his birth father were undeniable. They were brothers. They had to be. Why had he never said anything? Why had he kept the truth from him? Why had he pretended to be someone else? As he thought about it, he remembered hearing people saying that the man had issues and was not normal. But he only thought that meant because of how he treated him as a child. He knew as he grew up that the man was too rough and too strict with him. Maybe now he knew why. Or now maybe it was more confusing. Ben had reached the gazebo without realizing he was even walking in that direction. He sat down and looked out over the mountains.

Barbara closed the photo album and stood up. She went to the coffee pot and poured herself a fresh cup. Life as she knew it had changed just a few months ago, changed again just a couple of days ago, and now, now it had taken a drastic change. One no one could have guessed. She looked up as the door opened. Steven walked in.

"Did you know?" Barbara instantly asked him.

"Know what? Where is Ben?" Steven looked around the room.

"Ben is out for a walk. Did you know about the man who raised him?" Barbara asked accusingly.

"What about him? I don't know a thing about him. The photos were mostly of you as you were growing up. I was hoping they were filling in some blanks, and maybe through them, you and Ben could connect closer. Why are you upset?" Steven walked toward his wife. Barbara stepped back away from him. "Baby, what is wrong?" Steven stood still. He had never seen his wife like this. He knew a lot about her and her past. What was in the photos he lovingly had put together that caused this change in her?

Barbara sat down and put her head on the island. She cried. Steven casually walked to her and put his arm around her. She allowed him to comfort her. He still had no idea what was going on. He was there for her no matter what had been discovered.

Ben burst into the kitchen. Sitting at the gazebo had only made him angry. The more he thought about what they had discovered, the more he hated the man who raised him. Maybe it would have been better never to see those photos. Maybe it would have been better not to know or think he knew what seemed to be fact now.

Steven jumped when the door slammed, and Ben walked in. Ben stopped when he saw Steven. "What do you know about the man who raised me?" He demanded.

"I don't know a thing. Barbara asked me the same thing and then broke down in tears without telling me what had happened. What's going on?" Steven stood up straight.

"Those pictures," Ben said, pointing at the closed album. "Those photos. The man who raised me seems to be our true uncle."

"What? How can that be?"

"That is what we want to know. That and the fact that there was a time we lived across the road from each other and never knew we were related, let alone twins! My life has been a lie. So has part of hers. Since our childhood, we could have been together if the people who raised us wanted us to be. For some reason, they kept it a secret. Maybe, just maybe, they didn't know, but something tells me they knew."

Steven was in shock. Now he understood his wife's meltdown. "I swear, I knew nothing about the man who raised you. I didn't know anything about you or of you until several months ago. How could I know about him?" Steven asked.

"Sorry. I'm angry. I feel defeated. I feel suddenly lost. I feel empty inside. Here I am finding my sister who should have made my life complete, and suddenly we find out a piece of our connected lives had been kept secret from us. We need to know if it was on purpose or if they honestly did not know. Even if the man did not know who Barbara was when we lived next door to each other, he could have told me that he was my biological uncle. Instead, he said to make things easier on all of us in the future to call him uncle so people would not question anything. He could have told me about my family. And if he was a blood relative, what did he know about Barbara being out there somewhere after our parents died? I have more questions than I ever had in my life!" Ben sat down at the island. He had to calm down. Having this reaction was not going to solve anything. It was not helping his new connection to his sister.

Barbara raised her head. She had heard everything her brother had said. She was just as confused as he was but knew anger would not help solve anything.

"Brother, it's okay. We need to be calm and figure out how to deal with this news.

"Where do we start? I've not spoken with my uncle in so long I'm not sure where he is anymore."

"Since I got married, even the first time, I have not been in touch with my foster families. It has been a while since I was in touch with my adoptive family. I hate to admit that."

"You have nothing to be ashamed of. There comes a time in our lives that we get out on our own, form our own families, and if the relationships with our former families were strained, we tend to break away from them."

"I know, but they gave me so much at a time when I needed to feel loved. When I met and married my first husband, they thought it was a bad idea and seemed to throw their arms up and quit trying. I expected them to stay in touch, get to know him, and love him. Instead, they got busy with their lives and left us alone. Maybe they thought that was what I wanted since I seemed to rebel against them when I fell in love with him."

"Do they know you are married to Steven now, and life is much better for you?"

"Yes, I did contact them. When I was going through my divorce, I called them to let them know. They never asked if they could help me, offered a place to stay, nothing. I guess they figured since I had made my bed, I needed to lie in it or figure it all out on my own. So, I figured it all out on my own. That was when Steven found me."

"Where did the two of you meet anyway?" Ben was still sitting down, and the thoughts of their mysterious past had slipped away for the moment."

"Funny story there. I was running away from my bad marriage. I flew out to Seattle one weekend just to hide. I found this quaint hotel in the center of town and settled in. Each day I would walk the area, sometimes for hours. One day I walked into the bar just down the street from the hotel. Steven was the bartender that night. We just started talking."

"And the rest is history, as they say?"

"Almost."

"No sparks immediately?"

"No, I wasn't looking. I just needed someone to talk to that night, and he happened to be the one I opened up to for some reason. I stayed until closing that first night, and after he had closed up the bar, we went for a midnight walk downtown."

Ben noticed Barbara's eyes took on a different look. "There were sparks that first night; look at your eyes. And I see that smile." Ben smiled, knowing his sister had found love that night.

"I have them now, but not that first night. I was in pain. I was lost. He listened. We exchanged phone numbers and emails at the end of that night, but he never called. I had to return home two days later and never got the chance to see him again. I went to the bar, but they said he was off those days, and they had no way of getting in touch with him. I just assumed he was avoiding me."

"So, how did you reconnect?"

"About six months later, my doorbell rang. I never received many visitors, so I assumed it was just kids playing or solicitors. I peered through the peephole and could not believe my eyes. I opened the door, and we immediately fell into each other's arms. I slowly backed up so we could close the door, but it was several minutes before we let go of each other."

"So that was when you became inseparable."

"That was it. We sat and talked for hours that night. I asked him why he had avoided me after we first met in Seattle. He told me that he had an emergency and did not want to burden me with what was going on. He said he felt I was a damsel in distress when I was there and that he would forget about me and that I would forget about him."

"So why did he track you down?" Ben was more curious now than ever. His sister had a mysterious life. He wanted to know more.

"Steven told me that as much as he tried to forget about me, I was all he thought about and talked about to anyone who would listen. He said his co-workers at the bar told him to find me so they would not have to keep hearing about how he should never have let me go. So he tracked me down as soon as he could."

"He came thousands of miles across the country. That was some impression you made on him in a short amount of time."

"I know. Now, look at what Steven has done for me, for us." Barbara reached for the photo album. "Little does he realize that now we have more questions."

"That's it!" Ben suddenly stood up. "Steven!"

"What about Steven?"

"Don't you see? He was able to track you down across the country with nothing to go on but your phone number and email address and what other things you may have told him that first night. Now, he went to all the trouble and research to get these photos for us." Ben pointed to the photos.

"Yes, and?"

"He has a talent for finding out information. We can ask him to help us determine if the man who raised me and your foster mom knew anything back then. And if that man is not my adoptive father but is my real uncle, maybe we can find out what he knew or knows about what happened the night of the accident and the days that followed."

"You are right. Another thing to investigate is if he adopted you, why not have you call him Dad? Instead, he wanted you to refer to him as your uncle." Barbara stood up and hugged Ben. "We have a mystery sleuth in our midst. We need to use him and his skills."

Chapter Sixteen

Possibilities

In the days after Ben and Barbara first viewed the photographs, they continued to spend time together discussing their lives growing up. They filled Steven in on all the details of their time together at the property near the creek. While they both remembered similar things while living there, there were differences.

Ben soon recognized that some of his memories of his time with his uncle could be considered abusive behavior from the man who raised him. One night, he fell asleep thinking about it and woke up with memories of threats, punishments, and time left alone. He could not remember why he was left alone so often. He was thankful that Barbara and Steven had decided to stay a little longer to help Ben and Barbara find answers to the questions that continued to surface. Maybe Steven could also help him discover why he was left alone so often.

After being in the area for over a week, Steven and Barbara talked one night in their hotel room. Steven knew his wife had something on her mind that she was keeping inside.

"Babe, what's been on your mind? I know learning about your past life and the connections with Ben have been overwhelming at times over the last few days. I think you have something more going on in your brain?"

Barbara was sitting on the sofa in the sitting area of their hotel room. She looked over at Steven, sitting on the other end, and smiled. He knew her so well. She had always been amazed at how well he understood her. Her heart beat a little faster as she thought of how much he loved her.

"You know me so well. I cannot hide much of anything from you. You know me better than I know myself sometimes."

"So, tell me what you are thinking."

" Oh, Steven, I don't know how to say what I've been thinking. But I guess it is best to blurt it out and hope for the best."

"Yes, that has always been the best as I see things. So spill it. I can take it."

"Are you sure?" Barbara asked as she formulated the words to tell him what she was thinking. She was afraid he would say she was crazy to even think about it. Or he could agree and make her dream come true. It was a dream she had recently developed, but a dream, nonetheless.

"I want to move here." There she said it. She winced, awaiting Steven's response.

"I had a feeling you were thinking about that. I have been thinking about it also and doing some research to determine its feasibility."

"You have been thinking the same thing?"

"Not as strong as you have been. But I could tell soon after we had arrived that you were going to love it here. The more you talk with Ben and the family, the closer I think we both have become to them."

"Would you even consider moving here? Close by, not that we lived at the hotel all the time. Is there a chance that you could find work locally?

"I've spent hours looking into places to work. Nothing has come up yet, but I have not given up. I was going to surprise you by finding a job and then telling you that we would stay so you and Ben could have the time you deserve as brother and sister that you missed out on as children."

"That is amazing; you are amazing." Barbara reached over and leaned in to kiss him. She had no idea how she would voice her desire to stay here in this quaint town and get to know her brother. She certainly was blessed to have a husband who knew her and knew her so well.

The phone rang in their hotel room. Steven reached over to answer it and winked at Barbara as he said hello. "Yes, I understand, Sir. Yes. I would be honored to come to see you in your office. Today, at three?" He looked at Barbara, who nodded her head. She had no idea what she agreed to but felt she could handle it

"Yes, I will be there at three this afternoon. Thank you, sir." Steven put the phone back in the receiver and walked back to Barbara. She had only heard his half of the conversation but was anxious to hear what the caller had said.

"I have a job interview!" Steven said as he took his wife by her hands and lifted her to stand with him.

"That is awesome! Where?"

"Well, it takes me back to where I started working, but it is at least something."

"Back to where you started? The job is local, isn't it?" Barbara stepped back from him.

"Oh, yes, the job is local. It is as a bartender."

"Why as a bartender? You have come so far in your career. Why go backward?"

"It's just a place to start. I need to get my feet wet working in the area."

"Yes, but I don't understand." Barbara stopped talking. She knew she needed to trust her husband. He had never steered her wrong before. He had been good to her. He had taken bold steps before, and they had led to success. She needed to trust him now.

"Honey, trust me," he took her hand and raised it to his face to kiss it. His way of reassuring her.

"I do. I trust you. You have always known what you were doing, and it always turned out the way it should." Barbara leaned against him, and his arms wrapped around her as they always had. The love between them was never doubted.

"So, since I have a job interview this afternoon, I think we need to get to the manor so you and Ben can talk more while we are in town. Just in case we cannot stay as we hope."

"Sounds like a good plan to me." Barbara backed out of their embrace and went into the bathroom to prepare for the day.

An hour later, they were parked at the manor watching a few of the guests walking down the steps to go on their adventure.

Ben met them at the front door. He was on his way to town to pick up some supplies for a repair he had to make in one of the rooms.

"Hi Sis, how are you? I'm headed out for a few minutes. Do you want to come with me?"

Barbara looked at Steven.

"Go, I have places to go in town, but this will give you time alone with Ben."

"I'm ready. Where do we need to go?" Barbara turned from Steven to Ben as she spoke.

"Just to the hardware store. You would think by now that I would have all the tools and supplies I need to fix just about anything. But, no, this time, I don't."

Ben opened the pick-up truck door for his sister. He smiled as she sat down and buckled her seat belt. As he closed the door and walked around to the driver's side, he waved at Steven. He owed a lot to that man. He had brought him his sister. And now, maybe he would be able to help them find the truth about their father, the man who raised him, and the lady who Barbara was so fond of all those years in her foster care.

As Ben drove slowly into town, it gave them more time to talk. He had always wanted a sister, but it was better than expected now that he had one.

"So, what do you think about the man who raised you? Do you think he could be hiding something?" Barbara did not mince words. She was getting right to the bottom of the reason for her visit.

"I never suspected anything when I was little. As I got older and then on my own, I felt that the man was hiding something. For years I did not have contact with him. He refused to come to see me. And after a while, I stopped trying to include him in my life. I had given up on him. It wasn't until I was in therapy with Joe that I realized something was missing in my life."

Barbara caught the word, therapy. "Why were you in therapy?"

Ben realized there was a lot about his life that his sister did not know. "Oh, there was a time in my life that Heather and I were headed for a divorce. I agreed to see a therapist with her, and after our sessions, I started going on my own when we realized there was more to my life and background than I knew. That was when we started looking for the rest of my family." Ben stopped talking as he parked the car at the home improvement store. "I will continue this later." He said as they got out of his truck.

Barbara nodded her head. It was hard for her to comprehend Heather and Ben ever having marital issues. They seemed like a perfect couple.

After purchasing the items he needed, Ben drove the two of them to the local dairy bar. Ben continued his story while they sat inside and enjoyed their ice cream treats.

"You see, many years ago, Heather and I were in a car accident. She almost died. If you notice, she walks with a slight limp. That is my fault. Or at least I thought it was my fault. To make a long story short, we went to therapy to heal our marriage. The therapy worked, but it opened up a new can of worms. As I felt more connected to Heather and her family, I felt disconnected from my past. I felt I had missed or forgotten a lot of it. I knew I was adopted and that my parents had died in a car accident, but I felt more."

"I understand that feeling. That was how I felt before Steven found you."

Ben nodded his head. "Yes, I am grateful for him finding us." Ben looked outside the dairy bar and noticed a rainbow in the sky. He had not even known it was raining while they were inside. He smiled.

"Why that smile?" Barbara asked. She was facing away from the front window and turned just in time to see the last of the rainbow. "Ah, I see. A rainbow makes you smile."

"Rainbows always make me smile. They remind me that there is light at the end of the tunnel no matter what trial I am going through. There is beauty after the storm. And in a roundabout way, there are solutions to every problem if you take the time to find them."

"I have always loved rainbows. The colors are so bright sometimes. And as each line is different, so are the promises within. We often have more than one issue we are facing, so God gives us a variety of solutions."

Ben sat back and looked at her. "I never thought of it that way before. That is interesting." He then continued with his story. "As I was saying. I felt I was missing a piece of my life. I spent hours trying to relive the car accident with my parents. The more I envisioned it, the more I did not remember our father being in the car. I was searching for our father to be still alive for a while. I never dreamed I had a sister."

Barbara had been listening to every word. She was deep in thought, deciding what she had felt as a child. "I always knew a part of my life was missing. I never thought of either of my parents being alive. Besides you not remembering him in the car, what else makes you think he could be alive?"

"Oh, I don't think that way now. I figure it was you I was supposed to find."

"But you may be on to something." Barbara finished her ice cream and stood to throw away her napkin. Ben stood to follow her, and they kept walking until they reached the pick-up truck.

"What are you suggesting? Do you think he may be alive?"

"Well, look at the photos we've found from when we were toddlers. Then look at the photos of the man who raised you. We both agree they look similar. We need to find him and see what he says about our lives as children. I think he may know more than he ever told anyone."

"What about the foster mother you had when we lived by the creek? Do you think she knew anything?"

Silence overtook them as they drove. There was no question about the lack of conversation. It was a silent mutual agreement to be in thought.

When Ben pulled into the parking lot at the manor, he broke the silence. "What should be our next step? Shall we talk to Steven about searching, or do you want to talk to Joe, our family therapist, to see what he can pull out of us?"

"This Joe is the family therapist? Interesting." Barbara slowly walked up the steps to the manor. "I say we talk to Steven first."

"Whatever you want to do. Talking to Steven may help us when we talk to Joe. I should call Joe and set up an appointment soon."

"Ok. We may have more time to talk to Steven than we thought."

"How so?"

"He had a job interview in town this afternoon."

"That is awesome!" Ben stopped and turned to her. "Does that mean you are moving here?"

"That is what we are discussing, yes."

Ben wrapped his arms around his sister at the doorway as Heather opened it, and the two boys ran past everyone.

Chapter Seventeen

Family

Barbara's life changed dramatically in the weeks following Steven's job interview. Her life had been full of moving and changes and new people in her life and old ones leaving. The last time she moved was when she and Steven married. At that time, she was planning never to move again. She was content where they were and the life they were living. That was until Steven opened her world beyond her imagination.

Steven had immediately accepted the job offer from Terri. Her assistant had been the one to set up the interview, but Terri was the owner and was the one doing the hiring. It was a step down for him. It was back into what had started his career, but it allowed him to do something else for his wife to bring her joy. He would deal with the hardships of the job if they arose. Terri had dreams for her business and saw Steven as an asset. His knowledge and connections would prove beneficial to her.

Terri had made her decision to hire Steven even before she interviewed him. She had read his resume and did a reference check on him at one of his former places of employment. She knew he was the one for her business. She had visited the bar where he had once worked a few years earlier. It was located across the country at the best bar and restaurant she knew. Anyone who had once worked there was a good match for her. Despite any wrongdoing he may have done, she admired him. The staff she met while there had been the friendliest. The food was perfect. The service was memorable. She was thrilled to have one of their best people on her team.

Barbara was shocked when she found out what job Steven had accepted. It was the furthest thing she would have expected. And she asked him why he took it without discussing it with her.

"I don't understand why you would say yes to her so fast. You have not done the research; you have not looked for other jobs available."

"I know I may have jumped quickly at this, and I am sorry I did not talk it over with you first. But, listen." Steven held Barbara's shoulders to hold her in place while he spoke. "I know it seems irrational and nothing like how I usually accept a job but look at it this way; it gets you here with your brother."

"We could have waited. I could have stayed here while you continued to work at home while looking for something better here." Barbara protested.

"Yes, we could have waited, but you will understand when I explain the ultimate offer."

"I'm listening." Barbara backed away from Steven and sat on the edge of their bed in the hotel room. She was tired of living at the hotel but thought she'd be home soon, so she never complained.

"In the course of our conversation and as she went over my resume, she noticed the work I did in Seattle. Yes, it was many years ago, but it was where I started. And it was how I learned to work my way up by knowing so many people and companies."

"And how is that going to help you here? Here you are just a bartender."

"For now, yes. I will work as a low-man in the business, but Terri and I talked about her goal for the Downtown Café, and my job is so much more than what it seems."

"What are you talking about?" Barbar leaned back and crossed her legs. Was this something she could support? Or was Terri just a big dreamer and using Steven?

Steven sat down beside Barbara and took her hand into his. This may take a little encouragement to get her to accept what he was about to tell her. "Well, Terri wants to expand the Downtown Café. She wants to improve it, build a stronger clientele, and draw in more visitors. You understand that need."

"Yes, I understand the need to find ways to bring in more customers. So, what is her plan?"

"You know that backroom area of the Café and the section in the back that rarely gets used? I think your brother said that was for storage? Terri wants to utilize that space to expand the business."

Barbara was quiet. It made sense to take advantage of the newest change to the town and the approval to have a bar in town. With it, Terri had been able to hire Steven. "I did find it strange that there was no bar in town."

"The newest ruling has changed that, and Terri was the first one to apply and get the license for her café to serve alcohol."

"That is awesome. I am glad for Terri. So how does being her bartender open the road for a better job later? She has more up her sleeve, doesn't she?"

"Yes, she does. She wants to build an addition to the café to have a lounge and hold special musical events."

Barbara's eyes opened further as she smiled. Now she understood the connection and the reason Terri had hired Steven. It seemed he had connections to everyone across the country in the music industry. Yes, he'd be starting over here, but she knew it would not take him long to build up the business for Terri, and maybe it would lead to something great.

Steven watched Barbara as everything seemed to click for her. "Still concerned?"

"Not in the least." She held up her hands for Steven to take and pull her off the bed. As they embraced, the phone rang.

110

"Never fails," Steven said as he reached for the hotel room phone. "Hello."

Barbara walked to the window and looked out while Steven was on the phone. She didn't hear what he was talking about, as her thoughts were about moving.

"That was Ben. He wants to know if we can meet with him at the manor for lunch. I told him we would be there."

Barbara moved away from the window. "Yes, of course. Let me get ready." Her mind was swimming with the stress of moving as she finished getting ready to see her brother. As they drove, she wondered what Ben wanted to discuss. Whatever his news was, she had news to share with him about them moving. She was smiling when they arrived at the manor. Life was good, stress and all.

Ben met them at the front door with a big smile.

"You look happy. No, you look like you are bursting with something to share."

"Oh, I have something to share, and you won't believe what it is." He said as he walked them into the great room.

"We're not meeting in the kitchen? This must be big." Barbara said as she took a seat by the fireplace.

Steven sat next to his wife while Ben sat in the recliner.
"

"I received a phone call this morning," Ben began. "And you won't believe who it was from."

"As excited as you are, I would say it was from the man who raised you."

"Okay, that was too easy for you, but yes. It was David."

"What did he have to say for himself. Did he say why he has been out of touch with you for so long?"

"He told me where he had been and added that he would be in our area tomorrow and wants to meet with us."

"Us?" Barbara questioned. "Why us and not just you? Do you think he has something to tell us about when we were kids? Did he know we had found each other? He must if you say he wants to meet with both of us."

"He didn't know we had found each other at first. He just said he would be in the area and wanted to meet with me. I told him that whatever it was about, he needed to know that we had found each other and had a lot of questions."

"What was his reaction?" Barbara sat forward. She looked at Steven and then at Ben. This could be interesting, she thought.

"I could tell he reacted to the news by how he hesitated before he said anything else. He then said he would like to meet with both of us."

"I wonder if he has come up with a great story for us or if he is ready to tell us the truth."

"What do you think the truth is?" Steven asked.

"I'm not sure. I am sure that David knew we were siblings when we lived by that creek. The more I think about it and recall our time there, what other reason would he have to keep me away from Barbara most of the time? Why would he punish me for playing with her and the other little girl."

"The other girl's name was Wendy," Barbara interjected.

"Yes, Wendy. You two were inseparable. I'm surprised that you two were not blood siblings. Whatever happened to her?" Ben asked. He knew that would change the direction of the conversation and delay his telling Barbara where David had been the last couple of years. But, he had asked, so he would wait.

"When they removed us from Annie and the creek, she was placed with a family that adopted her. We stayed in touch for a while but lost touch by the time we were in high school. We both got busy with other things. I often think of her and wonder where she is.

"Maybe when we finish finding out the facts about you and Ben, we can find Wendy," Steven said. He was getting good at finding things and people. He was also good at keeping secrets when best for those involved.

"So what did David say? Where has he been?"

Ben lowered his head. He didn't know if he was ready to share that news but knew it would come out when they met with David later.

"David has been in jail."

"Jail! Why?" Barbara asked as she sat up straight.

"Yes, jail for the last two years. It seems he got caught up in a fraud case. He had hoped he would not have to serve time, but he had a tough judge, according to him. He is out of jail but still on probation for five more years. And still has a hefty fine to pay."

"Wait," Barbara held up her hand to stop Ben from speaking. "He has a fine to pay, and he contacted you. Don't you see why he called you?"

"Why?" Ben began and then stopped. "You don't think he contacted me for money, do you?"

"I would almost bet on it, Brother. Just look at it. He has not been in touch for several years. Let's not even count the ones he was in jail; he was not in contact before that time, right?"

"True, it had been a while before that."

"Now he contacts you when he is being released from jail. I think, when we meet with him, we need to be careful and not fall for whatever he wants from us."

"You may be right, Sis. And then I told him about the two of us. I wonder what is going through his mind now."

"I would say it is ways for him to get out of the truth and not ways of how he can get money from you."

"It will be interesting to listen to him. He asked me to go pick him up when they release him."

"Okay. Do you want me to go with you? Do you think we should have some questions written down to ask? I know we have several, but they may all disappear when we meet." Barbara asked.

"I think that is a good idea. Go to the office over there. Sara always has a notepad on her desk."

"Thank you. Are you sure she won't mind?"

"She'll be fine. I do it all the time."

"Yes, but you are family."

"I see you have already forgotten; you and Steven are now family."

Barbara looked at her husband. "Family. Do you know how good it feels to be a part of such a great family?"

Steven reached for her hand. "I am so glad we made this trip. You deserve to be part of this family."

"Thank you," Barbara said as she rose to walk to the office. For once in her life, she felt she belonged.

Chapter Eighteen

The Missing Piece

David awoke on his cot and looked around. It was his last day to be held within these walls. Two years had been longer than needed, in his opinion. It was also his opinion that it was all a big mistake. He just had to get out to prove it. Before he was released, his last phone call before leaving had proven to be more than he ever expected. All he wanted was some help to pay the fine. Once his fine had been paid off, he would disappear again and leave him alone. Instead, Ben told him that he had connected with his sister. Now it was time for him to tell them the truth. The truth that they could handle. He doubted they could handle the actual truth.

Ben arrived on time to pick David up when he was released. It was hard to believe that this man could have been living so close to his home. And if he didn't live close, why was he in a local jail? Ben thought David had lived in another state all this time. Just another question to ask when they spoke.

David turned and took one last look at what he hoped never to see again. His life would never be the same. As he sat in the front seat next to Ben, he realized how true that thought was. His life would never be the same. He wondered if it would be better or worse when all was said and done.

"Hello, David. How are you?" Ben said, not knowing what else to say.

"I am good now. Getting out of there is the best thing to happen to me." David said as he buckled his seat belt. "Thank you for coming to pick me up."

"Where are you staying? You only asked me to pick you up, not take you anywhere."

"Well, I was hoping you would let me stay with you until I get my act together."

Ben almost slammed on his breaks. How could this man assume such a thing? He had not been in touch with the family for years, and now he wanted to move in? Instead, he said, "I am sure we can find a place for you to stay. First, we have some talking to do."

"Yes, I know," David said as he looked out his window to avoid facing Ben. He was not sure he was ready to talk.

"We have a lot of questions. My first question is, why the heck were you in jail? And why had you not called me when it happened."

"I didn't call you because I didn't want to get you involved at the time."

"Oh, but you want me involved now?"

"Now, I am a different person. My life changed while I was inside."

"Changed from what? A liar, a cheat, a scam artist?"

"I'm not a cheat. Well, not anymore. I was a liar and a scam artist. I admit that much."

"So, what got you caught and sent away?"

"Can we not talk about that just yet?"

"No, we will talk about it now before I decide where you will be staying. I may not want you spending time at my house with my wife and children. I may want you in a hotel out of town. Heck, I may want you on a bus to an unknown destination. But, I do need answers. First to the why and then to deeper questions."

"I know, and you deserve the truth about it all." David hung his head.

"Thank you. Now, start talking." Ben turned onto the highway and headed toward Bella Rose Estate.

David took a deep breath before speaking. "I got caught up in the wrong crowd several years back. I worked for a company that trusted me with confidential information, all their financials, and access to the safe. I loved the job. I had finally made it to the big league in business. As you know, our life when you were little was not the best."

"That is the other topic we need to discuss. But, go on with what happened at your job."

"After a while, the owner started spending the company money for his personal life. He asked me to cover it up. When I explained that I could not do that, he said he would find someone who would. I needed the income for my lifestyle, so I put up with his dealings. I started to work the numbers for him, and he pulled me further up in the company. Before I knew it, I didn't even think we were doing anything wrong." David stopped talking as he thought about the past.

"Then what happened?"

"Then we got a visit from the government, and my boss got taken down. He has a few more years of jail time to complete and a fine that he will never be able to pay."

"How did you get away with such a light sentence?"

"I cooperated with them and handed him over. They gave me a lighter sentence because I helped them put him away."

"Did you learn your lesson? What are your plans for work now? Can you even get a job anywhere?"

"I am not sure where I'm going from here. I have the fine to pay and am on probation for the next five years. My parole officer will help me find work. I need to stay out of trouble while under her watch. I have an appointment with her tomorrow."

"Ah, I can assume you need a ride to see her?"

"I will find a way to get there. I don't want to burden you with my troubles. Well, beyond picking me up today."

"Why did you call me, anyway? You've not been in touch in years."

"It is time for me to make amends with my past. That is something I learned while in jail and going to therapy. I have to, no, I want to start over with a clean slate."

"That would be nice. First, we need to discuss why the past was such a mess." Ben pulled onto the driveway leading to the manor as he spoke.

"You live here?" David asked when he looked around and spotted the manor.

"I live in one of the smaller houses on the property. My wife is part owner of this land and business. And no, before you get any ideas, you will not become a part of this."

"I was not thinking that. I was thinking you have done well with your life considering your childhood."

"Yes, I have done well for the most part. It has taken several years to get here, and I don't want you or anyone to ruin it."

"I won't ruin it. Hopefully, I can help you understand your beginning."

"And that is why I agreed to pick you up and let you come here. I need, we need, answers." Ben parked the car and turned off the engine. "You have a lot of explaining to do."

"Yes, I do," David said as he unlatched his seat belt and opened his door to step out.

Ben walked to the manor's entrance with the man he had called his uncle as a child. Hesitating before opening the door, he looked at David. "Behave while you are here."

"It is the only way I plan to be," David said as he followed Ben into the massive great room of the manor.

Sara walked out of her office to greet Ben and David. After a brief introduction and conversation, Sara offered one of the rooms on the second floor to David to stay in while he searched for a place to move. She was thrilled to see Ben connect with David. Sara hoped this meant Ben could move forward with his life. She knew he felt something was missing, even after finding Barbara.

David settled in his room and stood gazing out his window. His room was located at the back of the manor with a view of the mountains. It had been so long since he had seen such beauty he felt glued to where he stood. A knock on his door interrupted his thoughts. He opened the door to find Ben, who said it was time to meet more of the family. On the way home, Ben had explained how the family met in the kitchen most of the time, and that was how he would introduce everyone. David forced himself to turn from the window and follow Ben downstairs. He had no idea what to expect. He only knew that it was time to make his changes and be honest.

The first to greet him was Maddex. Like his older brother, Marc, he didn't know any strangers. Everyone was a friend to him. Maddex reached up to shake David's hand. Marc was right behind him. Ben introduced his boys and sent them to sit at their table for some snacks. Ben introduced Heather, Andy, Karen, Barbara, and Steven. When David saw Barbara, his past rushed in. He had to look away for a moment.

As was true to their family, everyone started talking at once, asking him all kinds of questions. David did his best to answer the easy ones. He was there until he found a place to live; he had been in jail; he was turning over a new leaf in his life, and he wanted to get the truth out. Those were the easy answers.

An hour later, the only people left sitting around the island were Ben, Barbara, and David. It was time for the truth. David had not expected this time to arrive so soon. He hoped he would have had more time to get to know Ben and Barbara before they demanded answers. He also understood they were owed the facts as soon as possible. They had waited long enough.

"I guess it is time to tell you the truth," David said when he heard the silence and felt the accusations through the eyes fixed on him.

"Yes, it is time," Barbara replied as she poured herself a fresh cup of coffee. She offered Ben and David one and poured theirs before sitting back down. "We need to know what you know."

David felt relief. They only wanted to know what he knew. Maybe it would be easier than he anticipated.

"I will tell you what I know. Where do you want me to begin?" He had no idea what they already knew about the accident when their parents died. Plus, it had been so long ago that they may have forgotten some things.

"You can start at the beginning," Barbara said. David could feel her anger.

"Yes, at the beginning would be a good place to start. Even before the death of our parents, if you know anything." Ben looked at this man he had called Uncle for most of his life. He sensed there was so much more to him than they expected to learn immediately.

David took a sip of the coffee and then took a deep breath. "When your parents were in the car accident, it was a shock to everyone. No one knew what to do with you." He said. Looking at Barbara, he added, "And no one told me about you at that time." He took a sip of coffee before continuing.

"I was contacted a few days after the accident to come to pick you up. They had found out I was your father's brother and only living relative. I had not been in touch with the family in many years and didn't even know I had a nephew, let alone a niece. When I came to pick you up, you, Ben, were the only one I knew about that needed a home. They said you were the only one who came to them after the accident. I had no way of knowing any different, so I took you and went on with my life. I moved us to the property at the creek after a couple of years of living in town. My wife had left me by then. She had wanted to have children but was unable to have her own. When you came into our lives, you were a godsend to me. She could not handle it. You were not her blood, and she refused to accept you. I told her I needed to care for you, and she soon left."

"She left you because of me?" Ben asked.

"Yes, she did. I had a choice to make, and I chose to take care of you. I knew if she was unwilling to accept you, she was not the person for me."

"Wow. Thank you. You sacrificed your soulmate for me."

"Not really. If she had been a soulmate, she would have stayed. She did try, but in the end, I was left on my own to raise you."

"Is that when you moved to the house by the creek?" Barbara asked.

David was caught off guard. He was not ready to talk about that time in his life. He hoped those memories would never arise again.

"That is when I remember the most about my time as a child with you," Ben added.

"To be honest, yes, that was when I moved there. My ex-wife took everything from me when we divorced. I had to start my life over again, but I had you. The house by the creek was available, hidden away from city life, and I felt it was a good place to raise you."

"So what happened?"

"What do you mean what happened? It was a good life there."

"Not from what I remember," Ben said.

"Not from what I remember either," Barbara added.

David took a deep breath. His facial expression tried to hide his feelings, but it was obvious he knew he had some explaining to do. Sitting before him were two adults who deserved the truth as only he could tell. Well, maybe he and one other person. It was up to him to supply the missing piece in their lives.

Chapter Nineteen

Facts

The afternoon proved to be life-altering for Ben and Barbara. When they first found the photos that put them together years after their parent's death, they never dreamed the truth about that time in their lives would be so complicated. David's account of when they all lived by the creek still left them wanting more answers. Now they felt the need to find Annie and get her side of the story. David's was just one side. They also had each other's sides, but there was room for one more side in their case.

David retired to his room after telling his story. He knew Ben and Barbara would need to mull it over and talk about it. He hoped that the truth would give them the peace they needed to continue in their lives now that they had reunited.

"So, what do you think of his story? Believable?" Barbara asked as she looked at her brother. She imagined her face looked as confused as his.

"I am blown away. Yet, something still does not add up." Ben said as he squinted his eyes, looking for more answers."

"I agree. Let's review what David told us, Barbara said. "Maybe we can find something we missed hearing."

"David said he was called a couple of days after the accident. Why did it take so long to notify him?"

"Maybe there was no identification in the car. Maybe he was out of town at the time, and they could not reach him."

"Okay, I'll give you that thought pattern."

"My question is, why did he not say anything to Annie when he realized who I was?" He could have brought us together when we were still kids."

"Yes, I agree. There has to be a reason. When did he realize you even existed? He said he didn't know about you when he came to take me to live with him. Maybe he did know and didn't want to be burdened with having another child, so he never mentioned you to the authorities." Ben was trying to figure it all out.

"Or maybe he didn't realize it until we lived at the creek. Maybe when he talked to Annie something came out that made him put the pieces together.

"He could have said something to Annie and gotten custody of you." Ben was thinking out loud.

"True, but I would have lost the one person who willingly took care of me. But maybe if we had been together, we would have turned out better."

"Speak for yourself; I think we turned out fine." Ben smiled.

"I agree, but it could have been better. We would not have had to endure so much along the way. Especially me. I got so tired of all the foster families, and then when I was adopted, it was not much better. They tried hard, but it was Annie that I longed to live with. I felt connected to her. As bad as life was when she divorced and lost half of her charge of children. She did her best to care for Wendy and me."

"There is more to our story than he let on. He knew something back then but was afraid or unable to say anything."

Ben and Barbara were silent for a while. Each was lost in their thoughts. Ben stared into space. Again, he wondered why his visions did not include a man sitting in the car's front seat. His memories had not changed over the years. It was always the same. There was no man in the driver's or passenger's seat. And no man had come forward to claim him afterward. Yet, here was David claiming to be his uncle.

Barbara sat in silence. Her eyes closed. She had shared everything she could remember from that time in her life with Ben and with Steven. Hearing David's side of the story didn't change her views but did change some facts.

David was Ben's uncle. And David knew Barbara was his niece but didn't tell Annie. Something still felt wrong. Barbara wanted to know what was still missing. She still felt as though she was standing alone in her life. She had Steven, Ben, and his family, but why had she been excluded from the family she could have had if David had just said something.

"Why didn't he say anything to Annie to let her know who I was?" Barbara spoke, breaking the silence in the room.

"I know. I wonder that too. He certainly had plenty of time to do so. You lived there for what, two years?"

"I did. We were active in the area. Annie got involved and made a few friends while we were there. Heck, she and David had become friends. Or so it seemed."

"Yes, there were times they were alone and talking. I wonder what they were discussing. Did Annie ever say anything to you that had your question the way things were?"

"No, but then, we were very young. Maybe she didn't think I would understand. Maybe they both thought things were better if kept secret since we were so young and had already been uprooted from our families. She may have thought I could not deal with another move." Barbara thought back to that time in her life.

"That could be. But we were also so young that it may not have made a difference to us who we lived with. I think we need to find Annie."

I think you are right. I need to talk with Steven to see if he can work on that for us. After all, he did connect us to David."

"And he connected us after all these years."

"For not being a detective, he has been amazing."

"I know. I have no idea how Steven developed that skill. I don't remember him finding anyone else for anyone."

"I think we have more thinking to do and trying to recall living there. More than the time frame of when I saved you from drowning."

"It is amazing. I remember that so vividly. I wonder why that is?"

"I have no idea why, but it has come in handy so far."

"I'll say. Look at us. If it were not for Steven looking for my missing piece, I would still not have a life. I would still feel alone."

"Same here. But I think you agree—there is still something missing."

"Or somehow, the complete truth has not come out yet."

"You are right. I think David is still hiding something."

As they continued to talk, Andy came into the room to prepare a snack for the guests. They looked at him and wondered how long he had been there. They were so focused on their conversation that he could have been there a long time.

"Sorry, we just found out that David is my biological uncle on my father's side."

"Wow. That must be a shock to you." Andy said as he reached for the pantry door.

"It is, but it also has us thinking there is even more to him. We just don't know what it is yet."

"Good luck. Is there anything any of us can do to help?"

"I don't think so. We have decided we need to find Annie."

"The one foster Mom you had?"

"Yes. The one I had when we were about four. It turns out that Ben and I lived across the road from each other during that time."

"You what?"

"Yes, we spent about two years living across the road from each other and never knew we were related."

"Wow" was all Andy could think of to say.

As Andy was baking cookies for snacks for the guests, David walked into the kitchen. In the meantime, Ben and Barbara had gone for a walk to the gazebo.

"What are you making?" David asked.

"Chocolate chip cookies for the guests. I always make too many so the family can have some." Andy replied, making it sound like David was part of the family and not just a guest.

"They smell wonderful," David said as he walked out the door.

"Thanks. Oh, by the way, thank you for being here to fill in the missing piece of Ben and Barbara's lives. I know Ben has been lost for so long. From what he has shared, Barbara always felt that way too. Said she always felt like she was standing alone in her life. No one ever stayed very long until Steven came along. And even then, Steven knew something was missing but didn't know what it was at first. I am so glad he found you."

David looked at Andy. "You mean that?"

"Mean what? That I'm glad Steven found you, or that she always knew a piece was missing?"

"About Barbara always feeling like she was alone. She always had someone taking care of her. I made sure of that."

"You made sure of what?"

"Nothing, sorry. I was just saying that she seemed to be happy."

"Women are like that. They make you think everything is fine, when deep inside they may have a lot of turmoil in their lives."

"I guess you're right," David opened the door and walked out without saying another word. He walked with no destination in mind. He had to think. Maybe he needed to tell everyone the truth—the real truth.

Ben and Barbara sat on the bench in the gazebo. They saw David walking toward them but sensed he was just out for a walk; until he reached them.

"Hello, you two," David said as he stopped before entering. "Mind if I join you?"

"Don't mind at all," Ben said as he inched over to make more room.

"Thanks," David said, adding nothing more.

"We've been out here trying to digest the details you gave us earlier. Why are you out here? This is the place to go to think." Ben said

David took a deep breath as he sat down. He couldn't look at them for a moment. "I'm here to tell you both the truth."

"I thought you did tell us the truth. What else is there to know." Barbara asked, wondering what else he had to share.

"You both deserve God's truth. I couldn't bring myself to open up earlier. I was afraid."

"Afraid? Afraid of what? What are you still hiding?" Ben asked as he moved his body around to look at David.

"Afraid that you would not understand, not accept me, not believe me for whatever reason."

Barbara turned to look at David. "I think we can handle anything you tell us. If not, we will work through it. We're tougher than we look if you're afraid of a few tears."

"No, certainly not afraid of any tears. I am afraid you will tell me to get out of your lives. I know I was not in your life, Barbara, but this will be hard to swallow."

David then took a deep breath. He reached up to the necklace around his neck. David had never taken it off and was now regretful for it. He would like to add one more memory if they would accept him. This time he hoped it would be a positive memory. He let go of the necklace when he noticed Barbara looking at it.

Barbara looked at David but didn't say anything. She wanted to hear what he had to say.

Chapter Twenty

Confession

A breeze gently touched Ben, Barbara, and David as they sat in the gazebo. Barbara brushed her hair away from her face. She felt an odd sensation on her hand like someone had touched it, but no one had. A shiver ran through her, but she did her best to ignore it. She concentrated on David as he began to speak.

David sighed a deep sigh. He looked out at the mountains in the distance. The beauty of them touched his heart. He looked over at Ben and Barbara. What he was about to say was not the hardest thing he had ever done in his life. Once before, he had made a decision that had changed the lives of everyone he loved. The time had come to admit the truth. The sad, maybe even sick, horrible truth was about to be revealed. He did not know what it would do to the two most important people in his life. He just knew they deserved to know, even though it could have devastating results and he could lose everything he hoped to gain.

Ben looked at David in anticipation of what he was about to say. Ideas of the possible scenarios ran through his mind. He was preparing for anything from this man. He already suspected that his life had been a lie. What could be worse?

"Ben, Barbara," David began as he shifted his body to face them better while still sitting alongside Barbara. "I have something to tell you that may change how you feel about me and Annie and life in general. I have a confession to make."

Ben and Barbara focused their attention on him and what he was saying.

David looked at Ben. "It goes back to the day of the car accident you were in with your mother."

He waited for a reaction, but there was none, so he continued. "That day is one I will never forget. Ben, you are right in your memories that your father was not in the car when the accident happened. I know this because," he stopped talking as a lump formed in his throat. How could he just blurt out the truth after all these years? He stared at Ben. Could this man read his mind? Would he have to say anything else?

David continued. "You see, I am." He stopped again and looked away. He could not form the words he needed to say. A tear ran down his cheek. Now was not the time for him to cry, he thought. He wiped the tear as he felt Ben's realization come to light. He looked back at Ben.

Ben looked at him; glared at him; looked deep into his eyes like he had never looked at anyone's eyes before. Ben's eyes opened wide; he stood up, never taking his eyes off David. Rage built up in his voice; he pointed his finger at David as he spoke. "Oh my God! Barbara, this man, the man who had me call him uncle and ignored you." Ben stopped. He could not form the words.

Barbara looked at Ben and reached for his hand to control him. She looked from her brother to David. "What are you saying, Ben?"

Ben continued to yell at David. "How could you? How could you live that lie all these years? How could you do that to us?"

"Ben, what is it? Who is he?" Barbara did not yet understand but knew it was not good.

"Don't you get it, Sis? David is not our uncle who kept us apart when he knew who you were. He is not the uncle who ignored you all those years. NO! David is a fraud, a liar, a delusional man! David is our father!" Ben walked away to avoid forming a fist and hitting the man sitting with them.

"What!" Barbara's mouth hung open. Her eyes looked at David and then her brother in shock.

"Yes, this man has lied to me, to us, all our lives!"

David hung his head. He was trembling. His hands shook. He was waiting for a punch from his son. The truth was out. He deserved whatever his children gave him. "Yes, I am your father." He felt a sense of relief mixed with the fear of what his children would do next. Tears were flowing.

"Our father? How could you be our father and never tell us? How could you not come for us after the accident? Why the lies?" Barbara whispered as she slid away from David. She was in so much shock she could not speak louder even though the anger inside her was boiling, and she could not get up even though she wanted to get as far away from this man as she could. Her mind was a jumbled mess of emotions, none of them calming.

"I wish I could explain it so you would understand, but I don't think it will ever make sense to you."

"How could it make sense? You, you, You!" Ben was so furious and conflicted he didn't know what to say. Here sat a man he had agreed to call his uncle all his life. A man who had ignored the fact that Barbara was alive and so close he could have, and had, in fact, touched her, yet he never said anything to anyone! How could any loving father do that?

"David, why? Why? Why did you let me, your flesh and blood suffer ALL my life in foster care, being tossed around like a rag doll, dealing with abuse and pain, and the feeling of no love, no one caring, no one sticking up for me? How could you sit back and watch what I went through and not reach out to me? HOW, How, how could you treat me as if I was a stranger?" Barbara was by then standing and pacing. If it had been colder out, the steam would be visible coming off her. There sat her father! Her flesh and blood! He had been with them for a few days already, ate meals with them, and yet never said a word. "How long were you going to keep this lie? Did you EVER intend to let us know who you were?" Barbara paced to keep from grabbing David by his shoulders and shaking him to near death.

Ben walked over to his sister and put his arms around her. "Calm down, Sis."

"Why should I calm down? Aren't you upset over this, this person? I'm not even close to calling him a man, let alone my Father!"

"Barb, I understand your reaction. Yes, what he did to us was horrible. Yes, he is very low on my list of good people at the moment. And believe me, I wanted to deck him one. That is why I walked away. We do need to let him explain."

"I don't think anything he has to say to try to explain it will Ever calm me down. I lived through Hell for so much of my life. I stood alone, raised myself. I LONGED for a loving family. I ached for acceptance in my life! And now to find out I could have and Should have had that? NO, I'm not calming down!" She used her strength to pull away from Ben. She didn't even want to have anything to do with Ben at that moment. She wanted to be alone—oddly.

Ben watched as his sister stormed out of the gazebo and headed for the manor. He knew it would take her a long time to accept David. It would take him time to accept the truth. At least he had the chance to be raised by him, even if it was under the guise of being his nephew.

David had sat with his head hung low, crying, as he listened to his daughter yell and scream at him. He deserved all of what she threw at him and more. David hoped that time would heal what he had broken when his children were toddlers. He hoped he lived long enough to be accepted. He had given up on the desire to be loved by them. Ben might be able to love him, but his daughter never would. He regretted his life. When he saw Barbara storm off, he looked up at his son. His sorrow was evident on his face.

Ben turned to look at David when he could no longer see Barbara walking away. "So, old man, How did you expect her to act? What reaction did you expect from me? Are you satisfied with what just happened? Are you happy?"

David composed himself and looked up at his son. "I did not know what to expect from either of you. I knew it was time to tell you no matter what the results. I am prepared for anything either of you wants to do or say to me. I assumed she would react in anger. I did her wrong all of her life."

"And why Did you do that?" Ben raised his voice without realizing it.

"Because at the time it happened, it was the best thing to do."

"To walk away from your children? How can that ever be the best thing to do?"

"When you hear the whole story, I hope you will understand."

"I doubt we ever will, but I am ready to hear it."

"I am willing to tell you, but I think I'd prefer to tell both of you simultaneously. Maybe with your spouses by your side."

"I think that is a good idea. I will try to talk to Barbara, and you can only hope and pray she is willing to listen."

"I hope she will listen. It won't take away the pain she feels, but it may at least explain my actions to a point she can handle it better."

"I think you need to stay sitting here for a little longer. I am going to talk to Your Daughter." Ben emphasized the last two words of his statement. He wanted to drill it into David that he had a daughter. A loving, beautiful daughter that he had ignored for most of her life.

Ben placed his hand on David's shoulder to indicate that he should not move. Then he began to walk to the Manor.

David watched as his son walked away. He had no idea what was to come next. Would he have a relationship with his children after all these years, or would he even lose his son because of a lie he created so many years ago because he felt it was the only thing he could do? Only time would tell. He lowered his head and wiped more tears away. His life and his future lay in the hands, hearts, and decisions of his children.

Chapter Twenty-One

Reaction

Sara heard the side kitchen door bang as she sat in her office at the manor. She walked to the kitchen, where she found Barbara opening and closing the cabinet doors with as much anger as she had slammed the kitchen door.

"Barbara, what is wrong?" Sara rushed to her and grabbed her hands to stop her.

"I need a drink! Is there nothing to drink here?"

"It's hidden, but why do you need a drink?" Sara said as she let go of Barbara's hands, opened the cabinet door closest to the outside door, and took out a bottle of red wine and a stemless wine glass.

"One word – David!" Barbara sat down on the stool at the island while Sara poured her a glass of red wine.

"David?" Sara handed her the glass and sat down with her.

Barbara took a mouthful of wine, swallowed it in one gulp, and then took a smaller one before responding.

"Because he lied to us! He lied to all of us. For years!"

"How did he lie to you? What's going on?" Sara looked around to see if Ben was around.

"He, he, he confessed to Ben and me." Barbara pointed toward the door and took another large swallow of wine. She handed the empty glass to Sara, who added more wine, and reached for the other glass she had retrieved from the cabinet to join Barbara in a drink.

"What did he confess to?" Sara knew it would take specific questions or a lot more wine to get details.

"He confessed that he is not Ben's uncle."

"Ok. What or who is David then?"

Barbara just shook her head. She could not bring herself to say the words. She could only feel her anger and know that she wanted to kill that pain with alcohol.

Sara sat next to Barbara with her arm around her shoulders. She did not know the details causing this pain to her new family member but knew it was unacceptable. No one treated any of her family that way. No one.

As she poured Barbara a third glass of wine, the kitchen door opened again. Ben marched in. He walked over to Barbara, ignoring that Sara was right there. If he saw her, he did not indicate it.

"Sis, it will be okay. You need to calm down so we can discuss this rationally."

"Rationally? There is no rationale for this whole situation. He lied to us! At least he told you he was family, even though it was the wrong relationship. Me? Me, he left to fend for myself!"

Sara stood up and walked away a little to let the siblings talk. Their voices were raised, and Sara knew from experience it was best to leave the two of them alone. She walked away from the island but stayed within earshot. She was catching a word here and there but could not make out most of them.

"Ben?" Sara whispered from the entry to the great room. "Do you have this?"

Ben nodded and motioned for Sara to come back in. She needed to hear this as much as the rest of the family did. He was not about to keep secrets from the family he loved. He knew the pain of keeping secrets.

"What is going on?" Sara whispered when she got close enough to her brother-in-law. He may not be blood, but he had been family for several years and what affected him affected her.

"Seems David, my uncle? Well, my uncle is actually our Father." He gave no other details; he wanted his sister-in-law to hear it and maybe even offer good advice; he knew she had been through a lot growing up and hoped she had some wisdom to share.

"He's your what? Your Father?" Sara pulled out a barstool and sat next to Barbara. She put her arm around her, joining with Ben in their attempt to calm her down.

"No wonder she needs a drink. I may have to pull out the other bottles I have."

"Do you have anything stronger?" Barbara looked up and raised her empty glass.

"Funny. I should not even have this in here. Andy is a recovering alcoholic, so we keep this place as dry as possible. I occasionally need a drink, so I have learned where he never looks. Hard to do with him being the chef." Sara replied. She got Ben a glass and poured the last of the wine into his. "Never fear—I have more wine." She was trying to digest the news Ben and just stated.

Ben took a drink of his wine and set his glass down. He had kept his hand on his sister's shoulder. She had stopped sobbing and shaking. "Are you going to be alright?"

"How could I be?" She sniffled. "But, yes, I will be alright—as soon as he leaves!"

"You know he can't leave. I guess he could leave, but we need answers to so many more questions. If we make him leave now, we will never know anything and certainly never know his side of the story." Ben said he glimpsed at Sara.

Barbara sat up. Her brother was right. She had questions; mainly—why?

"He has been lying all our lives, Sara. He is our father but never said a word to either of us." Barbara said after controlling her sobbing.

"How could anyone do that to their children?" Sara asked without thinking.

"That is what I want to know. At least David raised Ben while pretending to be his uncle. He never attempted to find me and tell me the truth."

"Plus, we found out that when we were about four years old, we lived across the road from each other, and David never said a word. He let us play together but never told her foster mother and never tried to tell Barbara. Of course, she was only four, and she may not have understood it back then. But he could have told Annie and tried to get Barbara back into his guardianship."

"Yes, but if he had done that back then, the law could have come after him for fraud. Did you say David never adopted you? Or waited several years, right?"

"Yes, he never adopted me. Why?"

"If you were just his foster child, he got paid to keep you. Had he confessed, he would have not only lost that money, but they would have investigated the accident and eventually found out who he truly is. He could have spent years in jail."

"That is where he belongs!" Barbara said.

"You may be right, but for now, if we can keep him in good graces with us, maybe we can get the truth out of him. Maybe, there are underlying reasons why he did what he did all those years ago."

"You are right, Big Brother." Barbara smiled. Ben seemed like her older brother, not her twin, with how he was handling the news they were dealing with recently.

"So, may I get him and bring him into the manor?"

"Yes, you may. I'll do my best not to attack him when he comes in. I still want to beat the snot out of him for what he did to me for all those years."

"I understand. But I have witnessed some of the pain you have dealt with over the years. You can handle all of this."

"I will find a way. Go get him so he can start talking."

"Are you sure? Are you ready?"

"Ready as I will ever be." She moved her eyes to Sara, "Did you say you had more wine?"

"Yes, Barbara, I have more wine. But I think you need to watch how much you drink, so you are sober when David speaks?"

Barbara set her glass down on the counter. "Why do you have to make sense? I've been told about you."

"All good, I hope."

"Yes, of course. And I need that right now, I guess." Barbara stood up to take her glass to the sink. Before she could, Sara picked up the wine bottle.

"Good. We will pour you just a little to get you through the next hour. Then you are cut off, deal?"

"Deal. Thank you for being you. I would have ransacked this place and not stopped until I found that bottle or bottles. I get that way sometimes."

"We all do, reluctantly," Sara said before putting the wine bottle away in the corner of the cupboard.

So glad to have you as part of my new family. I hope and pray David gives you the answers you need, and you can accept whatever he says. I can't imagine his reason being a good one, but you never know."

"True, I can't imagine it either. Will you stay and listen to what David tells us?"

"I don't know if it is my place to be here. It is between you, Ben, and David." Sara gathered the other wine glasses and put them into the dishwasher.

"I want you to be here. I think the whole family should be here. That way we don't have to repeat the story to everyone, and everyone hears the same details."

"Let's wait and see what David says about who he wants here. Heather and Steven being here make sense. The rest of us are not directly related to the situation."

"I have not been here very long to watch this family, but in the short time I have been, I know you are all one big family. You are honest and open, and there is so much love here."

"Oh, if you only knew our back story." Sara shook her head as she smiled. "It has not always been this way. Our family has had its share of secrets and lies. We did learn from them, though, so we love a good story when it comes along.

"I want you all here. That should count for something." Barbara stood up. Her shoulders held back, her head up, the tears were wiped clean, and she was set to listen to the lies or the truth. Whichever David was about to tell them, she hoped it would be the complete truth.

Ben walked back into the kitchen alone. He had gone out to the gazebo to bring David back while Sara and Barbara had continued talking.

"David went to freshen up. He asked me to call for the family to be here in an hour."

"He wants the whole family here when he tells his story?"

"That's what he said. He said you and I deserve the truth, but he wants the family to know it too, which is why he asked for everyone to be here. "So let me get the family together." Ben was off to find Andy. He had already called Heather, and she was on her way to the babysitter with the boys.

An hour later, everyone was sitting in the great room. This conversation was more than a family meeting held in the kitchen around the island.

Ben and Barbara sat with their spouses. Their lives were about to change. It was up to David to make it a change for the better. Only he knew the truth. His children deserved to hear what he was about to say. They had calmed down enough to listen and make up their minds about him. Everything he had heard so far had been so positive about this family. Would it stay that way? Would he be accepted when he admitted everything?

Chapter Twenty-Two

Reasons or Excuses

David looked at the people seated around him. Their eyes focused on him. Their minds were full of questions he only hoped he could answer to their satisfaction. He needed to tell them the truth, no matter how bizarre it sounded. He had always heard the truth would set you free, but somehow, this truth would pin him down more. Whatever the outcome, he began to tell his side of the story.

Ben stood up before David had a chance to speak. "Barbara and I have just learned some shocking news. We called you all together to tell you the news, and David is here to explain it to us all."

Barbara reached out and took her brother's hand. He pulled her up to stand by his side.

"You all know that for years I felt something was missing in my life. I had no idea what it was. I thought, for some reason, that it had something to do with my biological father. I somehow felt he was still alive." Ben looked at his sister. Barbara smiled and nodded for him to continue.

"Instead, thanks to Steven knowing that Barbara was missing something in her life and doing research, we found out what we were missing was each other. We thought that was all there was."

"Then we found David," Barbara added, doing her best to sound calm.

"Yes. David. I grew up with David. He took me in and later adopted me. He told me to call him Uncle David. So I did." Ben looked at David. He was having a harder time holding back his anger than Barbara had.

David looked at his children. He wondered what Ben was going to say next.

"Today, we found out David is not my uncle," He looked at his sister and corrected his wording. "Not our uncle."

Everyone was silent as they looked from Ben to Barbara and then to David. Who was this man?

"Today David told us, get this, this man has lied to us all of our lives. This man? David? Is our biological father."

A pin could have been heard falling onto the floor.

"Now we are here to listen to him explain himself to all of us. Because clearly, neither Ben nor I understand any of it. And we doubt we could repeat whatever he has to say. So, our father, David, wants to explain it to all of us." Barbara moved her hand toward David to let him know the floor was his. Then she tugged at Ben as the two of them sat back down.

No one said a word as they waited for David to speak. They exchanged glances with each other. Andy looked at Sara as they read each other's minds. Here were more secrets that could ruin a person's life. They both shook their heads and redirected their look to David as he stood up.

David directed his attention to Ben and Barbara sitting next to each other on the sofa near the fireplace. He wished their lives had been different while they were growing up. The only thing he could do now was hope to improve their futures by confessing.

David took a sip of water and began his story. "You two may not remember the days before the accident. You have told me that you had been told that your parents were both killed in the accident. And Ben, you say you don't remember seeing your father in the car when it happened. And your memory of that is correct. I was not in the car that day. How they determined I was in the car and died that day, I don't know. The facts are I was out of the country that day. You see, you were too young to remember the days and weeks before that day. I had some business dealings that caused us to be in such financial trouble that your Mom and I divorced. I had moved away and then traveled out of the country to pursue a deal that would solve all of our financial issues. I wanted to make sure you were financially supported. Granted, the deal was not legal, but I was willing to try anything to care for the two of you."

"On the day of the accident, your mom was on her way to a new job. She had recently moved and didn't know many people where she was. She had taken you, Barbara, to the babysitter and was on her way to take you, Ben, to another person's house. For some reason, neither one could watch both of you. That was when the accident happened."

"When the babysitter heard about the accident, she contacted the authorities and told them that she had Barbara but could not keep her full time. When they told her Ben was in the hospital for minor injuries and asked if there were any relatives, she said she did not know of any. And she was right, there aren't any others. They asked about the father, and she said all she knew was that your mom was divorced and had no other information about me. Your mom had not been in her new location long enough for anyone to know much about her. Your mother had no identification on her. She had not changed her address or contact details to her new place. The former place was empty when the authorities went to the address they eventually found. And she had left no forwarding information."

"Something had to happen with you, so children's services took you, and the next day they placed you into the foster care system. The babysitter told the authorities that she could keep you, Barbara, but not Ben."

"So soon after the accident, you were placed in separate homes. Barbara, your babysitter, took you out of the state with her. Ben, you were placed with a local family. I returned to the states to find out what I could about both of you. I read about the accident in a local paper I received from home. It said that your mother had been killed and that one child, a boy, had survived. It also said that the man in the vehicle had been killed. No one asked if that man was me or not. They just assumed he was the father of the child who had survived. With no identification on either your mother or the man, there was no way to say or provide much more. The investigation was soon dropped.

"The deal out of the country had fallen through, and I had no money to spare. When I read the news and the details of the accident and that I had been assumed dead or at least missing, I came up with a scheme. I knew you two were young enough to never remember your parents. As the years went on, I figured you would not remember the accident. And since you were separated, I wasn't even sure you would remember having a sibling. So I recreated myself. I changed my name and other life details and signed up to be a foster parent, so I could get you living with me. Somehow, it worked after about a year, and you were placed with me. I was finally making some money at a new job, plus as a foster parent, I was getting paid to care for you. I told you to call me Uncle David. You complied, and that was what we became. People got to know you as my nephew. No one ever questioned how you ended up living with an uncle and not your parents. Plus, we never lived in one place long enough for most people to know us. I stayed quiet. I went to work and took care of you." David took a moment to gather his thoughts."

"Then came the time we lived in that house by the creek." He took a deep breath.

No one said a word. They were trying to digest all that he had already said. Ben tilted his head, and his eyes squinted as his facial expression indicated his disbelief in the man's story.

Barbara looked at David and shook her head. "So, you admit you forgot about me? You let me go into the foster care system and never looked back? You never questioned where I was, if I was ok, even if I was alive?" Her voice raised with each question.

"Barbara, they had taken you out of state. It was impossible to get information on any of the kids in foster care in those days. I had changed my name and gotten rid of anything that was my true identity. They were not going to give me any information. I was no one to them. I never told the system my true identity. I told Ben to call me Uncle to make it sound better than a young child calling an adult by their first name. People would have questioned us more if I had not done at least that much. And people often said we looked alike, so Ben being my nephew was believable."

Barbara was hurt even more and was crying. Her father had left her and never cared enough to come forward until now. Her heart ached. She felt contempt for this man. She almost questioned him about truly being their father now. Who's to say he was not still lying. But what would be the reason for lying now? In the same sense, what was his reason to confess now?

The room remained silent. Everyone sat expressionless in their thoughts. What was there to say that Ben and Barbara were not saying?

Ben broke the silence again. "So you are telling us that you did it for the money? You were so disturbed that your solution to make money was to use your child and the foster care system? Did you even love me? Did you love Barbara? Hell, did you ever even love our mother?" Ben was almost in tears as his voice cracked while asking these questions. How could a loving man do this to his family? How? To go so far as to change his identity.

David hung his head. "Yes, I loved you. I loved your mother. But when my luck ran out, and the only solution she and I had was to divorce and go our separate ways, my only thought was to make money. I had to make money to return to all of you and prove to her and you both that I loved you. It was not my intention to leave forever. Your mother did not know this, of course. To her, we were through. I had ruined her dreams of a happy life ever after with two children and a loving husband. She tried her best to get me to stay and somehow work things out. She had gone back to work; she was saving money as best she could. I was still spending it. Whatever I made, I spent. I was in a vicious cycle in my life."

"Why? How? How could you say you loved us and yet ruin us?"

A tear ran down David's face as the memories of his past life flashed before him. He knew what had caused it. He knew he should have been wise enough at the beginning of his downfall to control himself and put his family first. Instead, he had caused such pain he doubted he would ever get their love back. He shook his head. He realized at that moment that he did not deserve their love. Not then and not now.

"It doesn't matter now. Everything from my past that I tell you, my reasons and my truths, are excuses coming from a weak man who let the wrong people control my life. Your mother was the strong one. She deserved better. That was why I asked for a divorce from her. I knew she would find someone better to love her and to love you kids. Since I could not make things better in my life during that time. I hoped she would wait until I changed and I could ask her to take me back. I never wanted anything to happen to her. I never wanted anything bad for any of you. My leaving was to protect you."

"You say that, and I almost understand it in the beginning. I don't understand your actions after the accident."

"I was still under the influence of the fake promises in my life. I tried everything to make money. And I made a lot, but I threw it all away. When you needed me, I came home. The only way I could make it was to use the system. After several years, I turned my life around and put in to adopt you. They didn't know I was your biological father; they thought I was a foster dad who wanted to adopt you. So we worked it out, and I was able to adopt you. By then, I had a real job, making real money. I had stopped spending it. I was able to take care of you."

"This was after you knew about Barbara?"

"Yes, that was after we lived at the creek."

"Which raises my other question. You knew who I was when you saw me at the creek. Why didn't you say anything? Why didn't you come forward to the foster system during that time?"

"I lost a lot of sleep when you lived across the road from us. I was so afraid the two of you would look at each other and somehow know you were related. Maybe not twins, but that you would see or feel something. But you didn't."

"And you never told Annie?"

"Nope. Even after you kids went to bed, we often talked, but I kept the front that I was Ben's uncle. I never told her anything that would make her think differently. I saw how she cared for you. I heard the story of her divorce and sympathized with her. I let her lean on me. I began to have feelings for her and wondered what would happen if she and I got married. I pictured all of us living together under one roof. I would have my two children again. It would all be a lie, but I would be there for you."

"So what happened? Why did you not pursue her?"

"We were friends. Nothing more. She was not interested in anything more. Her divorce was fresh, she had not been treated well by him, and I wanted to give her time to heal from that. Then one day, I got up, and you were gone. Children's services had taken you and the other little girl away. I asked Annie what happened, and all she said was things were not working out for her, and she would be moving out.

"I remember we moved out soon after they left," Ben said. His mind was looking back to that time in his life. He was still so young, but he remembered a lot about the time at the creek. Now he knew why. He was with his sister, even though he did not know it then.

"Did you even look for me after that?" Barbara still felt rejected.

"No. I am so sorry. When I spoke with Annie, she said she was moving out because she had a better place, a good job, and she would adopt you. I believed her. She told me the only reason you and the other little girl had left first was so she could get everything set up in the new house first."

Barbara stood up and walked into the kitchen. She leaned against the kitchen sink and looked out to the mountains. A whole world out there. A big wide world. A world she was lost in, again. Once again, not counting that Steven and Ben were in her life, she was standing alone.

Steven walked up behind her and put his arms around her. He gently turned her around to face him and embraced her. She wrapped her arms around him and wept.

Ben walked into the kitchen as his sister dried her tears on a paper towel. "Sorry to interrupt, Sis, but David has asked you to come back into the great room."

"Why would he want that?"

"I don't know. But he said that he has another confession to make."

"You mean there is more? What else could there be?" Steven asked as he embraced his wife as she sank to almost sit on the floor. "I am not sure she can take much more." He helped his wife stand against him. She needed him more than ever.

"Believe me, I'm not sure what more I can take either, but I want to hear what he has to say. I need to know what more lies he has to confess."

"We will be back in there in a minute," Steven told Ben. "Give her a little time to compose herself."

"Ok. I will tell him."

Ben walked back into the great room, where everyone sat waiting. No one was saying anything. Ben told them that Barbara and Steven would be right in.

"I will tell you the rest when she gets here," David said.

Barbara and Steven walked in a few minutes later and sat back down.

"Thank you for coming back. I know you hate me for what I did, but there is more." David said and hung his head again.

"What more could it be?"

"Something that will make you hate me even more, maybe."

"Go ahead, spill it. It can't hurt more than it already does." Barbara held her husband's hand and hung her head. She did not want to even look at this man who was her father. It was bad enough that he ignored her most of her life; what could be worse? She waited.

'Yes, I need to tell you one more thing." David looked around at everyone in the room. He had their full attention. How could he not? What he was telling them was changing all of their lives in a way. It mainly changed his children's lives, affecting everyone who sat before him. He had learned that this family was strong in the short amount of time he spent with them. And it would take a strong family to help them through what he was about to tell them. He thought about what he had already confessed. Maybe this last confession would not be as bad as he originally thought.

"I've already admitted that I was your father. And that part is true. I am your biological father."

Barbara sat up and looked at him. She had a sudden image in her head. Her mind was recalling the imprint of her birth certificate. She stood up in protest. "Wait! If you are my biological father," she hesitated. "Your name is not David!"

David looked at her. His truth had been discovered, but it had taken him introducing the thought that enlightened her. "You are right. My real name is Benjamin Thomas."

Sara looked at Heather when she heard the name. It sounded familiar. Heather saw her sister's facial expression and looked at David, or Benjamin Thomas, whatever his name was.

"You're Benjamin Thomas Kane?" Sara asked.

"Yes." David was surprised at someone else speaking.

Ben interrupted them. "If that is your real name, who is this David person you've been using?"

"Long story."

"All we have is time, at the moment. Start explaining." Ben let out a deep sigh.

"David was my half-brother. I took on his name when I moved away from your mother. It was part of the details of recreating myself. David had died several years earlier. I know it was wrong of me to do such a thing. I did not think when I did it, but I could not go back once I started. I had moved out of the country, and it would have caused so many issues there."

"Caused so many issues there? What about all the issues you have caused in your own family here?" Barbara raised her voice.

"I know that now. I know I have ruined your lives. I don't blame you one bit, no matter how you may be feeling. I cannot change the past. I can only confess the truth and move on."

"I have a question." Sara leaned forward and looked at Heather. She knew Heather had the same thought.

"Okay, what is your question?" David, or rather Benjamin Thomas, had expected to hear from someone other than his children.

"If you are Benjamin Thomas, and your half-brother is David, you also have a half-sister Diane."

Benjamin Thomas hesitated as he looked at her. "Yes, I do."

"Your mother is Rhea."

"Yes, my mother's name is Rhea. How do you know that?"

"Not to minimize the wrong you have done to this family, but do you know your mother's history?" Heather asked as she leaned forward as Sara had. For them, this story was getting deeper and more interesting. Their world was getting smaller.

"Yes, she told me about it when I was a teenager."

Ben looked at his wife. He was trying to read her mind. Then his eyes opened wider as he suddenly put two and two together. His father, Benjamin Thomas, was the son of one of the unwed girls rescued by Rose and Robert, the grandparents of Sara, Heather, and Andy.

"You have got to be kidding!" Ben stood up and began to pace. He tried to absorb this new connection.

Barbara sat up in silence as she watched everyone's attitude change from anger to wonderment. "What's going on? Who is this Rhea person you all seem to know?"

"Remember when I told you what Bella Rose was initially?"

"Yes, a home for unwed mothers or unwed girls as you referred to them."

"Yes, one of the girls was Rhea. The baby boy she had while she was here was named Benjamin Thomas. Her firstborn is our father."

Barbara sat back, trying to digest this news. It was too much. She didn't want that connection to change their attitude toward what he had done to her. "I don't care who his mother was or is; he left me alone all those years, knowing full well where I was and how I was being raised." She looked at the man who had lied to her. She stood again and left the room.

Ben stood to follow her, but Steven held his hand up, stopping him. "You stay. I will go."

Ben looked at his father and the rest of his family sitting around him. No one spoke while they each absorbed reality.

Barbara and Ben were the grandchildren of Rhea, one of the first girls to stay at Bella Rose Estate. They had a connection to this place. Benjamin Thomas did too, but he felt unwelcome here because of his poor decisions as a young adult.

He knew his children would be accepted with their connection to Bella Rose. He also knew it would take them a long time to accept him if they ever did. He stood and left the room. None of the family stopped him.

Chapter Twenty-Three

Life After

Benjamin Thomas was gone. After the night of confessing to his children and their families, he knew his deceptive life when he was younger had cost him. He knew there was no sense trying to stay beyond his welcome. He had worn out his welcome, not just at Bella Rose Estate but also in the lives of his children. While the rest of the world around Bella Rose slept, Benjamin Thomas had packed his small suitcase, walked out the front door, got into his car, and drove away. He never looked back.

A week had passed since Benjamin Thomas's confession and disappearance. Ben and Barbara spent time together each day discussing what he had told them as the memories they shared from the time at the creek became clearer. They tried to remember more of the days around the accident and losing their mother, but they couldn't. They discussed their lives growing up and how they each felt something was always missing. Their bond grew more and more each day. They were each other's missing piece.

Heather caught herself watching her husband walk with his sister every day. She smiled each time she saw them together. This bond was what her husband had been missing all his life. Ben had been right, thinking his father had not been in the car at the time of the accident and that he was still alive. In the end, that was not the missing piece in his life. Barbara was the missing piece.

Heather again smiled when Ben walked into their home kitchen and noticed his big smile.

"What's that smile about?"

"Steven and Barbara have found an apartment to rent in town!"

"That is awesome! When are they moving? Not that I want them to move out of the manor since they moved in. It made more sense for them to be at the manor than in that hotel room for this long. I'm glad we had a room available."

"It's been amazing to have my sister so close, but you are right; they need their own place. I am thrilled that Steven was able to find work so fast."

"I am too. Glad it is working out for him to work with Terri. I think they will take the Downtown Café to a new level with the lounge they are adding."

"I agree. It will be nice to go there once in a while."

"Yes. An adult getaway."

"You make it sound like there is nothing else around here for adults to do."

"Dear, all we have done in the last several years has been with the boys. I could use an adult night out."

"Say no more. We will find a sitter and go out soon."

"Oh, that sounds wonderful. Now, will you help me fold these clothes, put them away in the boy's rooms, and then help me with supper?"

"Yes, we need an adult's night out." Ben laughed and reached for one of the boy's t-shirts to fold. Being a parent was great, but they were overdue for a break, even if only for a few hours.

A knock on the front door interrupted them. Ben went to answer it.

Andy was on the other side, ready to knock again.

"Hey, Andy, what's going on?"

"Nothing major. I wanted to invite you all over to the manor for dinner tonight."

"Ok. You could have called," Andy said.

"I know. I wanted to take a short walk. Needed a break for a few minutes."

"Why, what's going on?"

Andy motioned for Ben to come outside. Ben called out to let Heather know he would be outside for a few minutes.

"Andy, you have me concerned. What's going on?" Ben asked as soon as the door was shut.

"Well, I am about to my limit of keeping things quiet around here."

"What do you mean? Are you ok?" Ben stood next to Andy and whispered. "Anything I can help you with?"

"There is something you can help me with at the manor before dinner," Andy whispered back.

"Ok. I'll be right over. Let me tell Heather. She can bring the boys over when they are ready."

"Perfect. I'll meet you over there," Andy said and turned to return to the manor.

"Hey, Heather, Andy needs my help with something for a few minutes before dinner," Ben said as soon as he returned to the house.

"Ok. I'll be over with the boys as soon as I get them ready."

"Ok. See you in a few minutes." Andy reached over and kissed her on her forehead.

Ben closed the door behind him and walked to the manor. That was one thing he liked about living on the estate. They all lived close enough to walk to each other's homes. That was one thing that would be different when Barbara and Steven moved into town and their new apartment. His sister would be close, but not next door. There were no houses left on the estate, but there was extra land. He wondered if he could talk everyone into them living on the grounds along with the rest of the family. He'd ask Barbara about it first. She may not want to be so close to everyone.

Ben walked into the kitchen at the manor through the back door. He saw Andy sitting at the island with paper, streamers, and other decorations spread out in front of him.

Ben quickly tried to think about who was having a birthday. When no one came to mind, he asked.

"What are the decorations celebrating?"

"A big announcement."

"Oh? And what is that?"

Andy held up the main sign.

"Oh, Man!! Awesome!" Does anyone else know?"

"Not yet. That is why we are having everyone come for dinner. And it was last minute because we didn't want people asking us why we were having dinner together again. It has been a while, and it has always had a special reason since we've all gotten married."

Ben tried to remember the last time they had a family dinner, not for a special occasion. It had been a long time. Even with Steven and Barbara, it was always a special occasion, even if it was because she was his sister.

"I know Heather will be excited! Does Sara know?

"Nope, no one knows except us."

"Nice." Ben reached across the table and picked up a roll of blue streamers. Then he reached for the pink roll and started to drape them over and around things, so it hung down everywhere. He was having fun.

"You're doing a good job, Ben. I may have you help with the decorations at the manor. Oh wait, you already do help Heather with those. No wonder you are good at this." Andy was laughing.

It didn't take them long to have the kitchen eating area decorated for the big announcement that Andy and Karen wanted to share.

A few minutes after they had finished, family members began to arrive. Everyone got excited the moment they saw the decorations and started talking. It did not take long for Andy and Karen to stand together and announce that they were pregnant – again! They did not know if it would be a boy or a girl, but they had a special cake made that would tell them. As much as Karen wanted to know, she agreed with Andy to wait until after they ate. The wait time would allow the family to talk about it and guess the sex.

Andy had made a meal of baby carrots, tiny meatballs with spaghetti, and Brussel sprouts, otherwise called baby cabbages. When the time came, they stood behind the cake and had the family stand around the front. They held the knife together to make the center cut to reveal blue or pink center icing. A slow cut and gentle separation of the two sides of the cake revealed pink icing! They were going to have a baby girl! Karen was so excited she began to cry.

"Why the tears, My Love?"

"I'm having another girl! With all the boys in the family, I figured it would be a boy."

"I welcome the challenge! I'll have three girls to put up with, I mean, love." Andy reached over and kissed his wife with a piece of cake still in his mouth. He could not resist a good dessert, even when he did not make it.

Karen opened the envelope she had brought from her doctor to show everyone the ultrasound photos. Everyone looked at the photo, even though no one could tell if it was a girl or boy. They would believe the cake reveal.

A new baby in the family! And another baby girl! Plus, they welcomed Barbara and Steven into the family. Life at Bella Rose Estate never slowed down. Sara stood back and watched everyone as they enjoyed cake and ice cream. The children were eating at a small children's table they had added to the kitchen. Her daughter was growing. Ben and Heather's boys were full of personality and sometimes hard to keep up with. Andy and Karen had twins and now had a new girl to soon add to their growing family. She could not ask for more. Her parents would have been proud of all they had accomplished over the years. She missed them every day. More so when there was a special event in her life.

Chapter Twenty-Four

Remembering

A new family member. An extended family addition. Bella Rose continued to grow.

Sara took a rare day off to spend at home alone. Randall had a court case that would take all day. Gayle was in school. Sara had a chance at peace and quiet for at least several hours. After hearing the announcement of a new baby on the way, she decided it was time to sit back for a day, maybe two. In addition to Andy and Karen's new baby, Ben's sister and brother-in-law had been added to the family by moving nearby. Sara sat at her window looking out at the mountains while she sipped the last cup of coffee of the day for her. She smiled as she glanced up at the photo of her parents hanging next to one of her grandparents. They all would be proud of her and her siblings. After all, it had taken all of them to continue what those two couples had started. Sara raised her almost empty coffee cup in a toast to them.

"We did it, Mama!" Sara stood up and nodded her head. Yes, her family had done it. They had managed to reach the point in their lives where everything was going well.

Sara walked to the kitchen and placed her coffee mug inside the dishwasher. As she turned, she noticed the calendar hanging on the wall. She looked at the date. It had been so long since the family had a regular family meeting no one had mentioned what year it was and what it signified. This was the year they inherited the rest of what their mama had set aside for them. They had met Susan's requirements personally, and the manor was doing what it was supposed to do. Five years. They had all lived on the estate grounds for five years. The business at the manor was booming and expanding.

Sara twirled around and turned her music up loud. Life was not only good—it was amazing. Five years ago, she had so many doubts she often thought she would have a breakdown. Now, look! Her smile grew as she danced, alone to the music playing. It didn't matter what song was on. Today was her private day, and she was going to enjoy it. She would bring up the inheritance topic in a few days. With everything else going on, she knew that no one else had given it a thought either.

She never heard the phone ring as she closed her eyes and danced around her living room.

Barbara left a message on Sara's phone. She had left one on the phone at the manor as well, finding it odd that no one picked up at either place, but didn't worry about it. Barbara was sure someone would call her back. She wanted some information and needed to ask to use one of them as a reference on a job application.

Steven had left Barbara on her own in the new apartment when he went to work at the café. Terri and he had contractors to meet and a business to run. Steven loved his new job and the responsibility that came with it. He was thankful that Terri had seen his potential from his work at the lounge in Seattle. He had loved his job there, loved the area, loved and missed the people—to a point. It was also there that he found his trouble and lived a life that he was not proud to admit.

Steven sat waiting for the contractor to arrive and thought back to the days and the lessons he had learned. One lesson was to keep his mouth shut. As a bartender, he heard and saw more than most other people. His customers were always sharing parts of their lives with him. He was a good listener, and they trusted him. He often felt like he was used as a haven for people to talk, and, boy, did they talk.

He regretted the one bad decision he made while in Seattle. One of his regular customers opened up to him about making a lot of money and offered Steven a cut. The guy made it sound easy. Steven wanted to think about it, but the guy said that night was the only chance he had to make the deal and asked Steven if he was in or not; he needed to know at that moment. Steven should have known better, but it was a lot of money, and he could use some extra funds. All it took was a silent nod of Steven's head, and his life changed forever.

The night he regretted in Seattle would always be in his mind. That night, when Steven was cleaning up the lounge and closing, he was suddenly surrounded by thugs instead of the regular men. The night four men entered through a side door that Steven had left open. He knew what they wanted. His customer had explained what a normal pick-up would entail. The drugs were always hiding behind the bar in a fake safe. The customer had never told Steven how much the drugs were worth. Steven was just to be playing the pick-up location role. Nothing bad was supposed to happen. Men would come in, leave a large sum of money and take the drugs—easy money for all.

This action repeated for a month. Steven was getting a good cut for doing nothing but leaving the side door open and letting the guys inside. Anytime the guys came, Steven walked away and never looked at who it was. That was the deal.

During the second month of this happening, his customer did not show up one night. Steven was concerned because the man had never missed a night. Drug deal or no drug deal, the guy was always there. The night arrived for the next drop. A new guy came in, gave Steven the code word, and handed him a bag. Steven nodded and placed the bag where he always had, and later, he left the side door open as always.

That night four guys walked into the bar after closing. Steven started to walk away from the bar when a commanding voice yelled for him to Stop. He froze. He was in handcuffs before he knew it and taken to jail.

The judge went easy on him as he was not who they were after, and Steven freely gave up his customer's name. However, he lost his job, home, and chance to work in any lounge or bar in Seattle. After paying his fine and serving time in jail, he moved as far away as possible.

When he was younger, he rebelled against his parents and school and treated people with no respect. He graduated high school but dropped out of college within his first year. He spent time in local bars and learned to mix drinks. His first job was at a local pub. He easily picked up on the business and advanced to work at the higher classed lounge. That was when life went downhill after two years.

His move east was the best thing he had ever done, followed by or equal to his meeting Barbara.

A tap on his shoulder brought him back to reality.

"Hi, are you Steven Howard?"

"I am, yes, sir."

"I'm Adam from Wells Contracting," he reached out and shook Steven's hand.

"Hi, Adam. Good to meet you." Steven took a breath to clear his mind from the past. He felt a chill run down his back. Adam resembled his customer in Seattle.

"I have been told you want to expand the café and add a lounge."

"That is correct. Terri isn't here today, but she and I have discussed the details and need an estimate."

"Show me what you have in mind."

Steven and Adam spent the next two hours going over the space, the layout of the room, and designing and planning a lounge.

"I think we can do this. I will talk with my partner, Donovan, and work on that estimate today."

"Thank you. I will let Terri know to expect to hear from you in the next few days."

"We will do our best for you." Adam turned to walk away. He then looked at Steven but shook his head. There was something about him, but he could not put his finger on it.

Chapter Twenty-Five

Expansion

Adam drew up some plans for the expansion of Downtown Café. He took them to his partner Donovan for his feedback. During their conversation, Adam mentioned his thoughts of knowing Steven from somewhere. Donovan was familiar with the family due to working with Ben and buying the contracting business from him, so Adam's comment had him curious.

"What about him is familiar?"

"That's just it; I can't pinpoint it. I don't know if it is his looks, how the man talks, or what. I just got a weird sensation while dealing with him. Maybe I sense he is a bad fit for the business. I don't know. Terri seems happy having him work for her. It's not my place to interfere with that connection."

"Yes, best not to get involved with that partnership. Terri looked for a long time for someone she could trust to work with her. Steven entered the picture, and it was an instant business connection. The fact that he has a connection to the Bella Rose Estate family is a plus for this area."

After a few changes to the original plans that Adam had designed, they made an appointment to meet with Terri and Stave to discuss details, finances, and the time frame for completion.

The four made their way to the back of the café after closing because Terri did not want to disturb her customers. She said they deserved a calm and pleasant lunch break.

Adam laid out the blueprints he and Donovan had drawn up. Terri and Steven stood beside each other across the table from Adam and Donovan. Terri's first impression was a positive reaction. She liked everything she saw. She looked at Steven and noticed that he was not as enthused.

"I can tell you are not impressed."

"Oh, I am impressed. Something is missing."

"What could be missing? They have a bar area with plenty of stools, tables out from the bar; a lot of space to mix drinks; the sinks needed, storage space, refrigeration, and coolers. I don't see what is missing."

"A stage area. That's what this lounge needs! A place for music! I knew we had not discussed something when making the original plans! A stage!"

Steven stood up and looked toward the area for the lounge. He looked around and visualized a stage that could be viewed from the bar area and the café if it was built right.

Adam looked at Donovan and shrugged his shoulders. "Did I miss something?"

"No, I don't remember them saying anything about a stage. So you are in the clear." He turned to Steven. "We can add stage space. Where would you like it?"

"Well, I think if we could have it so the customers could enjoy the musical entertainment from the bar area and the café, that would benefit both sides of the business. Is there any issue with putting it between them?"

"The only issue you may have is when you close the café for the evening and keep the bar open."

"That is true. We only have the café open for a short time during the day. It is our lunchtime and early evening. We close it down fairly early."

"We could make the actual stage floor retractable." Adam was using his pencil to sketch other stage areas. "We can make the actual stage retractable enabling usage solely in the bar area or stretched into both areas. This change will also give much-needed space when needed for larger events. A retractable wall divider instead of a solid wall."

Terri looked at the new sketch. She was still concerned about separating the two businesses and saw the potential to keep both areas open during special events or musical performances.

Steven looked at the new sketches. He liked the idea of possibilities. He looked at Terri and nodded his head. "I like this new plan."

"I do too. The potential for more business if we keep a larger area open when needed. It also saves doing extra work than if we had thought of this after the remodel.

"Okay. Let Adam and I go back to the office and redraw this plan. We will contact you when we get the changes made and the estimated cost."

As Donovan and Adam were leaving, Terri and Steven turned back to cleaning the café so they could leave for the day.

Adam turned to Donovan as they were walking to the work truck. "Do you know much about Steven? You told me he was new to the family, and it was a good family. But do you know Steven's background? Do you know where he was before he moved here?"

"He married Barbara and connected her to her twin brother, whom she had not seen since she was a toddler. Other than that, I think someone said before that he lived in Seattle. Why"

"I think I know him. He did not recognize me. And his size confused me, but people are always losing weight.

"Where do you think you know him from? It is rare to put personal lives with work, but there are times that we have to. Donovan hoped their connection from the past was a positive one.

"I think I met him in Seattle. I worked part-time briefly at a pub there. Mostly I was a frequent customer. I think Steven worked there."

"Interesting. I love how small the world is sometimes. What do you remember about him? Since you know him, maybe we should give Terri a discount."

"I'm not positive it is him. I'm surprised he didn't say anything about knowing me if it is him."

"What makes you say that? You are right, though; he didn't seem to recognize you. Unless he is unsure and just not saying anything."

"He may not be saying anything because of our dealings together."

"Oh? That sounds mysterious. Care to elaborate?"

"Not until I talk to him about it. I think it is better to be left silent, especially if he isn't who I think he is."

Donovan nodded his head. He understood people getting a bad rap when they were mistakenly identified. He had seen it in too many shows on TV and in person. He respected Adam for his decision.

Steven went home after the meeting with Adam, Donovan, and Terri. He was hopeful that the ideas he had interjected would make a difference in the profits for Terri. Steven knew he was her partner in the overall business, but it was all about her success. If he could be of any assistance for her to succeed, he would be happy. Life had been full of circumstances that he had been the back person to push someone else to succeed. He had also been the person who, because of his willingness to help, had suffered because of it. He did not want to make that mistake again.

He also knew that Adam was a man to watch. He knew that Wells Constructing had come highly recommended, but he was unsure if it was because of Adam or Donovan. He needed to investigate their business. If Adam was who he thought he was, there could be issues. And if Adam was who he thought, he wondered why Adam had not said anything to him. Maybe he was mistaken, and Adam was just one of those people who had a double. He had heard that everyone had at least one double somewhere in the world.

Chapter Twenty-Six

A Forgiven Past

Terri and Steven agreed to the new blueprints drawn up by Wells Construction. Work began within a week of signing the contract. On the first day of work, Steven pulled Adam aside to talk.

Steven had done his research on Adam and the company after his suspicions of the circumstances surrounding Adam's past. He found what he had suspected, but he knew Adam had changed, and the company was good, so he never raised his concerns to Terri. She did not need to know their past. It was obvious that Donovan did not know Adam's history. If he did, he might not have gone into business with him.

Adam had been too busy to think about who he thought Steven was until he summoned him to talk behind the café on the first day of the remodel. Adam was confused for a moment and then feared what Steven would say.

"Adam, I have racked my brain ever since I first saw you here to talk with Terri and me about this remodel. It took me a while before the past crept into my head, and I realized who you were. Even then, I was not positive, so I did some investigative work on you."

"Okay. And what did you find?" Adam was defensive in his response. He stood with his arms crossed and his right leg bent with his foot resting against the back outer wall of the café.

"I found that you are indeed the man I thought you were. I also found out that you are now a changed man. A better man. One that can be trusted."

"Wow, thanks," Adam said and relaxed his stance. "I, too, recognized you on day one. Or at least I thought I did. I figured I would have heard about you not wanting me to work there if it were you. Since you did not say anything, I figured that maybe I was wrong in my assumption."

"No, you were right. I am Steven Howard, the man you wronged when we were in Seattle."

"Sorry, man. That was a bad time in my life, and I paid my dues for it. You were not as involved as I was, so you got away easier. I now have a record that will stay with me my entire life. When I moved East and found Donovan, it was a game-changer. He was on the wagon too. We met at one of the many meetings I still attend. We hit it off from the beginning and, after a while, decided to work together instead of against one another. I am so glad he and I are business partners. When I saw you and told Donovan you looked familiar, he asked how I knew you. All I admitted to was that we had worked together in Seattle. I told him I was not one hundred percent sure it was you. I did not want to make you uncomfortable, so I didn't say anything."

"I thought about keeping it to myself but knew it would eat at me for the rest of my life. My only concern is that you are now out of that lifestyle and are ready, willing, and able to do the work."

"Believe me, those days are long gone. Unfortunately, never to be forgotten, and as I see, it is never to be far from my eyesight."

"I will keep it all hushed if that is what you want."

"That is what I want; to keep the past in the past. No one needs to know the truth about me."

"Maybe not."

"Maybe? How could it be better to have that horrible time in our lives exposed? If I open up and share, it will pull you into this bad light. I was not alone in it when it went wrong."

"No, you were not alone. Your life story and how you got out of it and into a better world would make a great topic for the kids to watch on Wednesday nights."

"Me? My story? How so?

"I think your story would make a great topic of how life can be transformed."

"It takes determination. And sometimes it takes hitting bottom, so the only way to look is up. Who would listen to my story? I am just a man who had it all, hit bottom, and turned myself around. The climbing back up was not easy. It took someone like Donovan to believe in me to reach this far again." Adam admitted.

"Donovan knows about your past life?"

"He knows I was at the bottom, and he knows I was in jail for those five years. That is how we met."

"You met Donovan in jail? I didn't know he was in jail."

"Oh, no, he wasn't. Well, not as an inmate. He goes to the jail to teach the prisoners construction work. Then, he gives them temporary jobs to help get them started into a new life."

"I did not know that about him. I knew he used to work with Ben, Heather's husband, and took over his company. I guess I never learned more about him." Steven had a new respect for Donovan after hearing that. He subconsciously smiled.

"Why the smile?"

"What? Oh, I didn't realize the smile showed. I was just thinking about Donovan and you. I was concerned about the company doing the work for Terri and wanted it to be the best possible and a job done right. Now I know she made a wise choice."

"Thanks, Steven. And thank you for the talk. We will talk later about my story. Maybe I can change someone's life by talking about mine. I never thought about it. I was just so glad to get a fresh start in life. Maybe I can talk to Donovan about telling my story somewhere he goes." Adam moved toward the door to go back to work.

"Adam?"

"Yes?"

"I hate that you got me involved with those drug deals in Seattle, but I am glad it led me to the here and now. Life has a way of working out. Thankfully it usually works out for the better."

"Yeah, sometimes." Adam walked into the café. He smiled to himself and started to sing as he walked over to where the demolition of the old walls was beginning.

Chapter Twenty-Seven

History Opens Doors

Barbara and Steven were making themselves at home after their move. It was easy to do, considering how friendly everyone in the community was to them. Plus, the way the family at Bella Rose Estates had taken them in as part of their family, simply by her being Ben's twin.

Sara spoke to Barbara one day soon after they decided to move to the area to be close to Ben. She assumed Barbara would want to work somewhere. All the women she ever knew had wanted to work. It didn't matter what the pay was for most of them. It was a matter of feeling appreciated, loved, needed, and having a feeling of accomplishment in their lives. She assumed Barbara would be the same.

"Barbara, I know you have not been here very long, but I was wondering if you had thought about where you want to work? Steven has his job at the café. What would you like to do? What did you do before your move?"

"I have been trying to decide that very thing. You are right. I don't like to sit idle and get myself in trouble, or worse yet, go out and get into more trouble. I need a job. Do you know of any openings?"

"After hearing your story and seeing your passion for all those children in the foster care system, I thought something to do with children would suit you best. You could be a teacher, counselor, advocate, or liaison for abandoned children. You have been in their system, and you could relate to them better than someone who went to school to learn about them. You have felt it, and I am sure that would go a long way in finding a job in that field."

"I have been thinking of some way to work with children. You are right about my ability to relate to those who have no parent with them. Even if my job is to be with them while the children go through the system, I could do that. Do you know of anyone to contact who may have connections?" Barbara almost felt bad asking. She knew Sara had a lot on her plate. She didn't want to be a burden to her new family.

"I do!" Sara was thrilled that Barbara asked for her help. No matter how busy she was, she always had room for one more thing.

"Why does that not surprise me? Ben told me you know a lot of people in this area."

"Ben is correct. I make it my personal goal to learn about people as much as possible. I never know when knowing one person and what they do, or have been through, may be helpful to the next person I meet." Sara smiled. She had come a long way from a shy little girl.

"I never trusted people enough to find out much about them. As a child in the system, I also realized that it didn't matter how much I learned about someone; it would not be long before I was no longer in their life. So I gave up inquiring. I only trusted one person—me."

"I cannot imagine all that you have gone through. Life is so unfair sometimes. Being a part of this family has been a blessing. The family history we discovered has set us apart from most families in this area."

"Ben told me a little about what was discovered about Bella Rose. It is amazing what your grandparents did when they saw a need."

"I agree. Rose and Robert could have shut the door on that first lost girl and never given her a second thought. Instead, they opened their door and their hearts. And with it a long history of loving and caring people."

"I would love to hear more about those girls. First though, who should I contact about getting involved with children in need?"

"That would be Joe, Joe McBride, and his wife, Nicole. Joe is a counselor/therapist, and Nicole is a registered nurse at the local hospital."

"As I said, you know everyone. Maybe it is best if I don't know how you know a therapist and a nurse." Barbara shook her head.

"Oh, that in itself is a story Ben needs to share with you. It involved Heather and him."

"Ben and Heather know them? Of course, they do. This family is amazing." Barbara shook her head and smiled. She never knew anyone who had so many friends and connections.

Sara smiled. "Yes. You have a lot to learn about this family. I am so glad you and Steven decided to move here."

"I am thrilled that Steven found a good-paying job so fast. Since this is such a small town, we accepted that it might take a while for him. Instead, it almost fell into his lap."

"Connections. That's all I can say. It pays to get to know people. Don't be shy. Get out there and meet them."

"I will try," Barbara said and took a deep breath to soak in the energy she would need to put herself out there into the world's craziness. She had spent so much of her life alone and was told not to get close to anyone. Now, she had the freedom to reach out to others for positive reasons. It felt good.

Sara went into her office to get Joe's phone number. One for his office and one for his cell phone. She also jotted down Nicole's cell phone number. She returned to Barbara, who had moved to stand looking out the front picture window of the manor.

"It's a pretty place, isn't it?" Sara asked as she handed Barbara the piece of paper.

Barbara glanced at the numbers and folded the paper. She put it into her jeans pocket and went back to looking outside. "Yes, this area is so beautiful. I will always miss the water of that creek. We didn't live there very long, but it was the one place I never forgot. I never knew why that one place stood out more than any other place I loved in my life. Now I know it was because Ben was there. We may not have known our connection, but somehow our hearts did."

"I am so glad you and Steven have decided to move here. I know you are in an apartment for now but have you thought about whether you want to buy a house or build one?"

"We did talk to Ben about that, and he said we may want to consider building near Bella Rose."

"That would be wonderful. You know we have over ten acres. Maybe we could find an area on the property to build another house."

"Here? On this land?"

"Sure, why not?"

"We're not blood relations to your family. Why would you do that for us?"

"Because you are Ben's family. And from what we have found out, you and Ben have a connection to this place. So you belong here as much as Ben does."

"It is a very small world, isn't it?"

"Yes. History, family, the right place at the right time, or at any time, the people you meet when you meet—they all play a part in our lives. It is up to us to make the connections and see just how life plays out."

"I am glad we made the connection," Barbara said as she smiled at the view. Her dream was coming true. No longer would she have to stand alone. At least she hoped she never would again.

Chapter Twenty-Eight

Rachelle Returns

Sara was working in her office when the door opened without a knock. She looked up to see Rachelle smiling with a gleam in her eye. Sara immediately stood up and hurried around her desk to greet her with a big hug.

"How are you, girl? We have missed you so much! I know it was for a good cause, but you could have called, emailed, sent carrier pigeon, something!"

"It is so good to be home. You know I would have been in contact with you if I could. But, something about a four-month honeymoon, a wonderful man in my life, and suddenly no one else seems to matter." Rachelle said as her face glowed with happiness.

"Hey, I'm not sure how to take that. But I know you. By that look on your face, it was amazing! How is Bob, by the way? Where is he?" Sara looked past Rachelle.

"He is taking all of our things to the apartment. I wanted to stop in and let you all know that I am back and ready to get back to work."

"I am more than ready to have you here. We have had some interesting things happen while you were away."

"Oh? Good things, I hope. Please, no bad news. I don't think I can handle bad news when I first get home."

"It is all good news. I will fill you in when you get back to work. The main detail is we have new family members."

"Who had a baby?"

"Ha, no one, yet. No, Ben found he had a twin sister! She and her husband have moved here." Sara smiled and walked away as if it was nothing special to discuss.

"Wait, What?" Rachelle followed Sara further into the office and sat down in the chair in front of the desk. "Speak to me. Tell me more."

"I thought you had to get your things into the apartment?"

"The heck with that; Bob can do it. What do you mean Ben found he had a twin sister? How did that happen? Where was she? What is her name? Tell me. Tell me." Rachelle reached out to Sara's arm. She begged to know the details.

"Briefly. You knew he thought something was missing in his life, right?"

"Yes. And that he thought it was something about the man he called uncle and biological father."

"Yes, and that's another part of the story, but Randall was doing some research for Ben and found Barbara! She and her husband Steven came to meet Ben, and well, they never left. They decided to move here."

"Wow! Remind me never to go on a four-month-long honeymoon again! What else happened?"

"That is the gist of it. We can fill you in later with more details. Right now, get going to help Bob. Get settled in and as soon as you are ready, come back to work. Is tomorrow too soon?" Sara laughed.

"How about the day after? I think we have a lot to do at the apartment to settle in and a day to relax from our trip."

"Yes, and you will have to share all about your trip!"

"Oh, we're not sharing all the details." Rachelle winked. "We will give you highlights. We took a lot of photos."

"Looking forward to it. Now, get going. Talk to you later. Oh, and welcome home. You don't know how much you were missed!"

"I have missed you, too," Rachelle said as she walked out the door.

Bob was still unloading the car when Rachelle returned to their apartment. He smiled at her and gave her a brief hug. "How is everyone at Bella Rose?"

"All good, and then some."

"And then some? What did we miss while we were away?" He knew something must be going on. He and Rachelle had not known each other very long when they decided to marry and go on a whirlwind honeymoon. He had learned almost everything he now knew while they were away. Bob loved her even more because of what he had learned. He learned her life belonged to Bella Rose and the family there. He was now a part of the bigger picture of the family.

"We have more family to meet."

"More? Who had a baby?"

"That is what I asked. No, not a baby. It seems Ben found out he had a twin sister. She and her husband have moved here."

"Wow. Interesting," Bob said as he closed the front door. The last of their luggage was now inside. "I can't wait to hear this story."

"Me either. This family continues to amaze me."

"They amaze me, and I don't know them that well."

"We will get caught up with everything in time."

"In the meantime, we need to unpack and settle in here."

"Yes, we do. When are you going back to work? I have to be back on Monday."

"I told Sara I would be back the day after tomorrow. I hope you don't mind." Rachelle realized maybe she should have asked him first. She still was not used to being married.

"That is fine. I know you miss being there."

"I do." Rachelle let the rest of her thoughts drop. She loved Bob, and he didn't need to know just how much she missed her Bella Rose family. Being away for so long and worn on her.

Bob and Rachelle spent a few hours unpacking and putting things away. At lunchtime, Bob suggested they go to town for something to eat. They had eaten out for months and needed to buy groceries before they could cook. Rachelle was all for it and suggested going to the Downtown Café.

"Sounds good to me. We've not been there for a while. I heard it has new owners."

"I heard that too. I know it was closed for a while but should be open again by now."

"We will find out," Bob said as he opened the door for Rachelle.

They arrived at Downtown Café and noticed the sign. "Remodeling, Don't Mind Our Dust."

"Well, that is interesting. We're gone a while, and so much has changed." Bob said as he opened the door for Rachelle to walk inside. He followed, and they both noticed construction work being done in the back of the café.

"What is going on?" Bob asked the lady behind the counter.

"I am adding a lounge area in the back. Please excuse the mess." Terri replied.

"That will make a great addition to this town. Hi, I'm Rachelle. This is my husband, Bob. You must be the new owner." Rachelle said and reached over the low counter to shake Terri's hand.

"Yes, I'm Terri. Good to meet you. Are you new in town?"

"No, I work at Bella Rose. In a roundabout way, I am part of the family there."

"It is really good to meet you. I am getting to know the family. I own this place, but Steven is my partner here. It is an amazing family."

"Yes, it is an amazing family." Rachelle changed the subject and asked what was best on the menu. Terri suggested one of her new sandwich meals and took their order when they both agreed on that and a sweet tea to drink.

Rachelle and Bob found an empty table and sat down to wait for their meal. Rachelle looked at her husband. "I have no idea who Steven is. Terri made it sound like he was part of the family."

"Maybe he is the husband of Ben's twin?"

"Ah, that could be. I will ask Sara. I don't want to sound like I don't know who a family member is." Rachelle laughed.

"True," Bob said as Terri brought their meal to the table.

"I hope you enjoy your meals. If you need anything, just let me know." Terri said, then turned away from them and walked back to the front counter to take an order from another customer who had just walked in.

"She is a sweet lady. I wish her the best with her new expansion. It will be nice to have a lounge in town."

"It will. We needed a place like that for a while."

"I never thought so until we were on our honeymoon. Those pubs we visited were so much fun." Rachelle admitted.

"They were, and the musical entertainment at them was a nice addition." Bob looked at Rachelle and smiled. "We did have a great time traveling, didn't we?"

"Yes, we did. I may want to do more in the future."

"I can arrange it. Anytime you want, let me know."

"Do you mean it? How can we afford that?"

"Oh, you of little faith. I have ways to make extra funds to pay for the trips. Plus, my investments over the years. We are doing ok, my Love." Bob leaned over and kissed his bride.

"I love you more every day," Rachelle said, then took another bite of her sandwich.

They both fell quiet while eating and watching the other customers come and go.

"I guess it is time to get back to the apartment. We still have a lot of things to do." Bob said after they had sat and relaxed a few moments longer in silence.

"Yes, it is."

They stood up, waved goodbye to Terri, and walked outside. Bob looked around before they crossed the street to their car.

"Let's go for a stroll through town," Bob reached for his wife's hand.

Rachelle looked at him and smiled. She placed her hand in his, and they slowly walked the length of the town, taking in all the sights, the stores, and the people as if they were visitors to the area. They were still in the honeymoon phase.

Chapter Twenty-Nine

Family Togetherness

Rachelle was back home, Barbara and Steven had joined the family, and Andy and Karen were only a few months away from having their third child. The business at the manor was going well. Sara knew it was time for another family meeting.

With the family as large as it was becoming, it was obvious that the family would no longer fit around the kitchen island. Sara moved the meeting to the hall of the church. This would give the kids ample space to play and not be underfoot by the family or the guests.

Andy did his usual and made a special meal for everyone. Karen had found time in her busy life as a mother of twins to make a cake. Everyone helped carry the food to the hall. Since they had constructed their event hall like most church halls, it was fully stocked with their kitchen needs to serve their family.

Sara looked around after everyone had arrived. What a crew it had become. The main meeting was meant for the immediate family, but she knew it was time for a family get-together. This would give everyone time to get to know each other.

While the kids were directed to get their plates of food and sit at the children's table, the adults mingled and talked amongst themselves. The family was together under one roof. Sara and Randall, Heather and Ben, Andy and Karen, Barbara and Steven, Rachelle, and Bob. Plus all the children. Gayle, Marc, Maddex, River, Ryan, and one on the way. What a blessing. Sara wiped a tear from her eye. Her parents would be proud of all the family had accomplished since their passing five years prior. Sara was overcome with a flashback of memories and how it all started.

When everyone was just about finished eating, Sara stood so she could talk to everyone. She smiled as she looked around.

"Hi everyone. It is so good to have you all in the same room at the same time. We have been so busy these past several months that we have not connected like we used to. I miss those times. I know I see you almost every day, but it is not the same. I would like to propose that we set a time to meet once a month, twice a month if you prefer. It doesn't matter if we have family business to discuss or Bella Rose business; we need family time. What does everyone think?"

"How about we do once a month for a family as a large family dinner and maybe game night. And once a month to discuss the business aspect of the manor. Any minor business can be addressed between the people involved or through emails," Randall suggested.

Sara looked at her husband. He still managed to surprise her. "I like that idea. I know this means that some of you will only be here for the family meeting and game night. I hope you understand. Does anyone have anything to add?"

Barbara raised her hand. "I am excited to be included in the family gathering. You have so much love to give everyone. And I am blessed."

Bob spoke up. "I am honored to be considered part of the family. So I will be here no matter how often we meet. Family time is important."

One by one, they all agreed to Randall's suggestion. They soon discussed what they wanted Andy to make for the next meeting. They settled on his famous lasagna.

After the next meeting had been decided, Karen brought out some games for them to play.

Sara went around to Andy and Heather and told them she needed to talk. She led them to the back corner of the room.

"We need to have a small sibling-only meeting soon. Can you both meet me in the office tomorrow morning?"

"What's up, sis?" Heather asked.

"I know we have been so busy that we have not been paying attention to what year it is."

"What do you mean the year? What am I missing?" Andy asked.

"Five years. We have reached five years since we all started our attempt to meet Mama's requirements in her last will."

"Heather looked at Sara. "Oh, five years! That means."

"Yes, that means we are due the rest of our inheritance." Sara finished.

"I will be in your office first thing in the morning," Andy said. "You are right; I had forgotten."

"I did too. We threw a lot into those five years." Heather said as she looked at the children playing in the opposite corner area of the room. Yes, a lot had happened. She felt a slight twinge of pain in her leg. Even that brought a smile.

"Okay, I will see you all in my office at ten in the morning."

"Perfect." Andy walked away to meet up with his wife and start cleaning up. Sara followed him to help. When they arrived, they found that their spouses had done all the cleaning while they were huddled in their private meeting.

They all returned to the table to play a game of Uno for a while. This lets the kids have more playtime as well.

An hour later, Heather went over to the kids' corner and told them it was time to put away all the toys; it was time to go home. The adults put their card games away and helped the kids get all the toys put away. When it was done, they all left the hall, with Sara last in line to ensure the lights were off and the door locked.

The next morning Sara and her siblings met in the office of the manor. Randall was also there to handle the legal aspect of the next step for them.

"As Sara has reminded you, it has been five years since Susan died and left you all with a challenge. You have met that challenge and far beyond. Susan would be proud of you. I had to remind Sara about it. Lucky for all of you, I had it on my calendar. He reached inside his briefcase and pulled out three folders—one for each of them: Sara, Heather, and Andy.

They each took their folders and opened them. Inside each one was a letter from Susan. Randall noticed as each one smiled when they pulled it out. He remembered the letters Susan had written to her children five years ago that started this. He wondered what she had included in these letters. He knew Sara would share her letter with him.

Also inside the folders were papers and another envelope. Inside the envelope was a key. They each had a key. They looked at Randall.

"I know—another key is involved. Susan did seem to have a thing about keys. Each key is to a separate safety deposit box at the bank. The boxes had all been paid for the past five years. It would be best to go to the bank by the end of this year to collect what is inside. The funds run out at the end of the year, and the contents inside will be removed."

Even Sara sat with her shoulders sunken. Why did her mother always have to make things so complicated? Why, even five years later, was she still playing with their lives? She wanted to cry.

Randall noticed his wife's reaction. "I know, it seems cruel that Susan is still making things difficult for you. But, I promise this is the last step in her game. I have no other files, no more secrets, no more records to ever give you from her. The only other instruction is for you each to read the letters before you go to the bank to open your safe deposit boxes.

"Thank goodness. I had forgotten the frustration we had five years ago. And now, with our lives busier than ever, we seem to be starting again with Mama's games." Andy said as he looked at the envelope with his name so neatly written in his mother's handwriting. He smiled. He missed his mother. He became solemn in his thoughts. Once again, as he had five years before, he regretted being the rebel he had been most of his life.

Heather looked at the key she had taken out. A tiny key that needed a mate at the bank to open a locked box with unknown contents meant strictly for her. What could her mother have for her? And why had they all had to wait five years? Then she remembered. Susan wanted her children to be together for five years. She hoped it would build their bond. And it had.

Sara looked at her siblings, lost in their thoughts. She suddenly realized that this was the year that everything could change for the family. They were no longer under Susan's time challenge. They were no longer staying together to satisfy their mother's requirements to receive their full inheritance. Once they all got whatever Susan had for them, they could go and do whatever they wanted. Bella Rose, as it was, could change.

Chapter Thirty

Belonging

The day after the family met in the event hall at Bella Rose, Barbara awoke early with a smile. Steven rolled over and saw her sitting up in bed and asked her what was wrong.

"There is nothing wrong. That is the most wonderful feeling in the world."

"Yes, it is. What makes you say there is nothing wrong? We have a lot going on and a lot of decisions to make. I have stress at work with the remodel and helping Terri." Steven could have gone on but stopped.

"Yes, we do have those things to consider and to handle. We will get through all of them. We have gotten through worse. At least I have gotten through so much worse."

Steven sat up in bed and put his arm around Barbara's shoulder. "Yes, we have. I know you have been through so much in your life. That is why, when Randall found Ben, I knew I had to bring you here. I hoped it would make your life complete."

"Complete? It has made me feel more than complete if there is such a thing. For the first time in my life, I feel like I belong. I know I have you, and that is wonderful. I know we have a future. I love you, and I know you love me. But last night, being included as part of the family. To such a large family. Do you understand how that has changed me? Do you realize I am a part of a circle that will never break?" Barbara had turned to face Steven. Her eyes were smiling. She was excited.

Steven smiled at her. He would never know his wife's intense feelings, but he did know that being part of a family meant forever. Steven came from a small intimate family. He reached over and kissed her forehead. "I am glad you are so happy. For us to be here is." He didn't finish his thought because Barbara did.

"Is perfect! It is meant to be in the here and now. Yes, I went through a lot of hell to get here. But I now think it was all worth it. Ben and I have our stories. We have the things we suffered through to find each other. It is that struggle, that search he did, that makes my being here much more amazing. If he had not felt the emptiness, that longing of an ache in his heart and searched, I still would be out there, maybe remaining alone."

"You had me in your life before that."

"Yes, I know, darling. I am talking about the time before you came into my life and rescued me from myself. I was miserable. I was so lost and alone. I thought no one cared. I thought no one would ever want me. We met, and it was the beginning. The beginning of what has climaxed into this big, wonderful world of family." She reached over and kissed her husband. He had changed her life, and she would always be grateful. He understood her need. He was her angel.

The sun was beginning to rise and shine through their bedroom window. Steven and Barbara had laid back down, cuddled in each other's arms. Barbara felt loved. She knew she was loved not only by Steven but by her family. Even the extended family had taken her in. She no longer stood alone. She sighed.

"Now, what is on your mind, my love?" Steven asked, raising himself onto his elbow and looking at her.

"Now it is my turn to find a job. You have your work with Terri at the café, and we can live on that, but I want to do something to contribute to us."

"You can do anything you want. You know you do not have to work, but I will support whatever you pursue."

"Thank you," she sat up in bed. "I think I need to call that Joe person Sara suggested. I want to be involved with children, possibly helping foster children and advocating for them as they begin their journey through the system. Maybe working on the system to improve it. We both know it is broken."

"You would be amazing with children. You have been through what they are facing. You could comfort them. Tell them it will all work out."

"That's just it. Sometimes it doesn't work out. I can be as positive and encouraging as the next person, but in reality, you and I both know the issues that need fixing."

"Yes, I know there are many ways it could change and be better for the children. That would take a lot of work. A lot of bureaucratic dealings."

"I know. That is why I need to be serious about the decision of my future work." Barbara stood up and began to get dressed for the day.

"I see you will start your process before the sun has fully risen." Steven stood up. He knew his wife. She wasted no time beginning her work on it when she had an idea.

"No time like the present. But first, it's coffee time." She smiled before walking out the bedroom door to make a fresh pot of dark roast coffee for the two of them.

Steven was not far behind her after he quickly dressed. He had the day off but wanted to check on the remodel's progress. Terri had closed the café for the week during demolition. She told Steven he would still get paid for the week as she knew he would stop by often to check on the workers. He hoped to spend the week with his wife, traveling the area and house shopping.

"Ahhh, fresh coffee! You are amazing." Steven said as he took the full mug from her.

"Are you talking about me or the coffee being amazing?"

"I have been caught." Steven took a sip of coffee. After swallowing, he reached over and kissed Barbara on her forehead. "Why, you, of course!"

"Good save, Mr." Barbara winked at him and walked to the front window of their apartment. She sipped her coffee and was deep in thought when Steven walked up behind her and put his arm around her shoulders.

"What do you say we take today to go house hunting?"

Barbara turned into his embrace. "Are you sure? Are you ready to find a house?"

"I am. I know this part of the country is our forever town. We need to put down roots of permanence."

"I like your plan. Let's do an internet search first to see what might be out there."

"Perfect." Her agreement made his day.

As the morning continued, they searched for a new place to call home on the internet. Nothing fit what they wanted. They found that they were looking for the same thing with only a few differences if they could find the perfect house.

By noon they realized they had forgotten to eat breakfast. But instead had contacted a realtor and set up times to look at a couple of houses and discuss details of what they wanted her to help them find.

They stopped by the café to examine the progress of the demolition. Steven took time to talk with Adam. Work was on schedule, and Adam said that Terri should be able to open by the weekend—the excess dust they were creating would be cleared up.

After their stop, they took time to grab a bite to eat in the next town before meeting their realtor. Barbara took a deep breath before stepping inside the office.

"Are you okay?" Steven asked when he noticed her hesitation.

"I am fine. A little overwhelmed, maybe, but so ready to make this change. Let's go do this." She reached for the door before her husband had a chance to be a gentleman.

Chapter Thirty-One

More Letters

The siblings waited a few days before going to the bank to open their safety deposit boxes. Each of them took time to be in private and read what would most likely be the last thing she had written to them. It would be her final touch in their lives. Her memory would live on forever, but the words she wrote would be her final farewell. The siblings knew their mama's message would be heartfelt.

Sara found time alone, as she always managed, in the office of the manor. It was where she had read the first letter and where she read some of the journals. The office was her physical connection to her mother. They had worked together inside those walls for several years, not to mention the number of years Sara lived there as a child learning the love of family and the business. When visitors were not keeping her busy and daily business was set aside, Sara often felt the presence of her mother around her there. Reading this final letter was not going to be any different. She knew the letter would touch her. Her tissues were handy, with one already in her hand when she took the antique letter opener and sliced the seal, revealing the stationary her mother always used. She took a deep breath and began to read.

"Dear Sara,

If you are reading this, I know you have reached the goal I set for you and your siblings. I imagine it was a struggle at times for each of you. I hope that you were strong and held the family together. I know that thought puts a lot of pressure on you, but I believe you are the one who made these five years work. I believe in you. I always have.

You may wonder what I have in store for you now that it has reached the end of the five years. You may even hate me for this. For all of this. For the past five years. For the demands I made for you to reach this end. For the way I may have died. I don't know when or how I died. I know that it is unexpected; even when expected, the exact moment is unknown, and that final breath you see and may have heard is always a shock. I hope for your sake you were not there for that.

I ramble—an old habit of mine. Let me get to the point. I hope you are reading this before you open your designated safety deposit box. If you remembered to follow the original process, you knew to wait. The contents of your box hold the key to your future.

You are looking at this page funny. I can sense that. I know you very well, my oldest child. You always were the one who wanted a controlled life. Everything was put away where it belonged. Life for you needed meaning. You could not take it day by day and accept whatever may come your way. You wanted advance notice, a warning of what was to come.

I hope you have overcome that for your sake and those around you. If you haven't and they have stayed by your side, realize how much they love you. You are very blessed.

Your future is in your hands now. I have had control even from the grave for the last five years. Of course, I could be wrong, and somehow, you had convinced the attorney and the banker to jump the hoops I set up. You are capable of doing that. I raised you to be a strong and independent lady. I sometimes regretted that over the years. Your life would be so much easier if you took a kinder, gentler approach to each day.

You and your siblings have a choice to make now. You can stay as you are, as I requested you to be—all living on Bella Rose Estate's property. Or you could jointly decide to sell the estate and each move on with your lives. It is now up to you.

It is my hope and prayer that you stay as you are. I imagine you are all successful in the business. I trust that you have been there for each other every step of the way. I pray that you have moved forward and have families of your own. I pray you have found your soulmates in life, and life is beautiful for you all. Yes, I know life can't always be a bed of rose petals—that sometimes a thorn sneaks in to hinder the beauty of perfection.

Go to the bank with the attorney and the bank president and open your box. Remove the last of your inheritance and, most of all—enjoy life. Never stop loving each other and the people you bring into your world. Make everyone you touch feel special. You have that gift. Stay positive and encourage everyone to keep smiling, my daughter.

I love you. I know you loved me. Now go, bid me farewell. Thank me or hate me; it doesn't matter now. Life goes on. Live it. Love it. Laugh with it. Experience it.

Love.
Mama

Sara clutched the letter to her chest. She felt her heartbeat and, for a moment, imagined it was her mother's heart beating through the letter. A tear ran down her face. Before she realized it, she was doubled over sobbing. This connection with her mother was her final goodbye.

Heather put Marc and Maddex to bed before telling Ben that she was going to the sitting room to read the letter from her mother. The sitting room in their home was a small, padded seat at the window overlooking the mountains. Just a small intimate space, perfect for one person to sit, read, think, or gaze at the beauty outside. She had often sat there when they first moved in. It was her small sanctuary, and even her boys knew to give her space when she was there.

Ben hugged her and held her close before she reached the bench. "I love you, babe. Don't ever forget that."

"I love you too." Heather was ready to cry before she opened her letter. It pained her to know this was the last contact from Susan. She sat, opened the envelope, and carefully removed the familiar stationery. Unfolding it, she began to read.

Dear Heather,

You have reached a milestone in your life now. It may not be a birthday or an anniversary, but it is a time in your life that may come with change.

Since you are reading this, I know that you have endured the five-year stipulation I wrote in my will for you to survive as siblings living and working on the same property and the business. I know that you found your baby brother sometime along the way, and everyone has made amends. I know that you have made a living for yourselves during those five years. I am proud of you.

You were my middle child. In so many ways, you fit the depiction of such a child. I hope you didn't feel the pressure of being the one in the middle. So often they feel neglected, lost in the crowd of a family. You did sit back and let the world go by you at times when you were growing up. You kept silent and hid away in your own space. You may still be doing that. I admire you for that. Life was always so busy that I forgot to take care of myself. By now, you may know all my secrets and know that life was not always difficult, that others loved me and cared for me. You may also feel a bond with me that your siblings don't. I felt that with you. I felt a connection as I watched Sara take off on her own at a young age. Her mind was always someplace else. Andy quickly became a rebel, and I often felt like a failure. I had no control. But with you, you were my homebody. You were the one who took it all in. You quietly sat back and watched as the world around you lived.

I hope you have overcome some of that and you are taking life by the reins now. I hope you have continued to love the man of your dreams, your soulmate. You and Ben made such a loving couple from the very beginning. I hope he stood by you and helped you heal after I died.

I also hope your family grew. You always had such a way with children. They easily bonded with you and loved you. I hope you have at least one more.

'You have talent, Heather. Use it—your natural ability to organize parties and decorate your room and home. I hope you have expanded on that and used your skills to make others happy. Your smile was always contagious. Keep smiling.

You know there is a safety deposit box for you at the bank. That is for you and your family--Ben and your children. Use it wisely.

It is now up to each of you to decide what to do with the rest of your lives. You are each now in control. I was still controlling you for the last five years. Or, at least I was trying. If you found a way around all that I had set up for you, more power to you. If you have followed my instructions *and desires so far, you have come a long way since I died. You have thrived and grown. I can only imagine what you all have done with Bella Rose Estate. I know you made it even better than I wanted it to be.*

You all may decide to sell the estate, and each go your separate ways. Or you may decide to stay as you are and continue to work together as a family as Bella Rose has since Rose and Robert built it. I have no control over what you will do now.

Now, my time in your life is up. You will keep me in your heart and your memory, but I will not be a burden to you. I have no power to tell you anything to do with your life.

Go. Make the best of your life, whether here with your siblings or on your own. I want you to be successful in all you do. I want you and your children to have the best. I want you to be happy and blessed.

Always know—I love you!

Love
Mama

Heather wiped the tears that were flowing down her face. She had forgotten the power her mother had over her. The last five years had blended into being a way of life. She had stopped thinking of them as being under her mother's control.

She smiled. That was Susan's intent from the beginning. To have her children so engrossed in living and being together as a family, they never remembered being under their mother's control. It had worked.

Heather stood up from the window bench and looked for Ben. She found him asleep in the recliner by the fireplace.

She smiled while she watched the man of her dreams sleep. Yes, he had stood by her—in the end.

She then realized that Ben was the only spouse her mama had known. Susan had missed Andy coming home, getting married, and having children. Susan had missed Randall and Sara getting married and adopting Gayle. She had missed—everything she wanted to happen. Heather wiped another tear and sat near Ben.

Ben stirred and opened his eyes. He reached for Heather's hand and pulled her towards him. She stood and pulled him off the recliner into a hug. In silence, he held her close while she wept.

Andy and Karen were rocking their twins to sleep in their comfortable home. Laying on the end table next to Andy was the letter from his mama. He glanced at it but knew it would have to wait. Instead, he watched his wife rocking River, who had fallen asleep in her arms.

Karen carefully stood up with River and took her to the nursery. Andy followed with Ryan in his arms. Once the babies were in their cribs, Karen and Andy walked out into the living room.

"You need to read the letter from your mama," Karen said.

"I know. I kept looking at it while I was rocking Ryan. I am almost afraid to open it."

"Why are you afraid? What could she write that would be so bad?"

"You don't know my mama. I was lost when she wrote this to me—well, not lost. I was being my rebel self. You know that. It was around that time when I met you."

"I remember it well," she winked.

"That time of my life changed my life. It was the best rebel event I had," he reached for her hand. "I guess I need to read the letter. Do you mind?"

"Mind? Why would I mind? I want you to read it. See what she has to tell you. I will be here for you."

"Thank you, my love." Andy hugged her. She was the reason he was still alive if anyone cared to know the truth. "You are the best."

"I know," Karen laughed and broke from his embrace. "Now, go read."

Andy walked over to the end table and picked up the envelope. He sat in the rocking chair, where he was rocking his infant son a few minutes before. Life had been a blessing. Nothing his mother had to say to him would change his joy. He opened the envelope and smiled when he saw his mother's known stationary. As far as he knew, it was the only one she ever used. He unfolded it and began to read.

Dear Andy,

My dear sweet son. My only son. My baby. First, know I love you. No matter what you have done in your life, no matter where you have been, I love you.

Since you are reading this, I know you have returned home. Per my request, you have changed your life to come home and live for five years at Bella Rose near your sisters and help run the estate. Thank you for sacrificing the life you were accustomed to.

You put me through a lot of heartaches over the years. From the time you were a teenager and quit school. The years you disappeared and had me worried. I learned early on to let you go. If I had tried to force you to stay, you would have rebelled worse. I did what I had to do.

When I wrote the first letters to you and your sisters that you were to read shortly after my death, I did not know where you were or even if you were alive. I am guessing you are fine.

My desire for you is that you are well. I hope you are home with your sisters helping them operate the manor. I hope you have found happiness. Five years may not be long enough for you to have made major changes in your life, but in time I hope you find true love and are blessed with a family of your own. A family is a wonderful thing.

I am so sorry that Glen never connected with you and that your biological father was never around much. I wonder if life has been such that you have found your biological father. I hope you have and that you get to know each other.

Andy, there is a safety deposit box at the bank for you. Inside is something that I hope will get you through life, at least for a while.

You may not have realized what this five-year mark means. If you recall in the first letter and instructions from my will, you and your sisters needed to stay for five years and make Bella Rose profitable. At the end of the five years, I never told you what I expected next.

The truth is, I have no expectations. I have no rules; I have no instructions. It is up to each of you siblings to decide what to do with Bella Rose. You can sell it and go your separate ways doing other things. You may stay and maintain Bella Rose as the family has run her since Rose and Robert built her. The choice is yours.

May you be blessed in whatever you do with your life.

Love,
Mama

Andy sat back in the rocker. He wiped a tear. He hated himself at the moment. He wished now that he had been a better son and had been home instead of running for so many years. Mostly he wished that Susan had lived to meet Karen and his boys and the one on the way.

Karen noticed that Andy had finished reading his letter and walked over to him. She asked if he was okay. All Andy could do was hand her the letter.

"Are you sure you want me to read this from your mama?"

Andy nodded his head because he could not speak. By the time Karen finished reading it, she was wiping a tear.

"I wish she had lived long enough to meet you and our family."

"I wish I had met her too."

Chapter Thirty-Two

Inheritance

After reading her letter, Sara called Heather and Andy and asked if they had read theirs and were ready to go to the bank. She told them that Randall had some free time that afternoon and that Rachelle would be handling the manor while they were gone. Both Heather and Andy agreed to meet and go to the bank that afternoon. None of them had any idea what was in the deposit boxes. It could be anything; it could be nothing.

Sara shook her head at the thought that her mama might have left them nothing. It would not be her way of doing things, but Sara could not imagine her mother having more money or assets to give to each of them.

They met with the bank president as they had five years before. He walked with them into the vault. He led them inside and added his key to each of theirs to open the boxes. He asked if they wanted separate rooms to look into their boxes, but they agreed they had nothing to hide and being together was fine. He and Randall left the siblings alone as they opened their boxes.

Sara was the first to open hers. She looked inside and found a padded envelope. Pulling it out, she found a journal and loose papers underneath it. She pulled everything out and placed it on the table. She looked at her siblings and opened the padded envelope.

Heather followed suit and had the same contents inside.

Andy was the last to open his. He did not expect to find the same thing in his box, so he was surprised when he opened it and found the same padded envelope, journal, and papers.

Inside each box were documents of investments Susan had taken out for each of her children. Over time the investments had earned interest and grown. After closer investigation and talking with the bank president, they discovered the money was worth close to a million dollars for each of them. The journal was the story of each of them from the day they were born until about age five, written by Susan. The loose papers were their birth certificates and other important papers she saved over the years.

When they finished at the bank, they went back to the manor with Randall. Life for each of them could change.

"Family meeting at the island?" Sara asked when they arrived at the manor.

"I think we need it," Heather agreed.

"I think so too, but we need to talk with our spouses first. If we meet to discuss our ideas for our futures, our spouses need to be involved. Do you agree?" Andy said.

"You are so correct, little brother. Let's meet back at the island in the morning."

"That will work for me. We can meet back here after we drop the kids at school." Heather said.

"Yes. Perfect." Sara agreed. She wanted to know what her siblings wanted to do, but they were right. Spouses needed to know what was going on. She was afraid with that much money invested by Susan for each of them that nothing was stopping them from the idea of selling Bella Rose and living off the investments.

She told Randall she needed to go for a walk and that she would meet him at their home. He understood her need and agreed.

Heather walked into her house and found Ben. He could tell by her facial expression that she was bursting with something to share. He asked if she was alright.

"I am better than alright. We are all better than alright."

"What do you mean? How do you know that?" Ben asked, walking up to his wife and hugging her.

"Why are you shaking?"

"I didn't realize I was, but when I tell you the news, you may be shaking too."

"Talk to me."

"Long story and details left out; I will tell you the important part. We, my love, are millionaires. Or close to millionaires."

"What are you saying? How are we rich?"

"Susan, Mama, the lady who gave birth to me. That is how. Somehow, she invested money for each of us siblings that grew to almost a million dollars in value over the years.

Ben looked at his wife. "You're not kidding, are you?"

"Why would I kid about that kind of money? No, I am serious. She did that for Sara, Andy, and me. There's more."

"More money?"

"No, more to discuss. Do you remember when Mama died and left the will five years ago with the odd stipulations for us to follow? One of them being for all of us to live here for five years operating Bella Rose?"

Ben thought for a moment. "Yes, I do. That is why we moved here. So what about it?"

"The five years are up. That is how we got the rest of our inheritance. It also means that we no longer are obligated to stay here and operate Bella Rose. Mama wrote in each of our letters that it was up to us what we did. We could stay as we are or sell the estate and go our separate ways."

"Go our separate ways? Doing what? Why would we leave?" Ben was confused and almost upset. He didn't want to leave. His life was finally together. He needed to stay.

"I have no idea what we would do either," Heather said with a laugh. She sat down at the kitchen table, and Ben joined her. They put their hands together.

"Then it's settled. We are staying," Ben said.

"I hope Sara and Andy feel the same way. I can't run this place on my own. I don't want to buy them out. I like things as they are."

"I am with you. If Sara or Andy want to sell it, we will discuss our options."

"We are all meeting at the family meeting place in the morning after we drive the kids to school. I am glad you are on board with me."

"How could I not be? You are my life!" Ben reached over and kissed her. He took her hands, helping her stand for a body hug and a kiss like they had not had in a while. Life was good.

Heather hoped Andy and Sara were making the same decisions.

The next morning they all met at the island in the manor.

Everyone's smiles made it look like they were hiding something.

Andy had made muffins and fresh coffee for everyone. Everyone helped themselves to both while talking idle chatter. Sara then called for them to sit down to discuss their situation.

Each of them took their turn, saying what was on their minds. At the end of the discussion, after all the questions had been raised and answered, they all agreed. They were all staying. Bella Rose Estates was going to continue being run by the Fairchild family. The next generation of Fairchilds, Kanes, and Williams, would be raised there. Life as everyone knew it would be the same.

The phone rang as a perfect ending bell to the family discussion.

Sara answered it, then handed it to Andy. It was Larry from Pennsylvania.

Andy took the phone call and, a few minutes later, was smiling as he hung up. He turned to his family and told them that Larry and Grace wanted to visit when the baby was born. They had not been to visit in a while, so Andy was thrilled that he would soon see his father again.

With the decision to stay and run Bella Rose, they each went on with their day as if nothing had changed. And it hadn't changed except for the fact that none of them had to worry about anything anymore. The Estate was doing well. Now each of them was also set for many years to come.

Chapter Thirty-Three

No More Silence

Silence. That is all Barbara heard when her mind woke up. Unwilling to open her eyes, she lay in bed listening. Still, there was only silence. She did not know whether to laugh or cry.

She had spent most of her life surrounded by silence or muffled sounds. To her, that was what life was. Silence and muffled sounds. Nothing directed at her. Nothing with deep meaning.

She smiled and opened her eyes. She sat up and stretched out her arms, welcoming the new day. Her life was no longer filled with complete quiet. The muffled sounds had long since disappeared. Her life had become peaceful, filled with family and love. Today was a new day, a new start.

She looked at the clock and climbed out of bed. The smell of fresh coffee lured her into the kitchen, where Steven poured her a fresh cup of black coffee when he saw her.

"Good morning, Beautiful. Did you sleep well?"

Barbara held the cup in both hands, absorbing its warmth before raising it to her lips and taking a sip. "Good morning. Yes, I slept well. Why do you ask?"

"Because today is a big day for you." Steven sipped on his mug of coffee as he flipped the eggs in the frying pan.

"Yes, it is. I have to get ready for it in a minute. Today I meet with Joe to discuss my options for working with him."

"I hope he has a few options for you. I know he works with several agencies, so he is a good source of information if nothing else. Hopefully, he'll have the perfect fit for you nearby."

"I hope so too. I would love to work with the foster care system. Work with the children and their placements. I know what I went through during my childhood and all the bad families I was placed with because not enough research was done on them beforehand. It may not be possible to spot all the negatives within a family, but somehow, I think a better job could be done."

"A lot of it may have to do with funding." Steven took the side known as 'devil's advocate.'

"I know. Even with the funds allocated for the research, things could be better."

"That is why I love you. You have such a positive spirit. You see a problem and know there is a solution. Even when most of the world lets it slip by with no hope of changing."

"Life can always be changed. It continues with or without change, but if there is a way to improve it, make things easier for other people, I think it is up to us to do what we can." Barbara finished her coffee and handed Steven her cup." Thanks, Babe. I need to get changed. I'll be back in a few minutes."

Steven knew it would take her longer than a few minutes, so he poured another cup of coffee for her.

"You know me too well," Barbara said, taking the mug and leaving the room.

An hour later, Barbara was sitting in Joe McBride's office discussing agencies needing passionate people working for them.

"There are so many agencies needing someone like you," Joe said after talking with Barbara and learning more about her background.

"Thank you. I wish I could help them all, but my passion is for the children. To assure they are treated right. To see that in their time of need, they feel loved."

"I have three things in mind for you to consider." Joe opened the top folder on his desk and handed it to her. "This is the first one. Not that I believe this one should be your first choice. This agency receives calls from couples and singles who want to become foster parents. It is up to the agency to investigate their background, meet with them, learn about them and their lives, and inspect their homes, the neighborhoods, the schools, and the neighbors. Then they do a write-up for the files. When a child enters the system, their case manager pulls files and does their best to fit the child in need with the best family."

"Is there no communication between the case manager and the person who had met with the family? Is it all determined by reading a file? Does the case manager meet with the family?"

"Those are the questions I would expect you to ask." Joe was impressed. "At this time, no. The case manager simply reads over the file and places the child. They meet briefly before taking the child there, and there is a face-to-face at their office before placement, but an in-depth look? No."

Barbara sat looking at the file. She flipped a page and saw an actual write-up. Despite the blackened-out names for confidentiality purposes, Barbara understood the write-up.

"This is not complete."

"What do you mean?" Joe looked at the papers she was referring to.

"There is no photograph of the family, the other children in the household, the family pets, the house itself, the landscape. I understand there is no need for photos of everything the child may encounter, but having photos helps the case manager feel if a connection is appropriate."

Joe sat back in his chair. This lady in front of him is just what the agency needed. And not as the one who went out doing the research. Barbara needed a management position to help the agency improve. Joe smiled.

"Why the smile? This is serious."

"Oh, I know it is serious." Joe sat up and leaned his forearms against his desk. "This agency needs you. They could use you to help them improve their system." Joe sat back and stared into space, fixated on Barbara.

"You are freaking me out. Why are you looking at me that way?" Barbara said, averting eye contact. She had a weird feeling running through her.

"How are you at public speaking?"

"What? What are you talking about, public speaking? I tell you an agency needs better communication between the researcher and the case managers, and you bring up public speaking? You are confusing me."

Joe stood up and started pacing the floor of his office. He looked outside and then at Barbara. "How would you like to be a trainer?"

Barbara started to speak in protest.

Joe held up his right hand. "No, hear me out on this." Joe sat down at his desk and pulled out four more files from his desk file drawer. "I am talking about speaking with all of these agencies, and I know there are more in other areas about how they can better serve the children they protect."

Barbara was speechless. Her day had begun in silence. Now came a quiet pause. Her mind was racing, So full of questions she did not know where to start. Her heart was overflowing with joy at this prospect. She could be helping so many future foster kids. And, of course, the foster parents and the case managers. And always in the best interest of all the children.

Joe watched as Barbara closed her eyes. She envisioned adult children approaching her and thanking her. She saw small children entering homes but turning to wave and throw kisses at their case manager for being there for them. She saw foster parents no longer filled with anticipation and assumption of things going wrong.

She opened her eyes several minutes later. "What else do you have to offer?"

He sat back and shook his head. He had been convinced she would take that first job he offered. "You don't want this one?"

"I am not saying I don't want this one. I am saying, what else do you have? You said you had a few positions to offer when I came here. I don't want to jump at the first one and miss out on something that could be better."

"Yes, I did say that." Joe reached for another file. "This one is for a case manager position. You would meet with the child, match them up as best you could, and if that one did not work out, you would move the child to a better home."

"And with little communication, it literally would be a case of doing the best I can." She handed back the file. "Next. Now that I see and understand the pitfalls, I want a better position."

"Well, the next position is one Sara told me about this morning when we spoke on the phone."

"Yes, and?" Barbara wondered why Sara had a job opening when she had sent her to talk with Joe.

"And... she wanted me to tell you that if you were not ready to work, or if none of what I had offered you fit what you wanted, she could use your help. She, Andy, and Heather could all use your help."

"How so? I don't see it."

"They are offering you the job of being a Nanny to all of their children,"

"Me? A nanny? Have they not seen all of my internet web pages and the trouble I can get them into?"

"They have, and they told me they would highly recommend you.

Barbara was flattered. To be responsible for six children, most under four, was a massive undertaking. She was not sure she was ready for that job. She held up her hand. "I am not ready to handle that many children full time. I appreciate their trust in me, but that is a lot. Sorry, Sara, but that is a no. At least for now."

Joe laughed. "I didn't think you would accept that challenge."

"Not that I would not help them out occasionally when they needed a sitter. But as a full-time position, count me out." Barbara said. "That is not who I am."

"Who are you, then?" Joe asked.

"I am the person who sees a need in a broken system. I want to discuss becoming the Director of Training."

"I was hoping you would want more information on that one. The agencies need someone like you. Someone who wants to help them improve and understands what the children go through in a broken system."

"So, who do I talk with about details?"

Joe stood up from his seat and reached out his hand to shake hers. "Meet Joe McBride, head of *Silent No More*."

"Of course, you are the person in charge. Why would I think it was anyone else?"

"There is one other person to include. My wife, Nicole. Together we are the head of *Silent No More*."

"Interesting name. Why did you pick it?"

"*Silent No More* is about children's rights for those that don't know about them or are too young to speak up. Nicole and I started this agency to be the voice of children. We found a breakdown between them and what the agencies who handle them can do. A breakdown of communication. A breakdown of betterment for them. Once they are in the system, they are forgotten. Love falls by the wayside as foster parents take on too many cases. Case managers are overwhelmed with clients, and it becomes a matter of how fast a child can be placed just to get them off the street and out of sleeping in an office somewhere. We needed someone to look at all the variables and fix them."

Barbara smiled. "You have found your person. I will do my utmost to work with you and Nicole to stop the silence. I certainly know what silence is. As an adult with a family and love, I have learned to appreciate it. As a child, I dreaded it. It meant heartbreak, sorrow, sadness, loneliness, and fear. It meant there was no love."

"Welcome to one more family, Director. When can you start?"

"I think we need to discuss details first. Although it is not a major factor in my final decision, what is the pay, the benefits, the office space… we have just begun."

Joe sat down and pulled out another file. This one had her name on it.

"Wait, that has my name on it already. How did you know?"

"Nicole and I just knew. We cannot explain it. We saw in you the person we needed and who needed us just by what we already know of you.

Chapter Thirty-Four

The Reopening

When Barbara finished meeting with Joe, she walked out of his office with her head held high. She decided to go for a short walk instead of going directly to her car. The world looked different to her now. The sky was bluer, the air fresher, and the people were smiling. Her heart was light. She had a purpose.

Her walk took her to the Downtown Café, where the remodeling was wrapping up. Steven had told her a week earlier that it was nearing completion. It had been a while since she had stopped in, so she turned and opened the front door.

She was immediately impressed. Steven had not disclosed any details of the work or design. She was about to sneak out when she heard her name called. She turned to face Terri.

"Hello, stranger. Steven talks about you all the time, but you never stop by. I was beginning to think you were a figment of his imagination." Terri said with a wink. "I know better than that, but it has been a while, girl."

"Yes, it has been a while. I have been working on the apartment, deciding what work I want to pursue, and we are thinking about finding a house to buy, so I've been searching the internet."

"No wonder you have not been here. You are busy. So have you found work yet? I could always use another hand around here if you need something."

"I found a job today. Don't tell Steven. I have not told him about it yet."

"Your secret is safe with me. I won't even ask you where you will be working. The less I know, the less trouble I get myself into. You know what I mean?"

"I do know what you mean." Barbara glanced up at the menu on the wall.

"Would you like something to eat? On the house, of course."

"I would love a Rueben sandwich. I don't make them at home. Always save them as a treat when we go out."

"One of my favorites, coming right up," Terri yelled her order back to the chef.

"So, you are looking for a house to buy? What area of town?"

"We'd like to be out at Bella Rose Estate. I want to be near my twin."

"Are you sure you want to be that close to your brother?" Terri laughed. "Sometimes, it can be too close."

"Not for us. We just reconnected not long ago for the first time since we were toddlers."

"Steven told me some about that. I am thrilled that you found each other. Family is important." Terri turned away to pick up Barbara's order. "You have a special man in that, Steven. I am sure you realize that."

"Believe me, I know. He spoils me, and I love it." Barbara smiled and took a bite of her sandwich. Terri asked if she needed anything else with her sandwich, then walked away to help another customer after Barbara shook her head.

After finishing her sandwich, she left without a word to Steven. He was busy talking with Adam and Donovan. On her drive home to their apartment, she noticed a house for sale. She pulled into the driveway and admired it. Before she could pull away, the owner stepped outside and walked to her car. He asked if she wanted to see the house and told her a little bit about it. Barbara declined his offer but said she would tell her husband. She drove away but could not get the house off her mind. She would tell Steven about it when he got home.

Steven got home late that night and was so excited to share news of the grand reopening that he never gave his wife a chance to say anything. Barbara patiently listened while she held in her big news. She knew that there were times in life that you stayed quiet until it was the appropriate time to speak.

"I have been talking non-stop. I'm so sorry. You had your job search meeting with Joe today! How did that go?"

Barbara smiled. She knew she had his attention now. She proceeded to tell him about the whole long process before telling her punchline of accepting the one job offer.

"You will be amazing at that!" Steven said. He walked into the kitchen as he spoke. "Time for a drink of wine to celebrate, don't you agree?"

"Sounds like a wonderful time." Barbara walked over to him and accepted the glass of wine he offered. They toasted to their future. Great things were about to happen.

A week later, Terri announced to everyone at the Café that she planned a big grand re-opening in two weeks. The remodel was complete, and the final touches and decorations would be up by then. Everyone was looking forward to it.

Barbara helped in her spare time with the final touches. Terri called Heather to help plan the re-opening. They found out that Adam was quite an accomplished singer and hired him to sing a few songs. He graciously agreed. Maybe his big break into the music world would come out of it. He knew very little about his new friends, and in the amount of time he had gotten to know them, no one had gotten to know much about him. He liked it that way. The less they knew, the better Adam felt. Steven knew, and that was enough. He trusted Steven.

The night of the re-opening arrived. Terri had advertised it for a couple of weeks, plus word of mouth helped bring in the large crowd. Terri had not expected so many people. She and Steven stood in the back and observed everyone as they mingled, ate the horderves, enjoyed drinks from the new lounge, and filled the café with laughter. Terri was thrilled with the turnout.

Adam sang a few songs to the karaoke system he had set up. When he finished his last song, other guests went up to sing other songs. The once-quiet café was full of life. Terri and Steven stood next to each other as they looked around the room and took in all the joy. Caught up in the moment, Terri reached over and touched Steven's hand. He immediately pulled away. Embarrassed by her action, she rushed away. He was not even who was on her mind.

Adam walked over to the bar and asked Terri when she wanted the party to end. He would shut down the karaoke to help slow the business.

Terri looked at Adam. His piercing blue eyes, thick dark hair, the smile that never ended, all of him made her smile. She smiled at him and told him what time to shut the music down. He turned to go, and as he did, his hand touched hers. She smiled, although he didn't notice.

The day after the re-opening, the café was open for regular business. Steven took to his new responsibilities with ease. Running the bar came naturally to him. He would be fine as long as he stayed clear of any illegal dealings. There was less temptation with Adam not working on the café's remodel. Steven knew Adam had changed his ways from their time in Seattle, but it was never far from his mind. He understood how easy it was to get sucked into something he did not want to do.

Chapter Thirty-Five

Broken

Downtown Café and Lounge was becoming a huge success in town. Terri and Steven hired more waitstaff and bartenders to cover the extended hours and accommodate the customers.

Barbara sat in her new office. She had been busy buying office supplies, decorating the room, painting the walls, and ordering office furniture a month before. Now she sat ready to start work.

First on her agenda was a meeting with Joe and Nicole. She had gotten to know them during the previous month. She enjoyed seeing them at the Lounge when it opened. It was one thing to know people in the work environment, quite another to know them personally. Knowing someone on both sides helped. Especially for the work she was doing.

Barbara had learned a long time ago that a person is not what they seem to be on the first meeting. Each person has multiple levels in their life. She liked to get to know as much about people as she could. That was her advantage in this job.

Joe and Nicole walked into her office while she looked out her office window. When Joe asked her which office she wanted, that had been her only requirement—a window with a view. There were several vacancies in the building. She had not picked the largest one; she picked the best one for her needs and claustrophobia.

"You have done wonders with this office space," Nicole said as she walked inside and glanced around.

"Thank you. I confess I had Heather help me. She is amazing. If you ever need a decorator or a party planner, she is your gal," Barbara said. She took a seat at her desk and motioned Joe and Nicole to sit opposite her.

"What have you decided to address first, the major agencies that place children or the children's case management teams?"

"I have decided to address the major agencies. I need to find out how they place the children that enter their system. I know the case managers look to them for guidance in their placement. I need to know how they select which children will be placed with which individual families. I am most likely wrong, but I assume the process needs help. Once I know what is lacking, I can put together specifics to improve the process."

"That seems like a big challenge," Nicole commented.

"It is, but starting small is not my style. Not when it involves children that need help and need love."

Nicole looked at Joe. "You certainly have selected the correct person for this position."

Barbara smiled when she overheard. "Thank you, Nicole. I only hope and pray I do you justice and make things better for the children. Lord knows, the way it was when I was in the system sucked. And from what I see, it has not changed much over the years. Children come in from all directions and are simply placed with the next family available. It doesn't matter if they are a good fit. That process needs to stop."

Joe was impressed. "Let me get you a complete list of the placement agencies. You will also need a list of the case managers and their agencies."

"Are there other people who deal with the foster system? Such as the police department, hospitals, shelters? Or do they all go through case managers?"

"Anyone in the human services business has the responsibility to direct children to the foster system. They generally go through a case manager. Not all do. A few of them contact the placement agency directly, which sometimes confuses the whole process."

"I would say it does. I understand the desire to go direct as it quickly gets the child into a home, but that does not guarantee a good family fit."

"You are correct. And it does not get a follow-up with the child. Many of them get lost in the system."

"My heart aches for the children. Of my foster families, I think a couple of them were temporary on purpose, but with each one, in the beginning, I hoped each new home was going to be my final home. I cried myself to sleep more nights than I cared to count. It was not until Steven entered my life that I felt true love. These children need to know and feel loved. They need assurance that adults in this world are fighting for them."

"Have you ever thought about public speaking?" Nicole asked.

Barbara looked at Joe. It was one of the questions he had asked her. She shook her head. "No, not until Joe asked me in my original interview. Why do you ask?"

"Because you have passion. A passion that these agencies need to hear and feel. They need to hear your story and then your plans to change things for the better." Nicole turned to Joe.

Joe looked at Nicole and smiled. "I already have made calls to set up a major event for a speaking engagement."

"Excuse me?" Barbara asked when she heard about a speaking engagement.

"We both believe you need to prepare a presentation for a speaking event to get the agencies interested and willing to be involved. Doing this will save you time. Instead of going to each one individually, you get them all at once. What do you say?"

"Say? I'd be a nervous wreck. But I see your point. Let me work on a presentation."

"I am so glad you accepted this position. The children will benefit from this even though they may never know it. The ones who have been through the system the former way will notice a difference. I hope it will mean children go through fewer foster families before they are adopted."

"That is my plan." Barbara stood to walk her guest to the door. Their meeting was over, and each of them had work to do.

Three weeks later, Barbara stood on the stage at the local high school in front of over a hundred people representing the local agencies and companies dealing with the foster care system in the area and surrounding counties. She looked around the room, trying to feel how they felt. She knew that what she was about to present would change them, how they did some of their work, and how they felt.

Barbara answered their questions for over an hour after she finished her presentation and learned of their concerns. She was physically and mentally drained when the last person walked out of the school.

Left alone with her thoughts and many written down, she wept. She had learned so much from them as she wished they had learned from her.

Steven walked into the auditorium finding his wife sitting on the edge of the stage with her head down. He did not notice her tears until he stood in front of her, and she looked up at him.

"What's wrong, babe? Did they not like what you had to say?"

"Oh, Steven. No. It was quite the opposite. They were responsive and very concerning. They had so many questions it was hard to keep up. I am drained."

"Do you think they will be willing to work with you on your goals and plans?"

"Very much so. You would not believe the hugs I received, the applause, and the overall feeling of this place as they listened. A few even asked if I had a committee set up or needed them to join me in the training process. It was amazing." Barbara had wiped her tears, and a smile had replaced her somber face.

"That is what you wanted. You wanted the agencies and people to be with you on this mission."

"Yes, it is. And I think, at least with this first group, that I have their support and encouragement. I told them I would have another meeting in a couple of weeks after I have talked to the second group."

"Second group?"

"This group was made up of the agencies that place the children. The next group will be for all the case managers and other agency personnel handling the children and placing them. That group is the one that may need more in-depth training."

"How so?"

"Because I plan on changing the process. It will take getting used to, but it will be better for the children. I don't want them to pick up a child in need and dump them into foster care with just any family. I want them to know more about the family first. I want a definite follow-up process, so no child goes neglected and forgotten."

"You arc an amazing woman, Mrs. Howard."

"Thank you, Mr. Howard. I owe a lot to you." She stood and kissed his cheek,"

'How do you owe it to me? I was not there when you were growing up and going through the system."

"No, but you were there for me when I needed it as an adult. You have shown me a love that no one else did. You proved to me that there is light at the end of the tunnel. I want each child to know that feeling while still a child. I want them to experience the love of family while they are still in the system. I want them to have a positive childhood through their unfortunate circumstances. I know it is possible—if done right."

Steven reached for Barbara's hand. "Come on, young lady. Let me take you out to dinner to celebrate your success and the future you are planning for the next generation."

"I don't feel worthy of a celebration. Not yet anyway."

"Whether you feel it or not, you deserve it. You have put your passion into this endeavor. I am proud of you."

Barbara smiled as she took Steven's hand and walked out of the school. Life was going to be amazing for them all.

Chapter Thirty-Six

New Life

"I think it's time."

That statement puts a couple into immediate action no matter where they are or the time of day. And it did just that to Andy when Karen spoke to them at three in the morning.

Her pregnancy had progressed without concern this time. When she was carrying the twins, she had to be careful. This time she handled the nine months like a champ. That phrase, though, always brought a bit of panic. When she said it, Andy jumped into action.

Andy made phone calls. Sara rushed over to take care of River and Ryan. Heather and Ben went to the manor to handle the morning guests. Barbara and Steven were on alert to help where needed. Rachelle and Bob were to help Heather and Ben. Giving birth in this family was an all-on-deck family affair.

Karen called Dr. George to let her know they were going to the hospital to have the baby. Everything was working according to plan.

Andy pulled up to the emergency room entrance and rushed to get a wheelchair for Karen. Her contractions had become intense on the drive, and he was not sure he would have time to park the car before she delivered. An orderly rushed out and helped Karen into the wheelchair and into admission. Another orderly motioned for Andy to park the car. Andy was ready to panic until he saw Dr. George, who motioned for him to park the car.

"You have time. Go." Dr. George motioned to the father-to-be. She was accustomed to this behavior from panicked fathers. She also knew that Karen still had time before their baby girl would be born.

Andy returned and walked with Karen while the orderly wheeled her down the hall into the pediatric area of the children's hospital. Karen moved from the chair to the bed with ease. Her contractions had subsided for the time being. When she lay back on the bed, another one came. The nurses attached the leads to monitor her vitals and her contractions. Andy watched in amazement. His panic subsided as he was no longer in charge of what would happen. He never had the desire to deliver his child alone. That was someone else's job. He sat in the uncomfortable chair and watched until the nurses had finished.

Dr. George entered the room to check on her patient. "We meet again." She said cheerfully. "Are you ready for one more?"

Andy sat straight up. "One more! What do you mean, one more? Are we having twins again?"

"Oh, no, no. Sorry. You are only going to have one child this time. It was enough to have two last time. The sonogram would have shown if you were going to have twins again."

"Ah. Okay. You had me concerned!" Andy's panic subsided. One more was all he could handle. He was not even sure they could handle the one extra. The twins were a handful and not even two years old! He closed his eyes to ponder his family. All was good.

A moment later, he heard Karen Scream. He knew it was time now. He remembered that sound. He rushed to her side and glared at the door. Two nurses quickly ran in, followed by Dr. George.

"Okay, it's time."

Andy stood to leave. Karen yelled at him before the next contraction and told him He was not going anywhere!

"You heard the lady, Andy. You are not going anywhere. You are going to help with this one. Let's go."

Andy walked around the bed and took hold of Karen's hand. He stayed by his wife's side; she would not let him be anywhere else. He smiled at his wife and felt the love between them without saying a word.

Fifteen minutes later, their beautiful and perfect daughter was born. After a quick physical, cleaning the baby, and documenting its vital information, the baby was placed on Karen's chest for skin on skin bonding. Andy watched this new member of his family open her eyes and look at her mama. Karen smiled and reached for Andy's hand. Her eyes said all he needed to hear. Love. Pure, sweet, forever love.

Karen gazed at her daughter. She had briefly seen her when they placed her on her chest as soon as she was born. Now she was clean and more beautiful. Her head of almost black hair, already three inches long, stuck out beneath the edges of her tiny knit cap. Karen removed the cap so Andy could see his daughter better. He immediately knew that their previously discussed name was a perfect fit. He replaced her cap to keep her warm and nodded to his beautiful wife.

The nurses left the room, closed Karen's hospital room door, and left the new family alone. For them, it was just another successful delivery and a new member of their patient's family. If they only knew how much this little girl would have from so many family members. Spoiled was just the beginning.

Karen handed their little girl to Andy. He sat beside the bed and gently rocked her while Karen fell asleep.

Mid-morning brought visitors to see the precious new bundle. The first to arrive were Larry and Grace. They had already headed to Tennessee from Pennsylvania when they heard that Karen had given birth. They had left late and stopped to spend the night in a hotel. Otherwise, they would have been there sooner.

Larry shook his son's hand, then embraced him. Congratulations, son. Grace had walked immediately over to Karen's bed and peeked at the baby while Karen nursed her.

"She is beautiful," Grace whispered.

"Thank you. We think so too. She is perfect in every way. Even with her look fitting the name we have chosen."

"And what name have you chosen for her?" Grace asked.

"Andy, Larry?" Karen called them to her bed quietly. She looked up at Andy. "Do you want to do the honors and introduce our daughter to her grandparents?"

Andy smiled. He touched his daughter and looked at Larry and Grace. "Dad, Grace, we would like you to meet Ravyn Grace Fairchild, your newest granddaughter."

"Hello, Ravyn Grace," Grace said as she gently kissed the knit cap on Ravyn's head. "Welcome to the family."

Larry turned away from everyone in the room. Andy turned to see what was wrong when he noticed his father wipe away a tear. He walked over to him and put his arm around him.

"Are you alright?"

"Yes, son. I am better than alright. You don't know what it means to me to have you name her after Grace."

"That name was an easy choice. Grace has been a part of Karen's life for many years, and she has become my second mother. We love you two."

"We love all of you." Larry wiped the rest of the tears and walked with Andy to join the girls—their girls.

The rest of the day was busy with family visits. The little family would be home the next day, but there was something about seeing the baby as soon as possible that everyone just had to do. Karen finally got some rest that evening when there were no more visitors. Andy spent the night helping take care of little Ravyn Grace. He smiled as he watched her sleep.

The next day the family gathered at Andy and Karen's house to welcome them home.

Larry told Andy they planned to stay at the manor to help with the children and the manor, wherever they could help. Andy told them they appreciated it. Two days later, they said they had some news to share. Andy looked at Larry and was immediately concerned. He was enjoying a happy time in their life; he did not want any bad news.

When all three children managed to be napping simultaneously, the four of them gathered in the living room to talk.

Larry stayed standing while the other three sat down. "I know you may be wondering why we have been able to stay here this long already. It may not have crossed your mind that we have been here longer than our regular visits. And you may wonder why I've not been on my phone with home and the business while I've been here."

"Now that you mention it, you have stayed longer than usual. I assume you arranged to have someone manage the business and lucked out at being here with us." Andy said. He had been so busy he had not thought much about it.

Grace reached up and took Larry's hand. They looked at each other without saying a word. Andy got an odd feeling that he did not like. What were they about to tell them? If one of them was sick, he was not sure he could deal with that. Not now. Life was perfect for all of them. There was no time for anything less or more, as the case may be.

"Andy, Karen, Grace, and I have sold the marina and the rental properties at Lake Wallenpaupack." He let that soak in a moment before continuing. "We have reached a time in our lives that we realize that if we don't stop now and enjoy the life we have left, we will never enjoy this life. You are looking at Larry and Grace—retired!"

Andy sighed with relief. Now that was news he could handle.

Chapter Thirty-Seven

Reconnection

Andy and Karen quickly got into a routine with all three of their children. The twins sensed that the new baby needed more attention from their mother than they did, and they easily took to Larry and Grace taking care of them. Karen loved having her friends around. It had been years since she had spent time with Larry and Grace. Her connection with them had begun so long ago. Her marriage and move to Tennessee had not been an easy one. She had felt like she was leaving her parents alone.

Andy was thrilled to have his father around him. When he first found out Larry was his biological father, he did not react very well. It took time and the telling of the back story to bond them. Now that Larry and Grace were there for an extended period, he wondered if he could talk them into moving to the area. One day, when things with the children were calm, he addressed his idea.

"Larry, Grace, you know how much I appreciate you being here to help with the twins. And I am thrilled that we have had this time together. I have to ask. What are your plans?" Andy asked. He knew the answer he wanted to hear but did not want to address that in the way he asked. He wanted it to be their sincere answer.

Larry and Grace looked at each other and smiled. Larry took Grace's hand. "Son, we had wanted to tell you this from when we arrived, but Ravyn Grace took center stage, and we did not want to take you away from that joy. But, we have been looking into buying a house near you."

Andy was thrilled and stepped toward them. They met him halfway in a family hug. "That makes me happy. I was prepared to invite you to move here, but I did not want to seem pushy, admitting I desperately wanted you to be here. And Karen will be beside herself."

"We thought you would like that," Grace said as she stepped out of the family embrace. "We have wanted to do this for so long, but we could not find a buyer for the marina. We finally found a young couple who not only wanted to buy the marina; they wanted the rental properties. They were perfect for it. So we signed the papers two weeks before we came here."

"Have you found any place here that you like yet?"

"We have. Just yesterday." It is a little house about fifteen minutes from here."

"That is amazing! Have you looked at it and made an offer? Are you ready to move?" Andy was ready for them to be his neighbors permanently. He knew the rest of the family would agree—it was about time.

"I think we need to celebrate your decision."

"I think we need to wait until we have found the perfect house to buy. We are not sure about this one yet. We can tell Karen and the rest of your family but save the celebration and party until later."

"Okay. As long as we can share this wonderful news with Karen."

"What wonderful news?" Karen asked as she walked up to them in her silent way. Andy hated that she could walk that quietly. She spooked him so often it was not funny anymore, although they always laughed when it happened.

"Larry, I will let you do the honors," Andy said with a big smile.

Karen turned to Larry and waited.

"Grace and I are officially retired. We have sold the business. And the best part is that we have decided to move here to be close to you and our grandchildren."

Karen had tears flowing before she realized it. She rushed over to them and threw her arms around both of them. "That is wonderful news! When are you moving?"

"We are looking for a house nearby, and then we can move. We have most of our home in Pennsylvania packed up already." Grace added.

"You are serious! Do you know how happy that makes me? The kids will love having you here. I will love having you here! Karen hugged them both as though she would never let go.

Over the next few weeks, Larry and Grace continued house shopping. They had toured so many homes the houses began to look alike. Grace was getting tired of not finding the perfect house. She and Larry had lived in one house their entire married life, and the search was wearing on her.

They had moved in with Andy and Karen to help with the children, and Grace loved being with them, but she needed her own space.

A month after deciding to move, Larry walked up to Grace and said he had found the perfect place. He wanted to take her to it immediately because the realtor told him it would not last. Grace looked at her husband, noticed his smile, and walked out the door with him.

They signed the papers and became new homeowners in a new state a month later. Within another month, Grace had their home looking as perfect as their home in Pennsylvania. Her smile had returned, and Larry noticed.

Larry was not the only one who noticed. Barbara noticed. Ben noticed. What Barbara and Ben noticed was the connection between Andy and Larry. Barbara and Steven quickly learned the history of Larry and Andy when they announced they were moving to Tennessee to be with family. She was impressed that they connected, and she noticed the love shine through them. It amazed her that Andy could forgive his father. That also made her think of Benjamin Thomas and his dealing with her and her brother. Could she forgive him?

Ben called Barbara one day and said he had something he wanted to discuss with her. She said she had something to talk about too. They met for lunch at the café.

After ordering their food and sharing some idle conversation, Ben brought up what was on his mind.

"I have been doing some serious thinking over the last several weeks since Larry and Grace moved here." He watched his sister's reaction. Assuming she could tell what he was thinking.

"Go on. I have been too, but what are you thinking?"

"You know the history between Andy and Larry, right?"

"Sure, it's part of the family history. Everyone at Bella Rose knows about it."

"I was already a part of the family when that was discovered, and Andy found out Larry was his biological father. I watched the emotions, the anger, the distrust, the hatred, then saw the change in them. Larry always wanted to be involved in Andy's life. Andy didn't know the truth until after he met Karen, and it took a while for them to bond. Now, look at them."

"They are close. Like a father and son should be. So, what is on your mind?" Their food came, which gave Ben a few minutes to form his thoughts.

"I have been thinking of Benjamin Thomas, our biological father. I think we should rethink our relationship with him."

Barbara took a bite of her sandwich while she listened. She smiled while she chewed. Her brother was thinking the same way she had been recently.

Ben continued talking as he ate. "I don't know how you feel about it. For me, he was there all my life. I just didn't know who he actually was. For you, he was never there. I understand if you still hate him for what he did to you."

"I have been thinking about that." Barbara interrupted him. "I know I hated him at first. He left me. He knew where I was most of the time and never contacted me. I may never understand that."

"I know, Sis. In my opinion, you have every right to feel that way. I was wondering if we need to give him another chance? He is our father. He is getting older. We have not spoken with him in months. I don't know why I have this feeling, but I do. I think we need to give him another opportunity to be in our lives." Ben said as he finished his lunch.

Barbara sighed. Her mind and heart matched her twin's. "I think we should. If Andy can reconnect with his father, forgive his mother and Larry and be one big happy family after all these years, maybe we can too."

"I will contact him when we get back to the manor." Ben reached out and touched his sister's arm. "Thanks, Sis."

"For what? I haven't done anything."

"Yes, you have. You opened your heart to a man who wronged you."

"A little, yes. I still have doubts and fears."

"Doubts, I understand. What are your fears?"

"My fear is that when we invite him back into our lives, and if I fully open my heart, it will get broken again, and I will be standing alone –again."

"You will never be in that position again, my dear Sister. I can promise you that. You have me in your life, and you have Steven. Plus, you have the entire clan of Bella Rose by your side. You are stuck surrounded by family now."

Barbara smiled. Her eyes filled with tears. That was a word she had longed for all her life – family.

Ben held her hand and smiled. "Never again, Sis. Never again."

Ben paid their tab before they walked outside into the center of town. The quaint little town they both now called home.

Chapter Thirty-Eight

Always Family

The time had come for another family meeting with the three siblings and the spouses. Sara originally thought the family meetings should be just her and her siblings. She soon realized that having their spouses included saved them from repeating the topics discussed.

They had begun to meet away from the manor for the family meetings, but Sara requested this meeting be in the kitchen at the island like they used to be. She had an idea that she did not want the general public to know.

Barbara and Steven agreed to watch all the children while the rest of the family met for their meeting. Sara also asked Rachelle and Bob to watch the children if they needed her. Bob eagerly said they could, then looked at his wife, who shook her head. She loved how Bob fit in with the family. He was always volunteering to help anyone who needed assistance.

Andy had made a simple supper for everyone as he used to do when the family was much smaller. Another trial dish before he put it in the food selection for manor guests. And if he received good family reviews, he would add them to his next recipe book. It had been a couple of years since his last book. Like had taken first place, and his cooking adventures had returned to what he knew instead of new dishes.

When they began to eat, Sara shared her idea with her siblings. "I have had a lot on my mind recently. With all the new people added to our family and Bella Rose Estate, I have been thinking," She began.

Everyone agreed there were several who were now part of the overall family. "What's on your mind?" Ben asked.

"When you are finished, I have my own news to share, if you don't mind."

"I don't mind. You are part of this family, and there are no rules to our meetings except to have fun." Sara looked at him. She was glad to have him in their family.

"A few months ago, we each received the last of our inheritance. I don't think any of us have decided what we are doing with it so far. I think we each have invested a lot of it. We have also deposited it to be safe and grow a little while we wait to decide on other things to do with it or if we need it quickly." Sara took a break and took a sip of her water.

"You are right. We've set some aside for a trip, but the rest is collecting interest and should be worth a good sum when the kids reach college age." Andy held Karen's hand. "With three kids, it will be needed.

Sara smiled. "Yes, you will need it for those three. They may be small now, but time flies, and they will be in college soon."

"Don't say that!" Karen joined in. "I like them being little."

"I have been in touch with my financial advisor, and he had an idea. You all know we have over ten acres of land on this estate. We have used several acres of it with the manor, our homes, the church, and the event hall. However, we have a lot of property not being used. Yes, it's nice to have all the land, but I think we have enough to offer a portion of it to Barbara and Steven."

Ben looked at Sara. "To my sister and Steven? That is an amazing gesture, but why?"

Sara returned Ben's look. "Because they are family now." She looked at Andy and read his mind. "Yes, Larry and Grace are family members now too, but they did not want to live so close to everyone. They wanted to be close but not right on top of us. I understand that. However, I did bring up the possibilities with Larry. He said it was best to live away from everything going on here. He never said why and I did not push for details. I figured if he wanted to share, he would. Soon after that conversation with him, they found their perfect home."

"So, what are you thinking? Offering Barbara and Steven a piece of land to build their own home?" Ben asked. He would love to have his sister so close.

"I think we can have them walk the property to find where they want to build. As long as there is nothing in the way, such as gas lines, power lines, whatever, I think we can sell them a half-acre, if not a little more."

Ben sat up straight. With this offer, he would have more time with his sister. She had been so busy with the new job that she had little time for him over the last month. He understood her being busy. He missed their conversations. Maybe with the new home, they could sit outside at either home and enjoy getting to know each other better. "I'm all for the offer," Ben said, not revealing his true excitement.

Sara looked around the island at Heather, Karen, and Andy. This decision was important. She wanted all of her family as close to her as possible. She could only imagine how much Barbara would want it. "So, everyone agrees to this?"

A look around the room told her they were all for it. She was glad about that. It was her first attempt to be a better person and to get out from behind the desk so much. She missed being with her family as they used to be. Funny, or maybe sad, how life gets busy, and the life you want seems so far away. Now was her time to shine.

Sara asked if they could vote on it. Every hand raised. Sara could not wait to see the smile on Barbara's face. She was forming a bond with her. Barbara may not be a blood relative, but Sara realized that family was made up of more than blood.

Sara pointed to Ben. "I am leaving it up to you to tell Barbara and Steven."

Andy raised his hand as if he were in school. "Yes, what can I answer for you?" Sara said when she saw his hand rise.

"Are we just giving them the land, or are we selling it?"

"We will be selling it to them at a very low cost. Barbara deserves it."

"Yes, she does. She and Steven have been house hunting for a while and cannot find the perfect one. They are renting but would like to be homeowners. Maybe it is because they are supposed to be living here near all of us.

"Could be. All I know is it has been on my mind lately, and I thought it was time to let you know my idea. I am open to feedback and maybe other ideas of what else we can do with the land. We can leave it as it is; I just think we need to do more with it."

"I think offering it to Steven and Barbara is a great idea, but I am biased," Ben said.

"I think it is a good idea too," Andy said. "Let's offer it to them now."

"They are watching all the children. We will let Ben talk to them after we all pick up our kids." Sara looked at Ben. "You had something to share with us?"

"Yes, I did. My news seems minor compared to what you just offered."

"Share it anyway. That is what family meetings are about; anything to do with our family. What is it?"

Barbara and I have seen how Andy and Larry get along with each other, and it has us thinking."

"We didn't always get along." Andy chimed in.

"I know, and that is why we are amazed and inspired by what the two of you have been able to do."

Everyone was looking at Ben, wondering what he had to say.

"Barbara and I talked the other day and have decided to give Benjamin Thomas another chance in our lives."

"That is awesome, Ben," Sara said. "Are you going to invite him here or go visit him? Do you even know where he is?"

"We are going to invite him here. Barbara can't get time off work since she just started her job and is thoroughly engrossed in it. I need to be here to help with the Manor."

"I think that is great news. If there is anything we can do to help, let us know. You all are family now."

"We will, thank you. Now I think we will leave to speak to Barbara and Steven. Thank you again for doing this for my sister and Steven."

"As I said, we are all family," Sara said.

Everyone helped clean the kitchen before they went their separate ways. Sara felt a peace she had not felt for a while. She was back to giving of herself. Life was good.

Chapter Thirty-Nine

Coming Together

Barbara and Steven were shocked at the offer from Sara and the family. When Ben told them, Barbara broke down and cried until there were no more tears.

The next day the three of them walked the property of Bella Rose to see where they might want to have a house. There was no vacant land at the top of the hill, so having a house built with a view of the mountains was impossible. They would need to build below the hiking trail, possibly near the road. They did not want to live too close to the road. They concentrated their search near the hiking trails and below the church, event hall, and flower gardens on either side of the paved road leading to the manor. Barbara loved the flower gardens but also the hiking trails. Ben told her if she built near the hiking trails, she could plant a flower garden. He even offered to help design the gardens.

Within a few days, they had chosen the piece of land they wanted. It was to the right of the driveway, below the hiking trail. Barbara had accepted her brother's offer to help her build a flower garden. She had talked with Andy about planting a few vegetables in a separate garden.

Sara had surveyors separate a half-acre from the rest of the Bella Rose property for Barbara and Steven. The property had direct access to the driveway, and the land behind their property line remained with Bella Rose.

Inspectors were called to ensure no hidden reasons against building a house there. When it was approved for them to be able to build a house on the land, they completed the paperwork, making Barbara and Steven property owners for the first time in their lives. Next came the task of finding a house design they both approved. That was more difficult than choosing the piece of property. Barbara wanted a simple house; Steven wanted a more elaborate one. He wanted the best for his wife. She had spent most of her life deprived of the best of everything. He offered to change that for her.

"I don't need the biggest and best. I just want a small cozy home to call our own. We have no children, and we don't need a lot of bedrooms. A good-sized kitchen would be nice, but the rest does not have to be huge." Barbara told Steven as they searched the internet for house plans.

"We need a living room large enough for the entire family," Steven laughed as he realized how big it might need to be.

"Okay, there is that. Most of the family gatherings are at the manor, but it would be nice to have everyone here once in a while. I will agree to larger size rooms. I am sticking to the idea that there is no need for several rooms."

"Open floor plan it is," Steven said.

"Agreed."

They continued to search until they decided to talk to Adam and Donovan about designing their own house. Maybe they could design a house to fit their needs and wants.

The next day Steven spoke to Adam. With their history and negative beginning years ago, long forgotten and forgiven, they had become close during the remodeling of the lounge at the café. Adam was thrilled to be asked. He loved drawing up blueprints for customers.

A week later, he had a couple of choices for them. One fit Barbara's wants, and another design was more elaborate per Steven's requests. They compromised after some discussion, and Adam returned to his office to draw the final blueprint.

Adam and Donovan began working with contractors to prepare the land when the blueprint had both Steven and Barbara's written approval.

Steven knew his wife deserved better than she thought. He called Adam without her knowledge.

"I want to request a special addition to the house. Barbara does not think she needs more than a simple small house. I know she is being humble and does not want anything elaborate. Our design has a front porch and a small deck along the back. Is there a possibility you can make the deck larger?"

"Of course. We can do whatever you want. I warn you she will notice it being built and the extra expense."

"If you can wait until the very end to build it, I think I can get her to go away for a few days of vacation while you build it. When we return, it will be a surprise."

"We can schedule the building around that. I am unable to tell you when that will be. It all depends on how the other construction work goes first. We rely upon the availability of supplies and the contractors we hire."

"I understand. We will watch closely, and I have a location in mind that does not require a lot of preplanning, reservations, or a lot of packing."

"Sounds good to me. What about the cost? She will notice."

"Let me take care of the extra cost. Bill the deck work separately, and I will see that it is paid. I have money set aside."

"We will do that. I will meet with you about the deck design later. We are getting the basement area dug and will soon begin construction. All of the supplies we need are in stock and should be delivered within the next week. It will be an amazing home for the two of you."

"Thanks, Adam. It means a lot to me."

"Our friendship means a lot to me. We had a rough start in Seattle."

"That we did. I am glad it is behind us, and that way of life is also behind me. It was a hard realization that I was ruining my life and the lives of others with the drugs."

"I'm glad you are here. Our history together makes this new connection more meaningful to me. I hope you feel the same way."

"I do. It means the world to me that you trust me."

"Always, my friend, always."

Adam disconnected the phone call with Steven and immediately pulled out the blueprint to add the decking design. His phone rang before he had time to put the pencil to paper.

"Hello, did you forget something?" He answered, thinking it was Steven calling him back.

"No, why would you think I forgot something? This is Barbara."

"Oh, sorry. I just had another customer on the phone and thought he was calling back. What's on your mind?"

"I want to talk with you about something special to be added to the house design for Steven."

Adam shook his head and smiled. He knew she could not see him and his reaction. "Ok, what would you like?"

"I would like a patio area built off the back deck with a fire pit. He works so hard and always puts me first. He deserves something special."

"We can add that. It will add to the time frame, but we can do that after the house is finished and you've moved in."

"Very true. Once we have moved in, maybe I can take Steven away for a few days, and you can work on the patio."

Adam wanted to laugh out loud but held it in. He had never had a couple so much in love they only thought about each other and not themselves. He hoped one day to have the same relationship with someone. "That sounds like a perfect plan. I will make a note of it. We can talk about details and designs later."

"Perfect. You and Donovan are the best."

"We try."

"Thank you for all you do. I will talk to you later."

"You are welcome, Mrs. Howard," he said, being polite and professional.

"Please, call me Barbara."

"Yes, ma'am," Adam said. "Have a great day, Barbara."

"You too," Barbara said and disconnected. Her plan was in place.

Three months later, Steven asked Barbara to go on a short trip with him to get away for a few days before moving in. She was reluctant, but when he explained that life would be full for them when they moved in and were setting up their home, she agreed. She worried about later asking Steven to take a short trip, yet there was no way around it.

Steven had made reservations in the Smoky Mountains for a long four-day weekend. A cabin in the woods with a view of the mountains and the town of Pigeon Forge. Since moving to the area, they had not been there, and Steven thought it was the perfect destination to enjoy the scenery and do some shopping for their home.

Barbara was amazed at the mountain view from their cabin. A regret about her new home was the lack of mountain views. She knew she could walk to see the view, but it was not the same.

While they were away, Adam and Donovan, and their entire crew worked on Steven's deck and the patio with the firepit that Barbara ordered.

The day finally came. Adam called Steven to let him know everything was complete and they could return home. They were so ready to see their home, even knowing they had a lot of work to do with moving their things in and setting up a home together. Their home—a connection

Barbara only dreamt about when she was a child. A permanent place to call her own.

Chapter Forty

Home Sweet Home

Barbara stood in her living room, looking around her home. Curtains were hung to accent the room's colors against the perfectly placed furniture. She slowly turned to take in everything around her. Gradually she walked from one room to the next, observing her surroundings. She smiled as she walked into the kitchen. She reached over onto the counter for a wine glass. Opening a new wine bottle, she poured herself a small drink and carried it into the living room —*her* living room. This place was her home sweet home.

It had taken her a lifetime to find this peace and serenity in her life. Her childhood had left her believing there was no such thing as true love, contentment, peace, stability, or any such thing as a home sweet home that would last a lifetime. Instead, she had been left with the belief that no one stayed in your life for longer than a few years, that each family or person you associated with would treat you differently, but all would walk out on you when the going got tough.

Over her younger years, she learned not to become attached to anyone, especially with all her heart. Giving her all to someone and trusting that person was the hardest thing she ever learned she could do. Until the day Steven walked into her life. The moment he walked into her life, everything changed for her and within her.

She smiled when she took a sip of her wine. Life had never been perfect until now. She had Steven to thank for that. He gave his all to her. He went out of his way to make her happy. He gave up his career to assure that she was with her family. He would do anything and everything for her, and she knew that. She was blessed.

The front door opened as she swallowed the last of the wine in her glass. She turned to find Steven walking in with a large bouquet of flowers and a helium balloon. She set her glass down and walked over to him. He set the flowers on the counter and let the balloon rise to the ceiling. They wrapped their arms around each other and hugged. They never wanted to let go of each other. Barbara felt his love for her when she rested in his arms. She hoped he knew how much she loved him. She had found her best friend, her soulmate in him. Life could not get any better.

"I have a surprise for you, my love," Steven said after they let go of each other.

"Another surprise? I am not sure I can handle more of those from you. What is it this time?"

"You, young lady, wife of mine, are going to join me for dinner at the best restaurant in town."

"The Downtown Café?" She looked at him, confused. "It is the only one in town. All the others are outside town or in the next town."

"No, not the café. We are going to the Wycliff."

"Wycliff? I never heard of it. Is it new in town?"

Steven smiled as he reached into his back pocket and pulled out two tickets."

'We need a ticket to get in?" Barbara asked when she saw what he was holding up."

"No, not a ticket to get into the restaurant. We need these tickets to get on to the ship where the restaurant is located." Steven smiled as he handed her the tickets.

Barbara read the information on the ticket. She looked at Steven in disbelief and shook her head. "We can't afford a cruise! Can we?" She asked as she looked up at him.

"Not only can we, but it is also paid for in full. We, young lady, are going on a cruise. You deserve it!"

"What about my work? I can't leave my people without their leader."

"I have taken care of that as well. We have to pack a few things, drive South to Florida, and walk onto the ship. We can do pretty much anything we want to for the rest of the week."

"What about?" She began to protest again.

He placed his hand gently on her lips to silence her. "No. Several friends saw my dilemma one day and suggested taking a cruise. Another friend works for an agency that plans cruises for couples and makes the arrangements. I took them up on their offer and found several discounts thanks to their help. The rest is history. A new chapter in our history of the life journey we share."

Barbara did not know what to say. Instead, she wrapped her arms around Steven. Life continued to be perfect. It was already getting better. Each day they did little things together to make the house their home. They attended local art shows and bought prints for their walls. They went to antique stores, attended flea markets and craft shows, purchasing things to decorate their home that matched their personality.

Steven was thrilled with his work at the café and lounge. Although many days were stressful, Barbara enjoyed her work even as she faced obstacles from some people concerning the ideas she suggested to improve the foster parenting process. She was confident in her pursuit of betterment for the children's sake.

A week before leaving for their cruise Barbara was not feeling well. She held it all in, not wanting to cause them to miss the cruise. She forced herself to hide how she felt. Steven never knew she was not her best when they left their home. And she was not about to miss this opportunity of a lifetime.

After a week away from home, Barbara never felt better in her life. The cruise seemed to be what she needed.

Whatever she felt before they left must have been nerves and anxiety.

Ben and Heather met them at the airport when they returned. While they were away, Ben had been arranging a surprise for his sister.

"Welcome home, you two!" Ben said when they were finally in the car after locating all of their luggage from the baggage claim.

"Thank you, big brother. You and Heather need to get away and take a cruise! It was amazing!" Barbara started telling them all about the things they did, the fun on the ship, the people they met. Ben could not fit a word in about his surprise. It would have to wait.

They were met by a 'Welcome Home' sign across the overhang at their front door. Flowers adorned the kitchen table. A special folded towel in the shape of a bear greeted them when they walked into their bedroom. Heather made their return feel as if they were still on a cruise. That night dinner was at the manor, where Andy had prepared a special meal for the family.

After dinner, Ben said he had an announcement to make that affected Barbara, him, and the whole family.

All eyes were on him as he spoke.

"As you all know, Barbara and I decided to invite Benjamin Thomas back into our lives."

Barbara sat up straighter. She was immediately curious. She had no idea where he was going with this conversation.

"While my sister and Steven were away, I took the liberty to locate him. Heather helped me find him and make the connection to Rhea, his mother, and our grandmother."

All eyes were on him, and the room was silent as they listened.

"They have never met. Most of you remember when Rhea and Laura were here a year ago. Rhea told us about her son she had while out of wedlock when she lived here as one of the unwed girls. Rhea said her son was adopted, and she never knew where he was. She told us about her other children, David and Diane, and Diane's daughter Laura.

"I remember Rhea saying she would like to meet her firstborn son if she ever could."

"She did say that. None of us knew where to look for our father after leaving here the last time, but we found him with some research done by Heather and me. We already knew how to contact Rhea. Now we have connected with them both.

Barbara was excited. "Are they coming here?"

"Yes. They are." Ben smiled at his sister. "With the assumption that you would approve, I took the liberty to arrange for them to come here to meet."

"Of course, you have our approval!" Sara said, not waiting for Barbara to speak. "This is exciting news."

"Thank you. They will be here in two weeks." Ben laughed. I knew you would approve. Heather assured me. So I have arranged to pick them up and bring them here to the manor to stay for a few days."

"They can stay as long as they want to. It may take longer than a few days to catch up with each other. They have a lifetime of missed life to share." Sara said.

"Thank you for that. I was hoping that would be the case, and I hope Rhea and Benjamin Thomas get along and forgive each other while they are here. I also hope Barbara and I can let him know we forgive him for all he did or didn't do in our lives when we were growing up."

"I think you and I both have agreed we forgive him. It is part of giving grace to others." Barbara said.

Chapter Forty-One

Mother and Son

Ben was thrilled that everyone at Bella Rose was excited about inviting his father and grandmother to visit. After the events that led to their father's leaving, he and Barbara talked about their feelings, about what he had done to them. They hated him in the beginning. He had lied to both of them. They believed that he had gone out of his way to avoid her, only to find out he had kept up with her most of her life. The knowledge of that had made Barbara even angrier at him.

In the end, they realized that they needed to forgive him. It did not matter what he had done in the past; he was now in their lives, and they still had time. Time to get to know him, time for him to get to know them. Know them for who they had become despite him.

Benjamin Thomas was surprised when he answered his phone and found Ben on the line inviting him to return to Bella Rose. During their conversation, Benjamin Thomas told his son that he was searching for his birth mother. He realized that it might be too late due to her age, but he said he still would love to know about her.

Ben told him that he already knew who his mother was and knew where she was.

"How? How do you know who she is?"

"It is a very long story. Trust me on this. Our family has done a lot of research. The history behind Bella Rose led us to find her."

"I don't understand."

"When you come to visit, we will explain it all. If you would like, I can arrange for her to visit here while you are here."

"Do you think she wants to meet me?"

"We know she wants to meet you. She has been searching for you longer than you have been searching for her."

"Did you tell her you had found me?"

"No. With the way things were when you left and how Barbara and I felt about you, we did not think she would want to meet the person you were. Since then, we have had some serious discussions amongst ourselves and are willing to give you another chance in our lives. We both agreed that if you wanted to meet her, we would let her know about you."

"Yes, I want to meet her. Ben, she gave me up when I was born. Maybe it's in my genes to give up on family."

"No. It isn't. Her circumstances were different, and she had to give you up. You, on the other hand, chose to do what you did. Do not get me started again thinking about how rotten a father you were. Let me think of the future we could have if we can all get together and work things out."

"That sounds good, son. Please let me know when you want me to be there."

"Let me talk to the family here and with your mother, and I will call you back to let you know."

"Thank you, Son."

"One last chance, Benjamin Thomas. One last chance."

Ben could not bring himself to call him Dad. That would still take time. And he may never be able to. He had spent his childhood calling him Uncle. When he found out the truth, he called him by his name. That may be the only way it would be.

Ben called another family meeting, telling them it would be a short meeting.

Everyone gathered at the kitchen island to hear what Ben wanted to tell them.

"Thank you all for being here on such short notice. Barbara and I and Heather have some news. You know we want to have Benjamin Thomas return and for us to forgive him and work things out between us. Barbara and I know it will do us all good to get to know each other for what is left of our time on this earth."

"Yes, we were waiting to hear when he would be arriving. Is there more?" Randall asked.

"Yes, there is. Benjamin Thomas told Ben he was searching for his birth mother. He knew he was adopted and never knew his mother. He told Ben that he had decided to see if he could find her after he left here. He assumed she was dead because of how old she would be," Barbara began.

"When I talked to him, I found out he wanted to know his birth mother. I told him we already knew her and where she was. He was shocked and, long story short, we have been in touch with Rhea, and she wants to come here to visit too."

"We told you before they were welcome to come."

"I know you did. I wanted to let you all know that it would happen, and in just two weeks."

"Oh, Ben, that is amazing. You and Barbara are amazing people to give him another chance. And then to have Rhea meet her son that she gave up for adoption! You truly are forgiving people. I am not sure I could do that." Sara said. Then she thought about all that this family had accepted, loved, and did for each other. They were blessed. Maybe Ben and Barbara were the best examples.

Two weeks later, Ben was at the airport to pick up his grandmother. Rhea had eagerly welcomed the invitation to meet her son. Her dream since the day she gave him up for adoption all those years ago was coming true. She had spent her life wondering. Wondering where he was. She hoped and prayed he had a great life. She wondered if she ever would be able to find him and have a relationship with him. She had come to accept the potential that she would die without knowing anything about him. And then Ben called her. She was thrilled beyond words.

Benjamin Thomas was driving to Tennessee to meet his mother and spend time with his children. A dream that he did not deserve. He treated his family horribly when they were young children and continued to do so after meeting them in adulthood. To be given another chance was rare. He would cherish this second chance.

The manor was cleaned for their special guests. The Café had notified its customers that it would be closed for one night for a special event. The event was a family party. While everyone could have met at the manor for the party event, they still had guests staying there that did not need to be included in the celebration. They could have met in the event hall, but that meant they still had to do all the cooking, serving, etc. And this was an all-family on deck, special event. None of them needed to be doing anything except family time. Everyone was excited. Rachelle and Bob had agreed to stay at the manor and handle all the guests that evening.

When Ben and Rhea arrived at the manor, everyone welcomed her with open arms. The family was so happy to have her there again. Sara hoped to have private time with her to ask her more questions about the manor and its history. For some reason, Sara felt there was more to know.

Benjamin Thomas arrived later the same day Rhea flew in. When he parked his car, he looked up at the front porch of the manor and noticed it was full of people. He smiled when he realized it was all family. He searched quickly for who might be his mother. It did not take long to pick her out from amongst the group. He hoped that all would go well. He had so much at stake. His future connections with his family depended on his behavior with them.

As he walked up the steps to the front door, he noticed the older woman had stepped to the center of the top step. He stopped to look at her. She stood still while she watched him. The middle-aged man was her firstborn. Her thoughts went to the day he was born. The tiny baby boy she instantly fell in love with, at the same moment, she had to hand him over for adoption. A tear escaped and slid down her cheek. She remembered she was one of the lucky girls.

Moments later, mother and son hugged. The rest of the world disappeared. It was a moment observed as pure love by the rest of the family standing on the porch.

History, the past, embraced with love into the present.

Chapter Forty-Two

Forgiveness

Sunrise came early at Bella Rose. Sleep had been almost non-existent for Ben, Barbara, Benjamin Thomas, and Rhea. Yes, even Rhea managed to stay up half the night talking with her son, grandson, and granddaughter. It was the best day of her life. It surpassed the day she got married. Surpassed each day she gave birth to her other children. It surpassed everything. The only thing that would make it better would be to have Diane and Laura there.

Rhea sat in the kitchen of the manor. Guests were always welcome to sit and join the family in the kitchen, but most did not intrude on them. Rhea felt at home there. It had been her home as a teenager, and she had never forgotten the love she felt and how she learned to love from Rose and Robert. Bella Rose brought her joy, even all these decades later.

Benjamin Thomas quietly walked into the kitchen. He had slept soundly but woke with thoughts of uncertainty. The fear he had that the reunion awaiting him would be brief and he would be sent on his way again was gone. Feelings he had never had before crept inside his head instead.

He regretted the way he had treated his children. All their life he had lied to them. He had avoided the truth. He had hidden from his daughter and lied while being in plain sight of his only son. He felt he had lived his life fighting against something he had no control over.

Now he faced reality. The reality was that his mother had abandoned him. He had grown up in a loving family. The only family he had ever known. He had learned that he was adopted late in life, and while he tried to hide his emotions about what his birth mother had done to him, he now faced facts. He attributed what she had done to him to what he had done to his children. They both had left their flesh and blood. He had wondered what she would have to say to him that would erase how he hated her. He understood why his children hated him. He tried to make it better for them. He could only hope that his birth mother would make life better for him. Their conversation the night before ended with a promise.

Rhea sat with a cup of coffee, reliving what she had told her son the previous night. No matter what she had said, there would always be that pain. Her pain. The pain he must also feel. The heartbreak that came with giving her firstborn up for adoption had never left her. She always wondered if he would understand if she ever had the chance to meet him and tell him the true story. Now, she had explained that it was not her choice. Yet, she felt in some way that she did have a choice. She had not been strong enough at a young age to voice her desires.

Rhea looked up to see her son. Benjamin Thomas stood a short distance from her. Her heart melted. The love she felt when he was born overtook her present. She swallowed hard and clenched her teeth to hold back her desire from within. All the years spent not knowing anything about him. All those nights that she cried herself to sleep when her parents made her give him up. The decades she longed to know where he was and if he was okay. Now, she looked him in the eye as he approached her.

Silence filled the room as mother and son, hearts opened, reached out to each other. Benjamin Thomas pulled his mother from the stool where she sat and embraced her. In an instant, with no words spoken, the decades of wonderment, pain, hatred, fear, and questions melted for them both. Their physical touch erased it all.

Tears flowed with no restraint. The wall of uncertainty collapsed around them. For a moment, all that mattered was that they were reunited.

Barbara walked toward the kitchen in the manor as her father and grandmother were still clinging to each other. She stopped in her tracks and stood motionless in the great room. Barbara did not want to disturb their family reunion. Thoughts flooded her mind as she watched them from a short distance. There stood two people who were her blood, her DNA, the reason she was alive. Two people whose lives she barely knew. She hoped the next few days would change that and that she could fully forgive. She had no reason to have anything against her grandmother. It was her father that caused her to live the life she lived. The wall she had around her was because of him.

Rhea broke from the embrace with her son when she noticed Barbara standing in the doorway. She motioned for her granddaughter to come in.

Barbara hesitated but walked in. As she got close, she felt relaxed. She did not expect to feel comfortable. She expected to be tense, cautious, nervous, anything but comfortable. Rhea reached out and took Barbara's hand.

"Good morning, my child. You are a sight of beauty and love." Barbara allowed herself to be drawn into Rhea's embrace as she glanced at her father before closing her eyes and feeling a love she had never experienced.

Gradually the rest of the family arrived at the manor for a late breakfast. After eating breakfast, Barbara and Steven invited Rhea and Benjamin Thomas to come to their new home. Barbara was proud of her home. She had finally reached a point in her life to feel loved and complete when they had moved into their house and made it their home. Now she had family love to share her heart and her home.

They drove down the driveway so Rhea would not have to walk the distance. She insisted she could have walked it, but they knew the walk back up the hill could be difficult for her.

As they approached the house, Rhea became quiet. Stepping out of the car, she looked beyond the house. Ben noticed it and walked over to his grandmother.

"What is it, Rhea? I can tell something hit your mind when you got out of the car."

"Nothing. I was just admiring the gardens behind the house."

"Oh, those. I plan to help Barbara make the best flower garden when the time is right to plant the other plants. She also wants to have a small vegetable garden. I think the other side of the house would be perfect for that. It gets enough sun and shade and is out of the public's view. That way, the guests won't think the bounty of our labors is for them."

"You all have done an amazing job with this place. I spoke with Sara when I was here the last time and expressed my joy in the work you all have done over the years. So many memories." Rhea said as they walked toward the front door. Rhea glanced into the woods on the other side of the house. No one noticed her gaze.

Barbara and Steven gave their guests a house tour. Heather had stayed at the manor to help set up a celebration held later that evening at the event hall. Even when the family was in town, special events were scheduled, and Heather had to work.

Rhea was impressed with what her granddaughter had done with the house.

"Your home is beautiful, Barbara. I am very proud of you."

"Thank you. It just comes naturally to me, I guess. I didn't even have Heather help me very much, and decorating is her specialty."

"Maybe you could be her assistant if she needed one, and you needed something else to do. I will tell you I am impressed with the work you do. You are amazing."

"I feel for the kids. They needed someone to help them, and I want to do what I can to be there for them and make the process easier and better. For everyone involved."

"I am sure you are making a huge impact."

"I can hope and pray. Would you like to see the landscaping that Ben has helped us do?" She asked everyone.

"I would, yes," Rhea said. She followed everyone outside. She did not want anyone to notice where her attention was focused.

Ben slowed down to walk with Rhea. He had noticed her glance earlier and wanted to see if she continued to look into the woods. She did.

"Rhea, what is it about the woods that intrigues you?" Ben leaned into her so no one could hear his question.

"Nothing. Why?" She lied.

"You keep looking in that direction. Is there something there that holds a memory?"

"I would rather not talk about it now," Rhea whispered and sped up her steps to be with Barbara.

The tour of the flower gardens and the planned layout ended. Rhea asked if there was a trail to the woods from their house.

"There is a hiking trail, but the entrance is closer to the manor than here."

"May we walk into the woods anyway?" Rhea started walking to the edge of the yard where the woods began.

"I guess. We never have. We always take the trail if we want to go into the woods for a hike. May I ask why?"

"Thank you. Let's go. Oh, and no, you may not ask. I will explain later." Rhea continued to walk. She was going to walk whether anyone joined her or not. She was pleased when everyone joined her. Their curiosity got the best of them, plus they did not want her to fall and get injured.

Chapter Forty - Three

Hidden History

Rhea led her family into the woods. She took her time, bracing herself against fallen branches and rocks. She looked from side to side as she slowly moved forward. Once in a while, she bent down and moved a small amount of brush to look beyond it. She carefully replaced each branch she moved. Her family followed in silence.

Rhea knew what was within the woods or what had been there many years before. She had not thought of it during her last visit. She had been busy with other things while there, and it had not crossed her mind. Arriving at the location of Barbara and Steven's house, Rhea noticed the edge of the woods that lay beyond their yard; it brought back memories.

The pathway she remembered was well overgrown. That did not stop her from following the route she knew.

"Rhea, our property line is just beyond that row of trees," Ben said to her.

"And just beyond those trees is a stone wall."

"There is?"

"There used to be. Are you sure about the property line?" Rhea said as she kept walking. Her age certainly was not slowing her down.

"As far as I know. Why?" Ben asked.

Rhea did not answer. A few steps further, just before they reached the stone wall area Rhea mentioned, Rhea stopped and scanned the ground around her.

Everyone followed her eyes. No one knew what she was hoping to find.

Rhea reached down and moved some weeds. She pulled them up from the ground and tossed them aside.

Everyone had caught up with her and stopped their chatter immediately after seeing what she revealed.

"What is this?" Ben asked as he looked at the ground at Rhea's feet. He knew what it was. He didn't understand why it was there or its significance.

"This is the cemetery where Rose and Robert buried the babies that didn't make it," Rhea said as she began cleaning off the tops of the two small grave markers at her feet. Barbara and Ben bent down to help look for the markers and clear them.

"How did you know this was here? Did all the girls know about it? How many babies didn't make it? Barbara asked as they were still uncovering them after finding five placed next to each other.

"I don't know how many there are. There were only a few when I left. I remember Rose and Robert speaking about it while I was here. They had just created this area, and while I was here, there was only one infant that did not survive."

Barbara had to ask, "Were there any mothers that did not survive?"

"Not while I was here, so I do not know."

"Look at this," Ben called out to everyone. He pointed to the ground in front of his feet. "This is a standard gravestone. The name Raymond is etched in the stone." He looked beside that stone to one next to it. "And this one next to him is a lady named Veronica. It seems they died close to the same time. I wonder how they are related to the Fairchild family. It seems odd that a standard gravestone would be here if you say this was for the babies that did not survive. You would think adults were buried in a traditional cemetery."

Rhea stood up. "I think that is all the markers for the babies. You may stop looking. If you want, you can search this place later, but I need to step away." She seemed not to have heard what Ben had said.

Ben suspected there was more to this place than she was admitting. Something personal. "What is it, Grandma?"

Rhea smiled, " You just called me 'Grandma.' Thank you." She reached over to Ben and hugged his shoulder. She shook her head. It was an indication she was not ready to talk about whatever was on her mind.

They all walked back to Barbara and Steven's house. After drinking some water, Rhea said she wanted to get back to her room to rest. They looked at her, wanting answers but agreed to take her to the manor to get some rest.

Rhea laid down on her bed. She tried to close her eyes, but her mind flooded with memories when she did. Memories that she had suppressed for decades.

She pictured herself when she was there as a child lying on her bed. On the other side of the room, her roommate, who had arrived the night before, lay on her bed moaning. Rhea knew the sound and what it meant and kept her ears open. The moan was louder a short time later, and Rhea knew it was time to bring Rose into the room. When she walked out the door, she met Rose on her way inside.

Rhea lay on her bed now and recalled the conversation. It was one she would never forget. It was a mixture of the roommate being in pain and Rose and Robert telling her what to do to deliver the baby. There was no separate room at that time to take her. And there was no time for Rhea to leave. Rose called her to help with the delivery. A short time later, the baby was born, but it was silent. It was the first time Rhea had ever heard of a baby being stillborn. She wept, as did her roommate. Rhea watched as Robert took the baby, wrapped it tightly in a tiny blanket, and left the room. Rhea never saw the baby again, and two days later, the baby's mother had left to return to her home.

Rhea put her head in her hands. The conversation with Robert the next day set the rest of her life into motion. She was told that the stillborn babies were buried at the edge of the property and would all be moved to a proper cemetery one day.

At the cemetery today, Rhea was faced with the reality that a proper cemetery was never created. A reminder that the babies who did not make it and were still on the property of Bella Rose never had a family that loved them. Besides the family and love Rose and Robert gave them during the brief time, the girls stayed there. The babies never knew the joys of living.

Rhea got up from her bed and looked out the window. Beyond the building was the rose garden. It was the one Robert had planted. She noticed the white roses in bloom. A smile came to her face. White roses are what Robert put on the gravesites. She knew this because after she learned of the cemetery, she made it an effort while she was in the area to visit it from time to time over the years she was nearby. Once Sara and the family took over, she stopped coming. The latest owners never knew she had a major connection to Bella Rose and that she knew what went on most of the time.

Rhea opened her eyes an hour later. She looked around the room. It took her several minutes to remember where she was and why. Her mind was fuzzy. She shook her head to empty the visions she still saw. That first stillborn was just the beginning. She had later learned that any time a baby did not survive, they were buried in that location. She was told that the mothers could not afford a better place, and usually, the baby's grandparents could not care for it, nor did most of them want to. They knew the life interruptions they caused. It was one thing to give your newborn up for adoption. It was another to know that you would never see your child because of something you did that caused some issues. Rhea wondered if the mothers or grandmothers could be reached or wanted to return.

Rhea sat up on her bed. She took a deep breath. She knew she needed to tell the family the story of the cemetery. She may be the only one still alive to remember the truth.

Ben saw his grandmother walk into the great room and asked if she would like something to drink.

"I'd like a stiff drink of something but will take a glass of water. Thank you, Ben." Rhea walked over to the rocking chair near the fireplace. She smiled before she sat down. More memories. Nicer memories filled this place.

Ben returned with a glass of water and a plate of chocolate chip cookies. "Here is a treat for you as well." He sat down on the sofa near her.

"Can you gather the family together again yet today? I want to share some memories and stories about Bella Rose that you may not know." Rhea took a bite of a cookie.

"Of course. I can make a few phone calls, and we can have them here for supper if you want."

"That will be perfect. In the meantime, after I finish this deliciousness, I want to go back to the cemetery we found."

"Are you sure?"

"Yes, I am sure. I will be fine if you are worried about my emotions."

"Would you like me to join you on the walk? Or have someone else walk with you?"

"I would like Benjamin Thomas to walk with me."

Ben was a little shocked, then realized the mother and son probably had a lot to discuss. "Of course, let me get in touch with him too."

"Thank you. You are such a blessing. I have no idea how you turned out so well with the way your father treated you."

"Determination? I don't know. He may have lied to me, but he was there as I grew up. I can look at it as how bad he was to me or how he at least tried. He didn't even try with Barbara. That is the sad part."

"I agree that is the sad part. I would have hoped he would have at least been there for both of you. Picking and choosing was something we had to choose when I was pregnant. The girls that were there were forced to give up their children. I never stopped thinking about your father and always wondered what happened to him, if he was adopted by a good family, and how he was as an adult."

Chapter Forty-Four

Untold Secrets

Ben called everyone and invited them for dinner at the manor. He told them Rhea had rested and wanted to talk about what they had found earlier. He also told them that he and Heather had a surprise for everyone. Everyone said they would be there. Sara did her best to make him reveal the secret, but he would not budge.

Heather arrived at their home a few minutes after Ben finished his last phone call. She and Ben were excited that they had been able to pull the surprise off without anyone knowing about it or seeing her when she arrived home. That was one disadvantage of living so close to all your family. It was hard to hide things and keep secrets.

Ben made sure that the rest of the family was already at the manor before he and Heather arrived with their surprise.

Rhea saw Ben and Heather walking up to the back door to the dining room. She gasped, which made everyone look. Benjamin Thomas did not know who the ladies were walking behind Heather. He looked at his mother, whose eyes were wide, and her smile was even bigger.

Rhea met them at the back door. "Diane! Laura! What a surprise!" She hugged them both. "Ben, how did you arrange this? I thought you girls couldn't make it." Rhea said in one breath.

"Hi, Mom," Diane said.

Benjamin Thomas stood there in silence when he heard what the older lady called Rhea. Standing in the room with him were his half-sister and her daughter. Two people he had never met and only recently knew existed. He could not stop staring.

Rhea took Diane by the hand and walked over to Benjamin Thomas. Ben had warned Diane and Laura of who would be there. He had not had the chance to warn his father.

"Benjamin Thomas, this is Diane, your half-sister, and Laura, her daughter. Ladies, this is Benjamin Thomas, my oldest child." She let the words sink in with everyone.

"Benjamin Thomas, glad to meet you," Diane reached out her hand.

"Good to meet you too, Diane." He shook her hand, then turned to Laura. "Good to meet you as well." He reached to shake her hand.

Laura shook his hand but looked at her mother. Her mother was smiling.

Ben broke the uneasiness he felt in the room. He knew that bringing his aunt and cousin would not be easy, but he believed Rhea needed it. She needed to have her family all under one roof. The unexpected discovery that afternoon did put a glitch in the festivities he had hoped for, but maybe it would bring them all together despite the coming news Rhea had to share.

"As some of you know, Barbara and Steven gave Rhea a tour of their home today. While there, Rhea wanted to look into the woods. It seemed she remembered something about that immediate area, so we joined her. None of us knew what to expect and what we found was a shock. We will let Rhea tell you what we found and what details she can about it. I have very little knowledge of what she knows."

Rhea stood from her seat and faced everyone. This was her chance to share the history of Bella Rose that she realized this generation did not know.

"Ben is right. When I stepped out of the car at Barbara and Steven's house today, I was immediately drawn to the wooded area." She turned to Barbara. "I will need another tour of your home because the only thing on my mind was the woods. I apologize."

"That will graciously be arranged." Barbara smiled as she replied.

"Now you are wondering what is in the woods that drew me in. History and memories. Family history drew me deep into that area of your property."

"You all know about the history of Bella Rose and how it began. You know I was one of the first girls to be rescued and stay here while I was pregnant and gave birth to my first-born son. You may also know that I gave him up as soon as he was born, and I barely got to see him. My mother made me give my baby up before returning home and getting on with my life. I did not want to give up my baby. I cried for months after that dreadful day. Due to my grief, Rose and Robert allowed me to stay here to recover more before going out on my own. Most of you know I have missed my son every day since. I never thought I would live long enough to see him."

"I never thought I would find my birth father let alone my grandmother," Ben said. These last few days have been life-changing."

"Yes, it has, son. Now about the woods. As you all know, this home began as a home for unwed mothers. As one of the first ones here, I was not privy to all the dealings they got into once I left. I followed the news about this area, but there was never anything about the woods of this property. I always wondered if any of you had found it. Today, I had to see if it was still there. And it is."

"Rhea, enough of the introduction; tell everyone what we found and its history," Ben spoke up in a kidding tone. Everyone there knew most of what she was telling them.

'Yes, of course. This place was for unwed young girls who could not stay with their parents. Some came on their own, and others had their parents bring them. I was one of the latter. My mother brought me."

" Stayed for a while after I gave birth and gave my son up for adoption. Other girls left immediately. Some girls left with their babies, most without. Some babies were given up for adoption. A few babies did not survive. They were either stillborn or did not live beyond a couple of days. Robert took care of those that did not survive. My roommate was the mother of a stillborn baby. I was in the room when she delivered." Rhea took a breath. She glanced at everyone's faces. She had their attention and knew she needed to continue. The hard part was the remaining story they did not know.

"After my roommate returned to her home, I asked Robert what he had done with the baby. He took me aside and told me that he had made a section of the property a makeshift cemetery. His plans were to move the babies to an official cemetery after their work became legal. When they began taking in the unwed girls, their work was not, and they had to do it all in secret. I asked him one day to show me the gravesites. He was reluctant but agreed when he realized I was mentally strong enough to handle it. Once I saw the graves and the little markers, I somehow felt at ease with their work. I trusted them more. Over the years, I forgot about the graves. Until today." Rhea lowered her head in sadness.

Diane put her arm around her mother. Ben looked at his father, who sat there in silence. Ben wondered what he was thinking.

The room fell silent. Sara could not believe there was a cemetery on the property. How could she not have known, and why was it not revealed in any property transfer, mentioned in her mama's will, or included in any of the other writings they discovered. She thought they had found all the secrets about Bella Rose and their family. Now, this. What else would they find, and when?

Sara looked at Randall. "Is there anything we need to do about a cemetery on this property?"

"I would consider it a family cemetery plot and just leave it as it is. The last thing you want to do is disturb a cemetery. You never know what spirits you will raise."

Sara lightly punched her husband's shoulder. "Don't say things like that. You know I try not to believe in ghosts and such."

"Maybe you need to believe," he said with a wink.

"I would like to go for a walk there tomorrow to see what we can do about the area," Sara stated.

"What do you want to do? We can't disturb it." Randall replied as he wanted nothing to do with calling any spirits from the past into the family. They had enough drama they had dealt with over the last five years. They certainly did not need more.

"Oh, no. We need to clean it up and make it a part of Bella Rose." Sara said.

"Are you sure?"

"Yes. It is a part of the family history. Robert made it special for those little bodies. He knew they deserved the best he could give them at the time. We need to make it special too."

Rhea had been listening. When she had control of her emotions, she spoke. "I can take you to it tomorrow. I love that you want to make it a part of the history of Bella Rose. You are right, Robert and Rose did everything they did for us girls, and it was all done in love.

After deciding what they would do with the cemetery, Sara and Randall said they were going home. Andy and Karen also left, giving Ben and Heather the great room to themselves to talk with Ben's family. He looked around at everyone. He had gone from sensing something was missing in his life to a room full of family. He smiled as he listened to everyone talking with each other. His father was getting to know his half-sister. His grandmother had held her firstborn's arm as her children learned about each other. Laura watched and listened. Heather was amazed at how life had changed, and the family had grown quickly. She noticed her husband's smile and put her arm around him.

"You are blessed, my love."

"Yes, I am. And I have you to thank."

"Me? I didn't do anything."

"You believed in me." He reached over and kissed her.

Rhea walked over to Ben and Heather. " I want to thank the two of you. If it had not been for your insight that something was missing in your life and your determination to find out what it was, none of this would have happened." She looked out over her family gathered around. "I would have died not knowing what happened to my precious little boy. My daughter would never have known her older brother. My son would never have known he had a little sister. You would never have known or remembered your sister. And my granddaughter would not have known what a wonderful loving family we all became despite the history details." She reached out and hugged Ben. "I love you."

"I love you, Rhea. I am blessed to have a wife that supported me and did not think I was crazy when I told her my life was missing something." He took Heather into the embrace with Rhea.

It was well past midnight when Rhea's family all said good night. She went to her room and softly closed her door. She walked over to her window, and even though it was dark outside, she gazed out as much as she could to see the stars. She had spent her life looking up at the stars. It was her connection to her family, even though, until now, she never knew where they all were. She just wished upon the stars that at some time each night, they were looking up as well.

Chapter Forty-Five

Restored

Barbara woke early from a restless sleep. She had tossed and turned so much that a few hours after going to bed, she got up and lay on the sofa so she would not disturb Steven. She still could not sleep, so she got up and paced the floor before she walked outside and looked up at the stars for a while. For some reason, the stars always had brought her a feeling of peace and contentment.

Steven got up early when he rolled over and reached for his wife, and she was not by his side.

"Are you okay?" He whispered when he found her sitting on the sofa, hugging a throw pillow.

"I'm fine. I had trouble sleeping and did not want to disturb you. Sorry if I woke you."

He shook his head and sat down next to his wife. "I reached for you, but you were not there. I got concerned. I was hoping the news about what is in the woods by our house had not spooked you."

"To be honest, it does a little. I think I will be alright with it once we all make it beautiful and maybe have a small ceremony for all those poor babies."

"That is a nice idea. I think Robert and Rose would like that too. I imagine they would hate that the cemetery has not been cared for. He did such a special thing for those innocent babies. And what Rose and he did for those unwed mothers is amazing."

"There were an amazing couple. Sacrificed a lot for all those girls. And for my grandmother to be one of them. I feel honored to be alive."

Steven held his wife in his embrace on the sofa and gently rocked her as she drifted off to sleep.

Everyone gathered at noon at Steven and Barbara's house. Rhea told them a little about what they might find before they followed her to the cemetery. It was a silent walk as they seemed lost in their own thoughts.

Rhea noticed the silence and appreciated the respect they gave the area. Until rediscovering it the day before, it had been decades since she saw the beginnings of the sacred place Robert had made for the precious bodies of loved babies. She looked to the sky to stop her emotions from showing.

Rhea stopped everyone when they reached the edge. "I know I told you what might be here. I can only go on what I noticed yesterday. I honestly think there may be more here for us to find. Don't be surprised by what you may discover."

Sara looked at Randall. What was she suggesting? Did Rhea know more than she was telling? Had she noticed something the others had not?

Randall shrugged his shoulders. He knew his wife well enough to read what she was thinking. He had to look at the area as a family member and attorney. He knew it could remain as a family cemetery and that nothing needed to be done legally.

Rhea bent down and moved some brush out of her way. She stood up and faced her history. A place that had changed her life when she was a young child. A place that had silently taught her the true meaning of pure love.

The family stood back, allowing Rhea time alone in this sacred place. A sense of awe filled the air. Barbara felt a chill. Sara rubbed her arms as a breeze gently touched her. Randall put his arm around Sara. Ben stood still, but looked around. He took in as much as he could see from his vantage point. It was not much, and he felt drawn in. He was the first of the family to step onto the grounds as he gently walked up to his grandmother. She felt his presence and rested her head on his shoulder as they stood side by side. Still, no one uttered a word.

"This is where love lies," Rhea whispered.

She broke her connection to Ben and turned to the rest of the family. It was time to start searching for and cleaning the gravesites. Then they would work to create the beautiful memorial garden that it was meant to be.

Everyone began to walk gently over the grounds. Brush, weeds, twigs, and leaves were pulled up and tossed onto a pile beyond the cemetery's edge. Grave markers were brushed off so names and dates could be read, if possible.

Ben wandered off on his own. He had noticed a different marker the day before. It seemed to be a marker for an adult instead of an infant. It was a large standard gravestone instead of a simple marker. No one noticed him leave.

He took his phone out of his pocket and took pictures of the site. For some reason, he did not want to share what he found. It seemed to be a separate section of the cemetery. Ben wondered if it was where it originated, and Robert was not the first to use it. Perhaps he found it and took advantage of the space. Ben did not know what to think. He could barely make out the name on the stone. He knew what he thought it had said the day before. A closer look now, and he was not sure. He would have to look closer at the photo he took. Do some research on the internet. Maybe search old newspapers for news that might explain it.

Sara stood up to take a break and noticed Ben walking back toward the rest of the family. She smiled but did not say a word to him. As she looked around, she realized that this space connected Ben and his family to hers before he and Heather met and got married. It was like they were destined to find each other. Without Ben in their lives, this would have less meaning. Without Rhea, they might never have found it or known its story.

A warm feeling came over Sara. She believed that everything happened for a reason. She believed that no matter what you do in your life, if something is meant to be, it will happen. All of this was meant to be. She shook her head. Why? Why so many babies that did not survive? Why did they have to die? Her family could have connected with Rhea without this part of her family history. What was she missing? There had to be more to the history, more to this sight than grave markers and sad stories of lost babies, broken hearts, and lives suspended in memories.

She glanced at Ben before bending down to continue clearing the ground. She felt a subconscious connection.

It took them a week of working in all of their spare time to clean the cemetery. Ben took it upon himself to purchase fresh plants, rose bushes, tulips, gardenias, iris, and garden decorations. He cleared and made a defined entrance, then placed a rose bush on each side of the gate at the fence he and his father built together. Rhea wrote a list of the names on the grave markers, including the dates. There were a few that she could not read, but she wrote the approximate date according to its placement. Robert had placed them in order of dates, which helped her know when the babies had been born.

When it was finished, the family returned to hold a memorial service. Rhea read all the names and dates. If she knew who the mother had been, she read those as well. Sara had given her the records they had found of the young girls who had stayed there to help complete her records. Heather said a prayer, and they had music softly playing while they sang a few songs.

When the humble service was over, they quietly walked away. Ben was the last to leave. He said he had a few plants to check on before joining them. No one questioned him.

Andy had made a late lunch for the family to be together one last time before everyone returned to their homes.

Rhea, Benjamin Thomas, Diane, and Laura were all leaving the next day. That morning had been a solemn time for the family, but the luncheon brought smiles and laughter back. Life was too short, as they all had witnessed, and it was time to celebrate the coming together of family and love.

Before Ben drove Rhea, Diane, and Laura to the airport, the family had one last meal together. A special request by many, Andy had made French toast, served with bacon, eggs for those who wanted them, and fresh fruit. And, of course, coffee. He had also made care packages for each of them to take on the trip. He included cookies, brownies, and peanut butter fudge from a recipe he had found amongst the papers in the attic. Rhea had taken one bite of the fudge and knew it was the recipe Rose had made. No one had made it like she did—until Andy.

Benjamin Thomas was also leaving that day to drive home. He promised Ben and Barbara that he would not disappear again. He promised his mother that he would stay in touch and visit her, Diane, and Laura.

Ben drove slowly down the driveway. Rhea had requested one last stop at the cemetery before she left. She was unsure she would ever be back and wanted one last look before saying her goodbyes to her past. It was a past that held sadness, heartache, and loneliness. A past that had led her through the joys, happiness, and love she found. And ultimately to finding her firstborn son and his family. She smiled as she walked amongst the gravesites. She knew that all the souls of these babies would live on in eternity. She had empathy for all the young girls who had suffered and lost. She wiped a tear as she walked away through the gate. Stopping to smell the roses brought memories of Robert and Rose that would never leave her.

Chapter Forty-Six

If Stones Could Talk

A month had passed since the discovery of the cemetery. Ben continued to work his magic within the fencing beyond the gate. He had not mentioned his discovery to anyone, even Heather. Somehow, he felt a connection he could not explain, so he avoided questions. When anyone inquired why he spent so much time there, he replied that it took meticulous care when plants were started, and he wanted to ensure they survived and thrived.

He built three benches and placed two on either side outside the gate. The third bench he placed facing the small grave markers of the infants, with the back facing the side where he had made his discovery. He then carefully cleaned up that secret area, keeping a hedge of weeds and brush between the two sections. He was not ready to disclose the treasure.

Ben had made repeated trips to town looking through old newspapers. He searched the internet for any information that could lead him to answers to who was buried under the gravestones. He had found three. The names were not completely legible.

The family had found two other gravestones when they found the infant ones and deciphered the names. They had not made a big deal of it, thinking they were related to the babies and simply had family that placed actual gravestones on their graves. As the dates were not legible, they could not tell. Which still left Ben wondering—who were these people?

Life at the manor returned to normal. Guests came and went. Heather continued to grow her event planning business while she and Ben raised Marc and Maddex.

Andy continued his chef work while he and Karen were busy with their twins, River and Ryan, and baby Ravyn. When Gayle had her latest birthday, Sara and Randall were introduced to a teenager's life. They were unsure what hit them but loved every minute of their daughter's life. Rachelle continued to help at the manor, and Bob continued his work outside the family business. Barbara and Steven settled in and became accustomed to having a cemetery in their backyard. Steven continued to work at the café lounge with Terri. Their business had grown when they added the lounge.

Ben and Barbara spent many hours together talking about their past lives apart. Ben always felt sorry for not being there for her, even though they knew it was not his fault. They stayed in touch with their father, yet somehow, Barbara never felt the father/daughter connection she hoped. He had broken that bond when he walked away from her as a toddler.

Ben and Heather had begun to take time away together, away from the kids and the rest of the family. There had been so much going on around them that they had lost some of their closeness. They were walking a trail in town one day when a man stopped them while they crossed the short bridge over a creek. The man said he recognized them. They looked at each other and shrugged their shoulders. He said he had seen them at the Café several months before. Then he went on to tell them that he had overheard one of their conversations about the gravesite. Neither one said a word as the man continued to speak.

He said his name was Charles and that he had recently moved to the area when his search for his ancestors led him to that part of Tennessee.

"I'm not sure we are the people you need to be talking with about gravesites. There are several cemeteries in the area. Which one do you need to find?" Ben spoke up while not revealing any information about the private family cemetery. Not many people knew about it, which is what the family preferred.

"That's just it. I don't know. I have searched several already. I have gone to every funeral home I can find. My next stop is the historical society here in town. That is where I am headed after my walk. It's just that I heard you talking about a cemetery when I was visiting a few months ago. I thought maybe you knew something that could help me. I was hoping this search would not take me long. I am on a short lease in town and need to get back to my family soon."

"I am not sure how we can help. I am not familiar with any of the major cemeteries. My family is not from here. My wife's family is." Ben responded, stating the truth about what he knew about the major cemeteries in the area.

Charles turned toward Heather. "Maybe your family could help in my search?"

"I don't know if they could or not," Heather said. She thought of her family. Had they not been through enough? Who was this man? She had heard enough about scammers in her life. She was not giving away any information until she knew more about him.

Ben sensed her hesitation. He turned to Charles. "Why don't we meet for lunch at Downtown Café tomorrow? You can tell us more of your story and show us what you have so far regarding your family and background. If we can help, we will, but I doubt there is much we can do."

"I will gladly meet with you tomorrow. Here is my business card. Feel free to check me out and make sure I am the real deal. I know there are a lot of scammers out there these days. I want to assure you I am not one of them." Charles handed Ben his card. Ben looked at it briefly, then handed it to Heather to hold.

"Thank you, Sir. We'll see you at the café tomorrow at noon." Ben reached out and shook Charles' hand before they went their separate ways.

Heather looked at the man's card as they continued to walk. "This looks legit. I will look up his information when we get back to the house."

"Good. I want to trust him, but I'm not giving away our family's secrets if he is somehow not associated with the cemetery."

"How would he be connected to the cemetery? Do you think he may be related to one of the babies buried there? Maybe one of the mothers is a relative?" Heather was searching for possible answers. She looked at Ben and saw something in his facial expression. "What do you know that I don't? You are hiding something." Heather reached out her hand, placing it on her husband's forearm, and stopped him from walking farther.

He stopped and looked at his wife. She did have a right to know. "I found something there."

"At the cemetery? What did you find?"

"More graves."

"What!" She turned him to look at her. "Where?"

Ben took a deep breath. "To the right of where the infant's plots are. I found them the first day we searched but kept quiet about them. They have traditional gravestones on them. I only found three. I have been searching for who might be buried there and have not come up with anything so far."

"Do you have any suspicions of who it could be?"

"None. I think the bodies are adults and not more infants because of the size of the stones."

"Interesting." Heather turned, and they continued their walk. "Can you show them to me when we get home?"

"Sure. I probably should have told you about them earlier so you could have assisted me in my search. It has been fun to find out as much as I did, even though nothing answered the main question as to who they are."

The next day Ben and Heather waited for Charles at Downtown Café. They doubted he would show up, even though everything Heather had discovered about him from his business card was true. They were ready to order their food when Charles walked in. He joined them when he saw them sitting at a table near the wall.

"Sorry I am a few minutes late. I had a call from my office that I could not ignore. They want me back to work as soon as I can finish my visit here." He sat down on the empty chair nearest Heather at the round table.

"We were almost sure you were not going to show."

"I did verify the information on your card last night, but we were wondering. How long are you planning to stay?" Heather asked, hoping he was leaving soon.

"I am not sure. I need to find this." Charles handed Ben a photograph.

Ben took the five-by-seven print and glanced at it quickly before handing it to Heather. "Do you recognize this?"

Heather looked closely at the image. To her, it was just a common gravestone. She tried to read the writing on the stone. "I can not make out the writing on it. Do you know what it says?"

"I do not. I think it was my grandfather's gravesite, but only because the photo and any information I have came from my grandmother. My mother gave it to me a week before she passed away."

"So sorry for your loss," Ben said.

"Thank you. Her death came as a surprise to my family. She had survived so much in her life we always expected her to outlive all of us." He took the photo from Heather and put it back into his jacket pocket.

"I'm sorry, I don't know where that is located. We don't visit many cemeteries. And the ones I have been to are what I call newer. That looks like an old grave, no offense."

"No offense taken. As I said, I think it has something to do with my grandfather or someone my grandparents knew.

It has to be significant since Mom gave the photo to me just before she died."

"I wish we could help," Ben said. Their food arrived, saving Ben from saying anything else.

Their conversation while they ate changed to local events and local history. Charles seemed genuinely interested and asked a few questions about the town's history and area. "Even if I don't find my answers in this town, I think I will be back. I may bring my family next time. This area is beautiful."

"We like it here. Of course, I was raised here, but Ben wasn't. Now it is our forever home."

"I can understand why. I am not sure my wife would like the mountains as much as she loves our home near the beach."

"Oh, I would love to visit the beach. The mountains are beautiful, but I've seen photos of the beach, and it seems mesmerizing."

"It can be. The storms can be dangerous, but we've survived so far."

They finished eating and sat for a few more minutes, talking. Charles told them he had one more cemetery to check later that day but would be returning home the next day. "Please get in touch with me if you find anything or if something comes to mind that may help me solve this mystery. You have no idea how not knowing a family secret has bothered me since Mom died."

"Oh, believe us, we know," Heather said as she looked at Ben and raised her eyebrows.

Charles shook his head. He was used to people trying to say they understood what he was going through, even when they had no idea.

Ben and Heather were on their way home when Ben turned to his wife.

"I know where that grave is."

Heather whipped her head around and looked at him. "You what?"

"I know exactly where that grave is. The one in the photo Charles showed us."

"Why, in heaven's name, did you not tell him?"

"Because I want to research it and him more first."

"So, where is it?"

Ben turned his head and looked at her.

Immediately, she knew.

"Oh, if stones could talk. We would have quite a story."

"I think we are going to have quite a story. In their own way—stones talk.

Chapter Forty-Seven

Family Questions

Ben called his sister the day after his lunch with Heather and Charles. He needed to share his assumptions with her, maybe more than he did with Heather. The graves were connected to both families, although he thought this particular one was from his and Barbara's family.

In his private conversations with Rhea, she told him about her father's confrontation with one of the local men. Her story suggested that she never saw her father again after the altercation. She had been told that the local man chased him off, and even her mother told her that because of that and other problems in their marriage, they had gotten a quick divorce, and he moved away.

The gravestone gave a different story.

Barbara met with Ben as soon as she could get away from work. She had not understood what her brother was explaining except that it was related to the cemetery. And if it had anything to do with it, she needed to know. She didn't mind living so close to such a place, but knowing the history would ease her mind on the nights that it bothered her.

She met him at the gate.

"What were you trying to tell me when you called? All I understood was it had something to do with a gravesite?"

"Yes, one particular grave. You know Heather and I met a man in town a couple of days ago and that we met him for lunch today."

"Yes, you told me. Charles, right?"

"Yes, he said his name was Charles. Heather checked him out, and all the information on his business card was true. He showed us a photo when we met, and I denied recognizing the image. I immediately handed it to Heather and drew his attention away from me. I did not want him to suspect that I knew anything."

"So, what do you know?"

"I know that we need to see what information we can find. I know that for whatever reason, Charles has a connection to that grave, and that grave is either connected to us or someone in my wife's family. For whatever reason, I suspect it is our family."

"Why?"

Because most of the graves are related to the infants that didn't survive."

"So it could be related to any one of those babies."

"True. Only Robert would know for sure. At least he is the logical one to know anything. However, I did find other gravestones there—ones to the right of where the babies are buried.

Barbara shook her head. "Oh? There are more?" She was quiet for a moment.

"What is on your mind, Sis?"

"I'm wondering what family we have become. I almost believe it was easier being in foster care and on my own. Life seems more mysterious since I have connected to more family."

"Never, Sis. We belong together."

"Yes, we do belong together. I am not sure about the rest of the gang we call ours now."

Ben laughed. Life was a lot simpler a year earlier. But he was thankful to have the mess he had as it meant he had his sister, father, and grandmother! Not everyone has that honor.

"Why are you laughing?"

"Life was easier before we joined this family. But what a ride we are on now."

"I agree. For most of my life, I was alone. Now I am surrounded by a large family. I have a great job helping people going through the same things I experienced. Some are going through what you went through. All of them feel like they are standing alone in this world."

"You can share your story and help them."

"I do tell them some of my stories. When I speak in front of groups, I share my story. The adults need to hear it to understand the need to get the children placed with the correct families."

"You are an amazing person, Sis. I admire you for being able to take what you went through for the good of others. Not everyone could do that. Many would hold a grudge and spend their lives hating the person who was not there for them. You took it to a higher level and have reached out to help others. You are a special person. I pray that you can help everyone you reach with your story."

"I can only hope I am a positive influence. Not all of them will have the advantage we did."

"I can't imagine you being anything but a positive influence if they know your story. You are proof of survival."

"Thanks, Brother."

They had reached the grave that Ben wanted to show Barbara. Ben pointed to the name on the stone.

Barbara strained her eyes to read the faded name. The years of weather had taken their toll. She could only read a few of the letters. The year was more visible.

Barbara looked at her brother. "What are your thoughts on this? Is it someone we may have known? What do you think the connection is to our family or this Charles person?"

"Well, Charles is about our age. If we look at the year, we can figure out this person would be older than Rhea. If we study the indentations for the name, look at the last name."

Barbara strained her eyes. She took her fingers and tried to trace the indentations. Nothing was coming to her in a full name. She looked at the last name closer and placed her fingers on the beginning of the lettering. When she finished, she looked at Ben. "Are you thinking what I think you are?"

"Have you figured out the name? If so, I may be thinking what you are."

Both of them had asked questions expecting answers without being specific about what they wanted to know.

Twins even separated at an early age and had a special bond.

"What are the chances that this is our great-grandfather?"

"You are seeing and thinking what I am." Ben smiled. At least she didn't think he was crazy.

"I think, somehow, this is Rhea's father. What I don't understand is why? What was the story she told us about him? That he had just disappeared, and he divorced our great grandmother?"

"That is the story she gave us. I wonder if she knows the truth, whatever that may be. I doubt we will ever know. The people who could tell us are gone."

"Maybe not," Barbara said. "Rhea is still very much alive."

"Don't you think she would have told us her life story? Don't you think she would have walked to the grave if she knew about it? I don't think she even looked in this direction." Ben looked at Barbara as he realized the facts. "No, she doesn't know about this grave. If she knew, she would have come over to see it while we were all here. It gives her pleasure to share her story with anyone who will listen."

"What is the connection to that man, Charles?"

"That part I am still trying to piece together. He said his mother gave him the photo just before she died. His grandmother had died a few years before that, so he had no one to question. At least we have Rhea. If only she could tell us. She may not even know the true story. If she does, why keep it a secret after all these years?"

"It may be worth calling her later to find out what she remembers." Do you think she will share her story?"

"I don't know. We may not be thinking straight either. We both tend to think outside the box, so we may have this wrong."

"I say we take a photo, send it to Rhea, tell her what we suspect, and see what she says. Have you told Charles about your find?"

"No, I didn't let it be known that I knew anything. Just in case he was not the person he says he is."

"You watch too much television." Barbara laughed. "For now, we need to get some rest. I will try to sleep, considering that the grave is closest to my house."

"It is nothing to give you nightmares over. You will be fine." Ben walked with Barbara as they left the cemetery. They would sleep on it. For now, it was their family secret—filled with questions.

Chapter Forty-Eight

Connected

Ben and Barbara met the next morning to write the note to Rhea and send the photo in an email. Then they went about their day while they waited.

It was evening before they got any response. Barbara saw she had an email from Rhea. Before she opened it, she called Ben to join her. He stopped what he was doing and walked down the driveway to read the reply that waited for them.

They both took a deep breath as Barbara pressed the computer key to open the message.

My Dear Grandchildren

I was confused by the photo that accompanied your message. It did not look like any of the graves of the infants, and I did not understand why you would send me a photo of a stranger's grave.

Then I read your message. To say that I am as confused as you are is putting it mildly. The story I told you when I was there about my father is what my mama told me all my life.

To read that my mama may have lied to me all my life is disheartening. However, your theory almost makes more sense than her story. I never understood how a man could leave his family, how my father could leave Mama and me. To just walk away with no further contact. In today's world, he would have had to pay child support, and from what I can remember, Mama never got anything after he left.

Do you think this grave is my father's? That he was killed for some reason? Maybe he was having an affair with a local woman, and they had a child? And that child is related to this Charles you mentioned? Maybe that is why the story I was always told is that my parents divorced, but I was never told why, even when I asked. Mama always told me that it didn't matter and that I did not need to know. Is there a way to find out if that is what happened?

When I think of that, it makes me angry. I need to think about that for a while. Do I want to know? If he did have a child with another lady... that means I may have a step-sibling out there somewhere. A person that, if my father had lived, I might have gotten to know. This breaks my heart. I am angry at him but sad to think what life could have been.

I have questions that may never be answered. Does his other child know about his other family if he did father a child? They may not know, and to learn of it now could damage their family. You may want to rethink researching to find the truth of who this person is in that grave.

However, you say Charles was given the photo by his mother, who got it from her mother. This action shows that the grandmother wanted her children to know something.

You have my blessing to continue your search. Please let me know what you find. Our family may be bigger than we thought.

Before I forget, I know the writing on the gravestone is hard to read, at least on the one you sent me. According to my mother, my father's name was Walter Brown.

I love you both. No matter what you find out,
we will always have our love. My heart says may
we forgive those who cannot ask for it, show
compassion for those who need it, and find love to
share through the truth.
Love, Rhea

Barbara finished reading the email out loud. She then moved her curser and pushed the print icon. She looked at Ben as they waited.

"I guess we have our answer. We need to keep searching for the truth."

"Yes, we do. Are you sure we want to know? When do we tell Charles?"

"We don't tell Charles until we are positive."

"Yes, we don't want to get his hopes up, and then if it is not the one in the photo or a family connection, he will have wasted his time."

"I am going to go home and do more internet research. Do you want to go into town and see if you can find more information from the historical society?"

"I will. At least now we have a name." Barbara said.

"Yes, we have a name. Now we need to see his connection to anyone in this area. And it could be that Rhea's mother made up a name as she did the story of what happened to him."

"I know, I thought of that. Let's hope the name is correct."

Ben and Barbara went their separate ways. They had a lot to figure out. Ben had a copy of the photo in his hand as he began his internet search.

Within minutes, Ben pulled up information about Walter Brown's birth and death. He pulled up newspaper articles. These included articles that brought to light what Rhea had suspected. Articles of the court case related to his murder. Ben also found Walter's obituary.

Ben scanned over the major details, looking for names of survivors. There, in plain sight, were the answers to all their questions.

Walter was survived by his wife Ruby, their daughter Rhea Brown, and his daughter, Carol.

Proof. Exactly what they needed to connect Rhea to Charles. A direct link to Charles's mother. Charles had previously told them that his father's name was Patrick and his mother's name was Carol. His father had left them before Charles was born, but Carol had given him his last name. He knew his father had left them, and his mother had remarried later in life. They never knew the truth about Carol's parents.

Ben called his sister.

"Hello, Ben, don't tell me you found something already. I haven't had time to talk with anyone in town yet."

"I don't think you need to talk to anyone unless we want a human interest angle. I found the proof we needed."

"How did you find it so fast?"

"Once Rhea gave us the name, it was easy. And if you look closely at the grave, you can make out the lettering."

"So, what did you find out? Was it as Rhea thought?"

"Yes, it was. I found an article about the court case involving the murder of Walter Brown. And I found his obituary."

"Oh, my. That puts a real twist on things. Both for our family and for Charles's. I wonder if he knew about any of this?"

"I doubt it. He didn't seem to have any information about his grandfather, just the photo his mother had given him."

"Okay. Now we need to contact Charles."

"No, now we need to call Rhea. She needs to know first. I found the article detailing the occurrence that caused his murder. All the details."

"All the details? That is either quite interesting or very sad."

"With our connection to him, I would say it is sad. I am glad most people today do not remember him or the story. Maybe it's good you didn't get a chance to talk with anyone in town. We may not want this information connected to Bella Rose."

"What makes you say that?"

"When you come back and read it, you will understand."

"I am on my way home. Be there shortly." Barbara said and closed her phone to disconnect from her twin. She shook her head at how interesting and full of surprises her life was now.

Ben and Barbara called Rhea as soon as they had the information that would change what she had been led to believe all her life. They were unsure she was ready to hear it and debated telling her. In discussing it, they decided she deserved to know. Or at least to ask her if she was up to hearing the facts.

Rhea answered her cell phone as soon as it rang, and she saw who the caller was. She thought they had more questions, although she did not know what else to tell them.

"Hello Ben, what may I answer for you?"

"Hi, Rhea. No, we do not have any more questions."

"Then why the call so soon after our conversation?"

"Because once you told us your father's name, I was able to pull up all the information we needed. The person under that gravestone is your father." Ben stopped talking and waited for his grandmother's reaction. He was unsure how she would react and began to wish they had waited to tell her until they could travel to see her or bring her back to the manor again and tell her in person.

Rhea was silent. That was not what she was hoping to hear. She wanted it to be some stranger who had wandered into town and had no family, no place to live, died of a broken heart, and Robert took under his wing and buried on the family plots. But no. It was mysterious, and it was family.

After a moment, Rhea spoke. "I'm here. I am in shock. Maybe denial is more accurate. I didn't want it to be him. I wanted my birth father to be out there still somewhere. You know, available if I chose to find him and learn the truth. Now I have no way of knowing anything for sure."

"The article sounds reliable. Maybe we can locate the journalist who wrote it. It might be a long stretch due to the person's assumed current age. But it would give me time to gather any extra public information."

"We also need to contact Charles and tell him what we found," Barbara added.

"Yes, you do. Can you give me a couple of days before you contact Charles? I also need to call Diane. This news affects a lot of people."

"Yes, it does. And somehow, we are tied to this Charles person. It would be best to learn more about him before bringing him into our family. He could be a scam artist. A man who knows exactly who is buried there and the connection to you. Your chance meeting may not have been so accidental."

"You are right, Rhea. I tend to think the best of people and never thought he might be after something in our family. What could he be after?" Barbara asked. She didn't know of anything that a stranger would want from them.

Rhea was quiet on the other end of the phone line. She was thinking about what Charles could want from her family. Nothing was coming to mind. "I do not know of anything we have that anyone outside of the family would want. Continue your research to see what he wants. If he is family, that may be all he wants to know. You said he knew nothing about his grandfather. Maybe he wants answers, as we do now. "

"Okay, we will. We will call back tomorrow whether we find out anything or not."

"I will wait on your call and hope I have more to give you. Maybe I can figure out what someone would want from our family."

They each said goodbye and disconnected. The twins had their work cut out for them.

Chapter Forty-Nine

No Longer Alone

Ben and Barbara spent their spare time researching Charles. They could not find anything negative about him. Everything he had told them, everything on his business card, every internet search to check his credibility came back perfect.

They called Rhea to let her know that Charles was who he said he was. And somehow, they were related.

Rhea told them she had talked to Diane and Laura to tell them what was happening.

They all agreed it was time to contact Charles and let him know they had located the gravestone and all the details that went with that news.

When they called his cell phone, they found out that Charles had returned to the area the day before. When they told him that they not only had found the grave but the history of it, he asked if he could see it in person and talk to them. "Since it is on your property, I thought I would ask before I showed up, and you thought I was an intruder."

They set up a time to meet at Barbara and Steven's the next afternoon. In the meantime, Ben and Barbara called a family meeting at Bella Rose to share the news with them.

"We wondered what was going on with you two. You've not been available for much outside of your jobs. While we do understand that, we are not used to secrets in the family. Ben, you know this all too well." Sara let them know she missed spending spare time with them.

"I know. The news we shared had to remain a secret until we solved the mystery. We did not need to involve any of you in this as it is our family, and we are," Ben started to say.

Andy held up his hand to stop Ben from saying more. "Wait right there. You are one of us. Blood or no blood between us, we are all family at Bella Rose. I do understand the need to work it out on your own. And appreciate taking it seriously. In accepting a new person into our family, we need to assure they are legit." Andy said as he poured coffee for everyone. "So tell us this big mystery you have solved without our help." Andy smiled. Their family was so full of secrets and discoveries over the last five years. He thought there could be no more to find.

"It involves the cemetery and Rhea." Ben looked at Barbara. "We have found that one end of the cemetery is where stillborn babies are buried. There is a section to the right of those that had three gravestones. As you know, we met this man named Charles in town one day, and he showed us the photo of the one grave. I did not react at that time because I wanted to make sure it was the same one I remember seeing when we cleaned out the cemetery."

Ben noticed everyone looking at each other and back at him. "I know I never shared with any of you that there were more graves there. I apologize."

"No need to apologize. We understand." Randall said, letting Ben and Barbara know that they were as much family as he was, if not more so.

"So what is the story? You said it was related to Rhea. Does she know what is going on with this?"

"Yes, Rhea knows. We filled her in from the beginning. What we had discovered sounds far-fetched considering when it took place."

"You have our attention. What is the story surrounding the gravestone?" Sara asked as she noticed everyone's attention was on Ben and Barbara.

Barbara began. "Ben and Heather met Charles several weeks ago when they were out walking. He said he had overheard their conversation about a cemetery a few weeks before and that he was looking for a gravestone in a cemetery but had no luck finding the one in the photo he had. He said he thought the grave was that of his grandfather and that his research had led him to our town. He had searched everywhere he could think of. He told them he had to leave town for a while but would be back. He showed them the photo. Ben immediately knew where it was but did not tell Charles."

"Charles gave us his business card, and we did some preliminary research to find out if he was legit or if we should run," Heather added. She then motioned for Ben to continue the story.

"Then we began researching the stone, the name, the date, and anything we could find out about the person buried there. We contacted Rhea because she was the only one we knew of with details about the cemetery. We sent her the photo of the gravestone, and she could read the name." Ben looked at Barbara.

"Rhea had been told all her life that when she was just a little girl, her father left them, and they never heard from him again. Her mother told her they had gotten a divorce, and he had just left. When she saw the name, she knew her mother had lied to her all her life. The person buried there is her father."

The room was silent for a moment while everyone soaked in the news.

"Rhea's father is buried in our cemetery? Why?" Sara asked.

"That is where it gets interesting. Her father, Walter Brown, was murdered in 1944 when he was thirty-one years old."

"Excuse me? Murdered?" Andy asked in shock. "Why?"

"Her father was in a relationship with a local woman, who also was married. The husband tracked him down and shot him."

"So how, or why is he buried here?"

"Rhea and her mother were still in the area or had returned to the area when the murder happened. Rhea's mother called on Robert and asked if he could be buried there because the townspeople would not want him buried in the county's cemetery due to the circumstances."

"Her mother wanted him here? I would think she would want him anywhere but here."

"I agree, but Rhea told us no one knew how her mother was. She had a forgiving spirit no matter how anyone did her wrong."

"Wow, that is more than I think I could do," Karen said. She glanced at Andy.

"Don't look at me. I'm not going anywhere," he reached over and kissed his wife."

"So, how does Charles fit into this picture?" Sara asked, trying to figure out the connection between him and Rhea.

"It turns out that the lady Walter had an affair with was pregnant at the time of his murder. Her baby was Charles' mother, Carol." Ben let that news sink in with everyone.

"That means Charles is related to Rhea somehow," Sara said, still trying to make the connection. "His mother and Rhea are or were step-sisters. Which makes him and your father cousins?" She asked, trying to make sure that was correct.

"Yes. Our father and Charles are cousins, making us Charles' cousin once removed if we are being technical." Barbara said.

"That is a lot to wrap your head around," Randall said. "Does Rhea know about Charles? Does Charles know that his grandfather is buried there and why?"

"Yes, he does. He was here yesterday, and we explained it all to him. He said he had to go home and figure things out. I am not sure what that means. He said he would be in touch."

"I'm not sure what our next step is or even if there is one. I guess we just leave everything as it is. Not much we can do. It's just that now Ben and I have a murder story in our family history."

"Be glad you don't have the murderer in your family. Speaking of which, do you know who the murderer was?"

"Charles said he heard that his grandmother, Pearl, never married. He never knew of a grandfather. But according to the article, it turns out the murderer was Ralph Swanson, her husband. He was sent to prison. We have no further information on him. We still want to research those details."

"Wow, just when you think life is getting routine, even dull, and boring, this news comes along by a chance meeting of a man while on your walk in town."

"We are still working through it. Poor Rhea now realizes that her mother lied to her all her life. She never knew her father was dead, let alone murdered. And she certainly did not know he was buried here. She said she remembers they moved quickly once, and she thinks this must have been when that move occurred."

"What a small world we live in today."

"That we do," Barbara said as she stood up and walked to the window. She looked out over the mountain view. Ben walked up to her as she gazed out.

"Are you okay, Sis?"

"I am fine. It is just that a lot has happened to me in the last several months to a year. I went from a rejected, only child, raised in foster care and being adopted, to belonging to a family of mystery."

"It is your family too, you know," Ben said as he held her in his arms.

Steven walked over to her and held her. Ben stepped aside to allow Steven to be the wonderful husband to his twin. He could not have asked for a better person to be in her life.

While Steven stood by Barbara, Ben told the rest of the family that they had contacted Charles and he was in town.

He added that Charles was coming out the next afternoon to see the grave and talk with them.

An hour later, the family had gone their separate ways to their homes. Barbara told Steven she needed some time alone but would be back.

Barbara stepped outside and began to walk. She headed up the hill to the hiking trail. At several spots, she stopped and gazed out at the mountains. From one location on the trail, she could view the cemetery. She stood on the short man-made bridge and stared down at the scene.

There was so much history in that remote location. Barbara was blessed knowing she was part of the family now. A piece of a loving family.

Barbara took a sip of water from the bottle she carried with her. Opposite the cemetery view was one of the several views of the mountains. The view took her breath away. A tear fell and hit her shoe. She smiled.

Three years, she thought. Three years changed her life. No longer did she have nightmares of her childhood. No longer did she have to count on herself for everything. She no longer had to hope and pray that her life would be uprooted at a moment's notice. No longer did she have to wish for a perfect life. Now she had that. She had love. She had* a family. She had a good life. She took a step and took in the silence of the woods. She was alone in the woods, but she knew she would never have to be standing alone again.

Chapter Fifty

Answers

Barbara awoke to the aroma of freshly brewed coffee after a good night's sleep. Steven had long since spoiled her on as many mornings as he could with fresh coffee. She smiled each time, no matter how tired she was from not getting enough sleep. She had not slept well for over a month. She tried not to believe that it was related to finding the cemetery so close to her home.

"Today is the day when Charles comes to visit, and we can determine if he has a hidden agenda for being here or if he simply wants answers. Now that we know the connection to the family and know that he is not a scammer, it may be easier to share information with him. Hard to believe your family is still growing. And it is with more adults being added, not babies." Steven said while he and Barbara got ready for the day.

"We don't need the addition of babies for a while. I am too busy with all the foster kids and agencies regarding placements. Also, it is *our* family, not just mine."

"From what I hear, you are doing a fantastic job too."

"Thank you. Today, however, we concentrate on the gravesite and Charles. It may be a day of sharing with Charles what we know, which will be the end of it. There may not be anything else to learn about him or the grave. You don't think Charles is after anything, do you?"

"I would hope not. All the information Charles gave us holds up. He is what he says he is. I think we can trust him."

"I think so too. Today may be a case of getting the answers for him and finding out more about him. By the way, how are things at the Café going?"

"They are going very well. Business keeps growing. There has been a substantial increase in customers at the lounge in the evenings."

"That is good. That's what Terri was hoping for."

"Yes, it was. I think she got more out of it than she expected too."

"How so?"

"She and Adam are quite an item now. He is there all the time when not working. He has convinced her to start a music night at the lounge for singing, bands, an open mic night, or something, at least on the weekends. In fact, the last rumor is that he wants to propose to her soon."

"Wow, that is awesome. All of it is great, but a proposal? I think they make a great couple."

"I knew you would say that. Please don't tell her about it. I'm not even sure I should know, let alone tell you."

"Aren't we now members of a family that does not keep secrets?"

"Yes, but we also know that some things need to be kept secret for a little while."

"Yes, I know. And trust me, I can keep this from Terri." Barbara walked to the living room with her empty coffee mug.

Steven followed her and put his arms around her. "I know you will keep this secret, and when the time comes, you probably will be there to help her make all the wedding plans." He kissed her forehead.

"I don't know about that. I'm sure she has other friends to help her with a wedding. Plus, she and Adam should make those together."

"You know as well as I do, the bride always needs a girlfriend to help. I have noticed that the two of you have become close friends."

"I guess we have. It helps that you work there, and sometimes I stop in to see you." She winked at him, then poured herself another cup of coffee. She brushed past him to finish getting ready for work.

"I know. But while you wait for me, I've noticed you talking with her."

"Guilty as charged. Now, I have to go into the office for a little bit today, and if I don't get going, I will be late for a meeting."

Ben and Heather talked about Charles' visit while they were busy getting the boys ready for the day. Ben had set most of the day aside to spend with him. He wanted to get to know the man better after discovering they were related.

Sara called Ben before he left the house. She wanted to know what the plans were for that evening with Charles.

"I don't have anything set in stone. I figured Barbara and I would meet with Charles and get to know him more, but I had no thoughts beyond that. And I plan to spend a good portion of the day with him before Barbara gets away from work. Why?"

"It has been a while since we all ate at the Downtown Café and Lounge. And none of us have been there in the evening for the music. So I was wondering if y'all want to get the family together and go have a party."

"A party? I'm not sure we will want a party. But I will take you up on the offer to go there tonight. It has been a while for us too. Let me check with Heather to see if we have any plans I don't know about."

"Sounds good to me. I have not called anyone else about it yet. I will call the others and see if we can pull off a spur of the moment celebration."

"I will let you know as soon as we are sure about not having other plans. I don't think we have anything going on. I have been wrong before, though."

Ben disconnected from Sara and went inside to tell Heather about the invitation.

"Sounds like a wonderful idea. It has been a while. Did she say the reason for the party?" Heather said when Ben told her about Sara's idea.

"Come to think of it, no, she didn't say. And you know me, I did not think to ask. Sorry."

"No worries. I may ask her later when I see her or call her. Just in case I need to bring anything."

"It's at the Café. What could you possibly need to take?"

"A gift for someone, maybe? I have no idea what we are celebrating."

"I will let you know if I find that you might need to bring anything."

Charles woke up late. He was normally an early morning person, but after he heard from Ben, he was anxious and could not fall asleep. He made up for it by sleeping later in the morning. He was glad he had not set a time to meet Ben that morning. As eager as he was to see the grave and learn about it and his grandfather, he was in no real hurry. He thought he would be once he found the grave marker, but he was holding back for some reason. He wondered if finding out who that grave belonged to was a mistake. He knew it was too late to back out now.

By noon Charles was ready to drive out to Barbara and Steven's house to meet Ben. As he drove the country road, he remembered what Ben and Heather had told him about the mountains. He was sure his wife would like it here even if there was no beach. He was amazed at the beauty.

He turned onto Rose Lane and headed towards their home. He had no set time to meet Ben and decided to keep driving up the lane to see what was there. In front of him stood the manor. As soon as he saw it, he wished he knew more about this family. He wondered how his grandfather could be connected with such a family. He was impressed by the building. And the gardens on the way up the road and around the front of the manor were breathtaking. He decided it was not a good idea to stop and get out. He pulled into a parking space and turned around, heading back to Barbara and Steven's house, where he was supposed to be.

Ben had watched Charles drive past his sister's house and wondered if he had gotten lost. He was about to walk outside to get him when Charles pulled into their driveway.

"Good afternoon, Charles," Ben said when he got out of the car.

"Good afternoon, Sir. We had no set time to meet, so I drove up to the top of the road. I hope you don't mind. That is quite a place you have here."

"It's not mine. It belongs to my wife and her siblings."

"It is still a nice place, and this area is beautiful."

"Thank you. I am the one in charge of maintenance and all the landscaping."

"You do amazing work. The grounds are beautiful."

"Thanks. I saw you drive past the house and was about to come to get you thinking you had the wrong place in mind. Glad you are here, though. Can I get you anything to drink while we talk?"

"No, thank you. Yes, we probably should talk, but I am anxious to see the gravesite."

"I understand. Let's talk about it first." He led Charles inside his sister's house and into the living room to sit down.

"What can you tell me about the gravesite?" Ben asked Charles.

"I know very little. My mother gave me the photo just before she died and told me that she had gotten it from her mother. I assumed it was a friend of my grandmother. I later thought maybe it was my grandfather from the name and date on it that I could make out, but it was not clear enough. All I knew was what my mother told me of what area of Tennessee it was located. She said that was all she knew about it."

"So, your grandmother never said anything about it or her husband? You never knew your grandfather?"

Charles shook his head. "I grew up with her telling us she never married and never wanted to. We just accepted it. It was not from the generation where women normally did that, but she was always a go-getter and maybe a slight feminist before there was such a thing."

"Interesting."

"What have you found out about it?"

"Quite a bit, actually. And it is not all pretty. My grandmother knew about this cemetery and was the only one we knew of to ask about it. So we emailed her the photo and asked her who it could be, and for any details she could offer us. At first, she was unsure about it but said it might be her father's grave and told me her father's full name."

"So it is your great-grandfather? How is that related to me?" Charles asked, not seeing how he would also be related to the deceased person.

"That is where the story gets interesting. Are you sure you don't want something to drink first?"

"Do I need something to drink?" Charles looked a little concerned.

"I am only talking about water or coffee. I think we can save the other stuff for later."

"Water will be fine then."

Ben went to the kitchen and brought them each a glass of water. He then sat back down and proceeded to tell Charles the truth about the gravesite and how the two of them were related.

"Wow!" That sounds more like a novel than real life." So, you are saying that the story my grandmother told us was a lie?"

"She is not the only one who lied. My great-grandmother also lied. She told her family that her husband ran off and left her and Rhea, and they got a divorce. She never told anyone about him being buried there, nor the story. I found the story and all the details online when I searched his name."

Charles was quiet for a few moments. Ben had just told him that his grandfather had been murdered; his grandmother had, in fact, been married but had an affair, and the man she had been married to was the murderer and spent the rest of his life in prison. No wonder his grandmother never mentioned a man in her life.

"What you are telling me is my mother is the child of my grandmother, who I knew, and your great-grandfather, who was killed?"

"That is the connection my family has put together. I think my wife or sister figured out you are my cousin-once-removed. Whatever that means. But that your mother and my grandmother, Rhea, are half-sisters."

"Talk about a complicated family!" Charles stood up and walked into the kitchen to put his glass into the sink. When he returned, he asked Ben if they could go to the grave.

Chapter Fifty-One

Celebrations

Barbara arrived home from her meeting in time to join Ben and Charles at the gate to the cemetery. Ben filled her in on what he had already told Charles, which was everything they knew.

Their conversation stopped when they reached the grave. Ben and Barbara stepped back so Charles could view it in his own way, with his private thoughts. He had not revealed to them what he thought about the story, and they wondered if he believed them. It was the truth. Sometimes the truth can be more unbelievable than a lie.

Charles stood looking down at the gravestone for a few moments. Then he squatted down and slowly moved his fingers across as he traced the name etched in stone. His thoughts drifted back over the generations. He wondered if the man buried here, who never lived to see his daughter, had loved his grandmother. Charles smiled when he envisioned the two together walking in secret in the woods, holding hands and sharing a love they could not allow. He wondered if that was why his grandmother said she never married. Or was it that she felt shame and anger toward the man she was married to, but who killed the man she truly loved.

Charles jerked up as the sounds of gunfire entered his mind. And the scene from an old western shootout formed. He shook his head and stood up. He turned away quickly and walked past Ben and Barbara back to the gate.

He leaned on the gate post and waited for them to catch up.

"Are you alright?" Barbara asked as she placed her hand on his shoulder.

"I will be. I just had a horrible vision while I was out there and had to wipe it from my mind."

"What was it? What did you see?" Ben asked.

"In my mind, I heard a gunshot, and the scene of one man killing another man ran through my head. It must have been so horrible if anyone had seen it happen. Do you know if anyone was a witness, or was it a private attack?" Charles became curious.

"As far as we can tell, it was a private attack that no one witnessed," Ben said.

" Good. I am glad no one had to see it happen. Glad for my grandmother too. Not that it happened, but that she didn't see it happen either. Sad enough to lose the father of your child. What a nightmare it must have been for her."

"I'm sure it was," Ben said.

"Are you going to be okay, Charles?" Barbara was concerned.

"I will be fine. Despite finding out the truth and how horrible it is, I can now rest easy knowing what the photo is about. And knowing my grandmother wanted us to know the truth about her and her love for the father of her daughter." He hesitated and looked off into the distance.

"What is it?" Barbara asked.

"I wonder if my mother ever knew the truth?"

"That you may never know. Hard to realize she never knew her biological father."

Charles smiled. "Well, while that is true. Also true is that the mystery is solved. Life goes on, and I want to celebrate." He raised his arm to the sky. "I am blessed to know that my grandmother had a man she loved and loved her. We always felt sorry for her for never being married. We never knew her story. Now I want to celebrate her love."

"We are all meeting at the Downtown Café and Lounge later for dinner and a celebration. Would you care to join us?"

"I would love to if you think it is alright with the rest of your family."

"I don't see why it wouldn't be," Ben said as he reached for his cell phone to call Sara.

When he finished talking with Sara, he told Charles that he was more than welcome to join them.

Sara hung up her phone and called Steven to let him know there would be one more person at the celebration. He told her he would add a setting, and everything was on target for the evening. Sara had a gleam in her eyes that matched her smile as she slid her phone back into her pocket.

Two hours later, the family was seated in the lounge area of the Downtown Café and Lounge. Terri had met them at the door and welcomed them all, including Charles. She walked them to their table and took their drink order. One of the new waitresses, who had recently joined Terri's staff, brought their drinks and took everyone's order.

While they waited for their food, they talked. Randall noticed Sara look toward the stage several times since they had arrived.

"What are you looking for? Randal whispered to his wife.

"Nothing," Sara tried to lie, but Randall knew his wife enough to know he should not pursue his inquiry.

After their meals were delivered and they began to eat, Ben asked Sara what the celebration was for. She told him that he needed to wait, but they all would find out soon. Everyone looked at everyone else. No one knew what was going on.

They all talked as they ate. Charles was listening more than he was adding to the conversation. He found himself smiling at how this family interacted with each other. Then he realized he was now a part of this family. It was a distant part, but a part nonetheless.

As the family was finishing their meal, the other guests in the café were also finishing. Sara noticed that no one was leaving. She looked around and did not recognize most of them, which was unusual. Then she remembered the reason for being there.

Steven had joined the family for the meal but returned to his lounge duties and walked up on the stage.

"Ladies and Gentlemen, I welcome you to Downtown Café and Lounge on this special night. My friend Adam and I invited you all here for a special reason. Many of you know Adam for the work he and his partner, Donovan, did to remodel this beautiful addition to Terri's place. Not all of you realize Adam's other talent. Adam is a great singer. We found that out here as he sang while he worked. He is the one who suggested we have the musical nights here, so if you have been to one of them, thank Adam. And here he is. Adam, the stage is yours." Steven waited for Adam to step on stage and handed him the microphone.

Adam held the microphone but didn't say anything for a moment. Instead, he looked around at all the people seated and smiled. They were all people he knew. Some from his past, but more from his present and the new life he hoped to continue.

"Ladies and gentlemen, as I look around this room, I see so many people who have been a part of my life. Some people have been part of my life for many years, some for only a few years since moving here. You all have blessed my life. And there is one person in particular who has blessed my life more than I ever thought possible." Adam looked around and gave Sara a look. Sara stood up and walked to the counter. She grabbed the hand of the person belonging to that blessing to Adam and walked her to the stage area.

"What are you doing?" Terri asked Sara, trying to get away from her grip.

"You need to hear what Adam has to say."

When they reached the stage, Sara let go of Terri's arm and returned to her seat. Adam reached out for Terri's hand.

"This is the lady who stole my heart and has been my blessing since the first day I saw her and drew up the plans for this place. She is the one who stole my heart."

Terri just stared at him. She wondered what he was up to. He had never done this before his show before.

"Terri," Adam began as he lowered himself to one knee. Terri looked at him with eyes wide open, unsure of what was happening. She had no idea what he was about to do until he began to speak again. She smiled as he spoke.

"Terri, my love, I know we have not known each other very long, but I feel we have an unexplainable strong connection. I know there is much to learn about each other in the days, weeks, months, and years ahead. We cannot continue to learn about each other if we are not together." He reached into his side pocket and pulled something out.

"Terri, will you give me the honor of becoming my wife and spending the rest of our lives together, learning all we can about one another? In simpler words, and those we have heard over and over all our lives, those simple words that changed the lives of numerous couples, I ask them of you." Adam opened the small box he held in his hand and let Terri see the contents.

"Terri, I would love the honor of spending the rest of my life by your side, learning about you, sharing our lives. You are my dream I never knew I had. Will you marry me?" Adam took the ring out of the ring box and held it up to the love of his life.

The room fell silent.

Terri looked at the ring, looked at Adam, and smiled. "Yes! Yes, I will marry you." Terri said. She smiled while she watched Adam place the ring on her finger. He held her hand as he stood up, wrapping his arms around her and lifting her off the floor. Neither one heard their friends and family cheering for them.

An hour later, when the guests said all the congratulations and went home, Adam and Terri sat at the bar, drinking one last drink. The sparkle in Terri's eyes was enough to light the stage. Adam's smile could not be diminished.

"When should we get married?" Adam asked as they toasted one more time.

"I have no idea. You managed to surprise me tonight. I realized most of the customers were people we knew, but it never occurred to me what was going on."

"I'm glad. I did have some help pulling it off. Sara and Steven were the only ones who knew what I was up to. And they did a fine job of keeping the secret."

"Yes, they did. I will have to talk to Sara about that! She's good." Terri laughed.

After they finished their drink and cleaned up the bar area, they walked outside. Terri still lived above the café, and Adam lived outside of town. They could have spent the night together, but Adam told her he would rather wait. It had been a big night, and they needed their rest. They both had work in the morning.

They kissed each other good night. Terri lifted her hand and looked at the beautiful ring that now dressed her hand. He had done well.

As she lay in her bed that night, she smiled. Life had changed for her since moving to the area. She had amazing people in her life. She had found her soulmate. Life was good.

As she drifted off to sleep, her mind had other ideas.

Epilogue

Standing alone had been Barbara's way of life. She had become accustomed to people leaving her. Sometimes they left suddenly, as her parents had when she was just a toddler. Each of her foster parents eventually left her by returning her to the system or the system taking her away. The last time she was removed from her foster mother was because another couple wanted to adopt her.

In the years she was with her adoptive parents she knew she was loved, but something was still missing, and she felt alone. As soon as she was old enough, she was the one who left them. She rarely spoke of them in later years. Her fondest memories had been with her foster mother, Annie. She would always remember her, and in time, she knew why. It was during her years with Annie that she had, unbeknownst to her or anyone, reconnected with her twin, Ben.

Barbara's life changed when she met and married Steven and discovered what was missing in her life through him. Her missing piece was her twin. A move to be near Ben brought her to the people of Bella Rose and their quaint town. A life she never dreamed possible was ahead of her; her future held an abundance of opportunities. Her life finally had meaning, love, and a large family. Her past had enabled the start of a new career. One that she knew would change the course of many other children.

Steven had changed his life around for Barbara. He knew she needed more than he alone could give her. In doing so, he opened up a whole new world for both of them. They met her lost family. They also met Terri and Adam and other new people who, if they were not already family by blood, soon became like family.

When Ben and Barbara discovered who their biological father was and that they had a connection to Rhea and to

Bella Rose, little did they know what other discoveries they would find.

A stranger in town brought more discoveries and connections to the family. Would the story behind the connection of Charles and Rhea cause tension or harmony? What other secrets lie in store for all of them?

Terri had moved away from the life she had known to start fresh. In doing so, she met Adam, who had also relocated to start a new life. Their bond was almost instant. They did not understand their connection, but Adam was not about to let it go. Terri thought his proposal had come out of the blue. Little did she know that he wanted to propose the day he met her.

Life for the two of them held great promise. That was IF Terri could get her past out of her mind. Her mind and heart had become a conflict the night she accepted Adam's proposal. What was the future she truly wanted to have? Was it too soon after her breakup with the other man in her life to make such a decision? Could she be happy with Adam? Or would her past hold her back?

So many questions remained. When life seemed to resemble normalcy, everyone realized they had little idea of what normal was. Life was full of mysteries, discoveries, and amazing truths. Was there a secret key to being normal?

Coming Next –

Two Unlikely Souls
The Mysteries of Bella Rose Estate
Book #5

Acknowledgments

Thank you, my fans, and readers, for your patience while I wrote this addition to the Mysteries of Bella Rose Estate series.

Thank you to those who touched my life and prompted some of the book's locations, character names, and storyline.

I have a shirt that says something like - I am a writer. Anything you say or do may be used in my next novel.

I will add that all it may take is how I see someone or something as I sit and watch people, which grabs my imagination. So to all of you – thank you for being who you are. If you see yourself in one of my characters…. You may be right. – Thank you.

Want to be in one of my next storylines? Let's talk.

Other books by Phyllis Dewey

FICTION:

Leaving Came Easy – The Mysteries of Bella Rose Estates Book #1
Secrets in the Attic – The Mysteries of Bella Rose Estates Book #2
The Hidden Truth – The Mysteries of Bella Rose Estates Book #3

NON-FICTION:

Her Turn - One Woman's Positive Journey Through Her First Year of Grieving.

www.ingramcontent.com/pod-product-compliance
Lightning Source LLC
Chambersburg PA
CBHW030407180626
46812CB00005B/1964